the Masks We Wear

LEE JACQUOT'

This is a work of fiction. Names, characters, businesses, places, events, and incidents, as well as resemblance to actual persons, living or dead, is purely coincidental.

Cover Design: AJ Wolf-AJ Wolf Graphics
Editing: Ellie McLove – My Brother's Editor
Proofreader: Rosa Sharon- My Brother's Editor

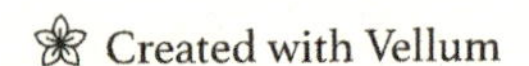

A QUICK NOTE FROM THE AUTHOR

The Masks We Wear is a standalone in the Emerald Falls Series. It is a steamy read intended for mature audiences. All characters depicted are over the age of 18. That being said, this book does include graphic consensual sexual scenes and physical abuse by a parental figure. It is a BULLY romance, and some scenes may be triggering for some.

This book is strictly a work of fictitious fantasy.

Reader discretion is advised.

To Vula, who didn't get to see this happen.

Twenty-five years ago, you wrapped my first story in cardboard and put it on your bookshelf.

You believed in me. Thank you.

ONE

Three Years Ago

"What do you mean you're moving here?" My childhood friend, Liliana, knits her arched brows, the vein in her jaw tics when she clenches it.

I don't understand. I thought she would be happy, excited even.

We've been best friends for seven years, and even though we only see each other in the summer because of my divorced parents, it's never hurt our friendship. When I'm here, we do everything together. We camp in the backyard, stargaze until the sun wakes up, gorge on popcorn and watch scary movies. My favorite thing about us, is when we talk, even when we run out of things to say.

But mixed in with all the good, there's also the crappy. Her parent's affair, my mother's unexplained medical issues, her father's abandonment... everything kids *shouldn't* have to go through growing up, we've handled together.

After what felt like forever, my mom asked if I wanted to move in with my father to finish the remainder of high school. She knew I liked Washington better, plus the school system has better opportunities for my future. Really though, Liliana was the first thing to pop in my head, and I said yes so fast I was scared I hurt my mom's feelings. But I was ecstatic.

Seeing Liliana during the short eight weeks of summer wasn't enough.

I want to be here all the time.

I thought *she* wanted me here too. Then again, I can't deny the subtle changes I've noticed before our eighth grade year—we lost half our summer when she went to a cheerleading boot camp. Ever since, she started dressing a little differently, putting makeup on and didn't want to eat junk food with me until two in the morning anymore. She said she had to maintain her physique if she wanted to remain on the squad. I didn't mention any of it to her, though, not even when she dyed her burnt caramel hair blonde and started wearing hazel green contacts.

I miss her chestnut eyes.

"What's wrong?" I ask, almost scared to hear her response.

Absentmindedly, I shake my head, ridding it of the thoughts. Liliana and I are best friends through and through. Every one of her secrets, every fear, every sad thought, all of it, belongs to me. I squeeze the small box in my hoodie—if not to make sure it's there, maybe for some luck.

I watch as she twirls a fake golden strand between her fingers, her gaze on the ground. My pulse strengthens with each passing second.

What is happening?

"You can tell me, Liliana," I whisper, giving her a soft, reassuring smile.

"Lily."

I tilt my head, my eyebrows furrowing. "What?"

"It's just Lily now."

"Since when?"

"I don't think you should move here, Spencer," she spits out.

What? A sharp pain echoes through my chest, and I rub at the ache. Liliana—*Lily* stands, brushing off her blue jeans.

My eyes follow her, too surprised to speak. Is that all she has to say about it? No rationale or explanation? But then again, her logic doesn't matter. I know it won't change the sting radiating through my veins or the sudden thinness to the air.

And I doubt anything will ease my throbbing heart.

Ugh. Why does she have to wear those crap contacts? I used to be able to read her like an open book. If she weren't wearing them, I'd be able to reason with her, maybe see where this bizarre change is coming from. Now, with those contacts that act like drawn curtains, I can't see anything, and I know she can't see *me*.

Did I do something wrong?

"Look, I gotta go, Spence. We have another practice."

Lily doesn't wait for a response and instead disappears through the gate combining our two backyards. I stand like a stick in the mud, fixated on the spot she stood until the sun's rays fade behind a row of clouds I hadn't noticed before.

Running a hand through the side of my hair, I slip the box from my pocket—the box I worked all spring to save up for, and open it. Even in the overcast, the small heart charm sparkles, attached to the James Avery bracelet she's been eyeing since last Christmas.

A heaviness moves into my chest, anchoring my racing heart in place. I swallow my thick saliva and look in Liliana's backyard to the treehouse we use to sleep in for days straight.

Today was supposed to be the day. The day she knew... when I finally told her what I've felt since I first laid eyes on her in second grade.

I make the decision quickly, before I think better of it, and go inside the gate, fumbling up the old ladder of the treehouse into the small space. We haven't used it in a couple of years, but nothing has changed.

An old black rug sits in the middle, posters of our favorite movies and animes pinned to the weathered walls. Two bean bags that are in surprisingly good shape sit in the corner. If I close my eyes, I can almost smell the popcorn and her lavender body cream.

Crouching down, I walk to a small chest where we keep all our secret treasures. It mostly contains geo rocks, a few trading cards, and a best friend contract we made in the fifth grade.

I sigh and slip the bracelet inside. Should she ever come here and look, she'll find *my* heart with it.

I don't need it anymore.

TODAY

I went back home that day, a cloud following me the entire five hundred miles to Idaho. It wasn't hard to piece together what happened. She was popular and needed to maintain an image, one I clearly didn't fit. After I figured that out, my decision was made. If she needed me to change, she wasn't worth it. Nothing is worth giving up who you are.

At least that's what I told myself every day for the rest of the summer.

My best friend in Idaho, William, filled most of my conscious hours with his presence. We overate pizza and watched way too many action movies while I moped. I couldn't help it. No matter what I told myself, I still cared, like a dumbass.

"Good guys don't get the girls," William would tell me, and I never understood why he thought it would cheer me up. It didn't. In fact, it did quite the opposite. I wanted to prove that I *could* get the girls. Even if they weren't the one I wanted.

That's when the dark streak happened. I put on some new clothes, developed a steady workout regimen—it didn't take much. I climbed the ranks fast, and the number of *girls* I got was probably on the unhealthy side.

But I didn't care.

I was proving William wrong and keeping my mind off of *her,* which is all I wanted. But the number of fights I found myself in, plus the countless times I was suspended, was not something I meant to happen. My grades never slipped—hell, I could miss a month and still pass my classes, but it was the look on my mother's face every time she came to school. Upsetting her was the worst kind of punch to the gut.

"I don't understand what happened to my precious boy. My sweet boy." That's all she would ever say. No scolding, no punishment. Just disappointment.

Nothing is worth losing who you are.

The two succeeding summers, I didn't go back to my dad's. Making excuse after excuse, but really I couldn't bear the off chance I might see *her.* So instead, we FaceTimed more, and my dad came to Idaho for visits.

Then my mom got her diagnosis: early stages of dementia. We chalked up all the signs to menopause, and in turn, prolonged her treatment. They say it's a common mistake, but that's bullshit. If I wasn't fucking around, and paid more attention, I would have noticed. It's just the karma for me doing the one damn thing I said I wouldn't ever do; breaking my mother's heart and conforming to a fucked-up society that determines worth by our chiseled abs or how big our dicks are.

And that same karma brought me back here to Emerald High. My father had us move in with him to help take care of Mom while also pushing me with my studies. My parents both know I would have dropped out to dote on my mom, and medical school would have been out the window.

Even though this is the last place I want to be, it's been fine for sixty-eight days. I've managed to return to my "pre-bad-boy state" and disappear with the sea of other outcasts, keeping my head low and eyes lower.

Until now.

The one day I was running late and threw on my dad's shoes by mistake, is the day I trip and land right at her feet.

"Fucking nerd."

The way her heel jerks under me, I can tell she wants to kick me, but when we lock eyes, she stiffens.

Lily still has the same blonde hair I remember from freshman year, only now, it looks a lot more natural. The same can't be said for those stupid ass hazel contacts. From down here, I can tell she's continued to watch her figure as it is the literal definition of a coke bottle, and I curse the way my dick twitches in my pants.

It's not fair she gets that reaction from me.

All this time, and it's as though a day hasn't passed. I'm still putty in her hands. The organ in my chest I haven't felt in ages picks up pace, thumping against my ribcage as though it's found its rightful owner.

I've seen her before, a few times from afar, but made sure to disappear before she noticed. It didn't bother me since the ache stayed dull. But this is different. My entire body fills with moths, flapping around in the dark, desperate for the light—something they haven't seen in three years.

When she recovers, so do I, fumbling to my feet like a dumbass and taking off before things get worse. Running a hand through my hair, I manage to rush away from the influx of hot air.

"If you're gonna be a jackass, at least know how to walk," an unfamiliar, high-pitched voice calls after me. It's grating, and I know it must belong to the cheap platinum Barbie next to her.

Jeers and snickers of nearby observers echo in the hallway. Well, if there's any way to announce my arrival, I guess this is as good a time as any.

Turning on my heels, I shove my glasses up my nose and look at the pale girl in her eyes. "If you're gonna be the school's blow-up doll, at least be a hot one."

My gaze flashes to Lily's before shifting back toward the AP hallway.

I can feel her eyes on the back of my head, in the endings of every nerve, and in the deepest, darkest part of my soul.

Fuck.

TWO

When the hell did he get back?

Scratch that. When the hell did he get so...delicious? Even under his thick orange flannel, the muscles in his back and biceps flex when he gets up. I also don't remember his jaw being so defined or his face being perfectly symmetrical. But his eyes are the same. A swirl of caramel breaks up the smooth brown in a way that almost feels hypnotic.

They pull me back to earth—reminding me who I am, what I was, the things I lost.

My biggest fears.

My greatest regrets.

"Can you believe that asshole? I mean, seriously..." My friend, and co-captain, Amora, drones on about her encounter with Spencer.

Spencer Hanes. *Holy Shit.*

I blink a few times—a failed attempt to capture one of the dozens of thoughts careening around my mind. The last thing I need to worry about is old secrets being dug up for anyone to find. And Spencer knows just where I buried them.

Finally grounding my head, I shrug. Talking isn't one of the things I often do, even when rattled. The less you speak, the less people know. I try to keep my face neutral as I wiggle my fingers and turn toward the front office.

"Where are you going? It's time for lunch." The sparkle in Amora's usually glossy eyes, dims. One hand is propped on a thin hip, while her face is pinched in disgust. She hates being alone with our cheer squad, though I haven't been able to figure out why. My dear friend is the biggest bitch they make in her five and half foot size, and she has no qualms displaying it.

"Bolwig," I call over my shoulder without stopping.

I've been putting the guidance counselor off for a while now, but two months into my senior year, I know it's no longer an option. At least, not a smart one. I have a feeling I know what she's going to say, and I've never been in the mood to hear it.

Rotating my increasingly tight shoulders as I reach her office, I can't seem to hinder my thoughts from returning to the mess that just dropped at my feet. Between Spencer and the uncertainty of my future, everything in my mind is becoming a tangled mess. Both unpredictabilities twist around each other like two weeds fighting for dominance in a garden. Both of them spread their tendrils around everything beautiful, threatening to overtake what I've worked so hard to cultivate.

I sigh—one thing at a time.

Ignoring the slight ache creeping behind my eyes, I walk toward Ms. Bolwig's collage-covered wall. Her office is littered with university pendants and pictures of prior students at graduation, probably her favorites. As I bide my time, attempting to keep my mind clear, I trace a finger over a few. Each one was taken on an impossibly sunny day, in an almost picturesque light. The many smiles shine back at me, and I wonder vaguely just how genuine their happiness is. No one is *that* happy. They're all just wearing masks, waiting for the moment they can take them off.

"Excited about graduation, Miss Conley?"

Ms. Bolwig's voice jolts me from my thoughts, and I whirl around to face her. The aging woman stands in the doorway; her signature clipboard hugged tightly against her massive chest. She twirls a fluffy purple pen between her short fingers as she gazes past me to the pictures.

"Yep." I pop the p, leaning on the wall. "Ready for the University of Kentucky."

The crows'-feet at the edge of her dull blue eyes make an appearance as she grins. "Ah, yes. Kentucky. Let's talk about that, shall we?"

Ms. Bolwig gestures a hand toward an empty chair in front of her pristine desk before taking a seat in front of her computer. She grabs a file from a stack and opens it with care, tracing the pages of what I assume is my permanent file.

It's clean, full of A's, a thirteen hundred SAT score, and not one referral. Captain of the cheerleading squad with perfect attendance since fourth grade. Even on that day, I would have given my left kidney to be at school. My file is—

"Uneventful," she determines.

I don't stop my face from crumpling. "*Uneventful?*" I repeat as though I've misheard her. I mean, I must have. I know it isn't the prize horse at the Derby, but it's still pretty impressive, nonetheless.

She nods her graying head slowly, still perusing the file. My fists clench at my sides, and I ignore the pain of my stiletto nails piercing into my palm.

"Can you elaborate, please, Ms. Bolwig?" The words are meant to be friendly, but coming through bared teeth, I know she hears the bite in them.

"You have an average record, but nothing to stand out for the program you're seeking at Kentucky."

My mouth pops open in protest, but she holds a hand up. "Cheer captain. Yes, I know. And winning regionals this year will do wonders, but you need to be more than a pretty face and a good *tumbler*."

She spits the last word out as if it's a curse. A good tumbler. Anger and irritation ripple down my body, and I could swear someone turned on the heater. I wipe my brow with the back of my hand as I search for the right words.

I'm smart, not like an Amelia Earhart, but I'm smart enough. Most notable of all, I am the best damn cheerleader and captain to come out of Emerald Falls since 1974. Which says something considering it's a big city with twelve different high schools scrambling for that title. I've brought more recognition to EFH than our most prized football players. Not to mention my girls rock out every damn appearance, which takes real leadership skills. I'm not just a good *tumbler*.

"I want to switch a course you're currently in. I know it's late in the semester, but Mr. Jones said he'd be happy to have you."

My eyebrows furrow. "Mr. Jones teaches AP Sciences..."

She huffs. "To be a slightly above average student, you can be rather dense, Miss Conley."

I bite my tongue to keep the retort from seeping out.

Whether I like her snide-ass comments or not, the woman is known for making things happen, and I need to get into Kentucky.

"He is taking his students to a competition. I think it would be just the thing to lift your head above the sea of other cheerleaders clawing their way to that university."

She keeps talking about some competition, but I'm not listening. The only one I'm worried about is regionals and all the practices in between. Cheerleading didn't come naturally to me. I had—have—to work on it every damn day. It's a commitment that most marriages don't have, and I bleed my soul into it each passing second. I deserve to go to Kentucky.

Go big, or go home, and I'll be damned if I stay here. Especially now.

I grimace but finally nod in approval. I don't intend to *claw* my way anywhere. I've put countless hours into paving the road myself, and I plan to walk on it in six-inch heels and a fresh manicure. Even at the expense of setting half my garden on fire to rid it of one particular weed.

She scribbles something on a pad before tearing it from the yellow backing. "Good choice. Take this to the registrar and hurry along. His period starts in ten minutes."

I take the paper from her gingerly, careful not to snatch it, murmuring a quick "thanks." My eyes drift to the pictures on the wall one last time before slipping out of her office.

This had better be worth it.

After leaving the registrar, I manage to slink past the cafeteria and down the AP hallway where I take a deep breath. As much as I want to focus on the shitty words of Ms. Bolwig, I can't help but wonder why Spencer acted like he didn't know me...

A tingle creeps up my spine, and my ears ring with the

whispers of what this could mean—the things people could find out. Image is everything here. I've spent a long time polishing myself to the perfect shine, careful to get inside all the nooks and crannies.

He can expose my rusted core in seconds.

Fear takes over, weakening my knees to the point I have to lean against the set of lockers on my right. The smooth metal cools my back as I take a few more breaths.

I can't let him say anything.

My wheels begin to turn, ideas forming on how I can keep my old friend quiet. There is one thing that might—

"Mija, how did your meeting go?"

I freeze, and my idea on the verge of creation vanishes, replaced by my shoulders tensing back up. Whirling around, my mother stands at the edge of the hall. She smooths down her navy uniform with one hand and holds on to an oversized trash bin with the other. A misplaced, warm smile spread across her face.

My eyes dart around, making sure no one is coming. She's never supposed to be here before five. By then, we don't risk the chance of running into each other. Sounds shitty, but if the Queen of Emerald High's mom was exposed as the school's head custodian, nothing I've done in this place would matter. I'd lose my spot faster than Amora's skirt after a game.

The curious part of me wants to ask how she knows I was meeting with Ms. Bolwig, but instead, I feign a bored expression. "Dandy."

Her smile fades, replaced by the snarl of her true form. "Such a stupid girl. I bet you won't make it to that cheer school."

I latch a finger around my necklace, pulling it side to side. "Hmm, see ya."

I don't wait for a response and turn toward Mr. Jones' class. The last thing I want to do is invoke her wrath and chance someone seeing. Straightening my spine, I flip my golden locks over my shoulder and open the door, letting the day's shit show stay behind me. At this point, I don't think it could get much worse.

Let's do this.

I've never seen a class of kids so engrossed in their work before the bell has even rung. Everyone's head is down, shoved in the pages of their journals, their pens working furiously across the paper. None of them even glance up from their notebooks when they hear me walk in.

A small girl with hexagon glasses and inky hair glances my way as I pass before looking back down. After a beat of silence, her head pops back up comically, and she elbows the boy next to her, motioning to me with her chin.

It sets off a chain reaction until all eyes are glued on me, a soft whisper floating around the room.

I'm used to the effects that come with being *Queen* of Emerald High, but it doesn't make it any less cringy.

Trying not to grimace, I stride over to Mr. Jones, who has his face glued to his computer. His eyes flash to me before returning to the screen. Like the four-eyed girl, he does a double take before standing too abruptly, knocking over what looks to be week-old coffee.

I recoil, terrified the dark liquid will land on my white suede heels, and watch him fumble to clean his mess. "I'm so sorry, Miss Conley."

"Not a problem, Mr. Jones." But even so, I take a few cautionary steps backward.

After wiping up most of the coffee, he ambles around the desk, rising to his full height, and straightens a wrinkled candy corn tie.

"Class, I'd like to introduce you to our newest member, Liliana Conley."

His confirmation that I'm joining the class sends an even louder murmur vibrating through the room, but I ignore it, holding up a hand in a light wave. "Please, just Lily is fine."

Mr. Jones beams at me, rubbing his stubble. "Of course. I'm going to pair you up with the lad back there."

He motions to the table on the far left side of the classroom, where the only student who hasn't looked up is scribbling in his notebook. Mr. Jones leans a little closer, dropping his voice to a whisper. "He's having a hard time adjusting to the idea of a partner, but I know you'll be able to work it out."

I raise an eyebrow in question. "Partner?"

He nods. "Didn't Ms. Bolwig tell you?"

Tilting my head, I wait for him to elaborate. The woman told me a lot, ninety percent of which has already been blocked out for the well-being of my mental health.

He shifts back, swallowing hard around his evident discomfort. "You'll be the fill-in we need for the science competition. We had a student move away."

My eyes widen of their own accord, and I feel my jaw tic, but I recover quickly, smiling at Mr. Jones. I knew there was a competition, but I didn't think I *had* to participate.

After granting him a curt nod, I stroll to the back and sit at the edge of the seat, setting my purse on the worn lab table and cross my feet at the ankle. A perfect ladies pose.

As if he's just realized I've entered the room, Spencer's mesmerizing brown eyes collide with mine.

THREE

Lily's pupils constrict under the light, letting her natural brown color peek from beneath the contacts. It's the first I've seen of them since middle school—when I knew her better than I knew myself.

There was a time when her eyes were the light leading me out of my dark ass cave. But that Liliana has come and gone, leaving nothing but a cutout of a basic bitch with a bad attitude named *Lily*.

I scoff, clenching my teeth at the thought of all the lost time I spent on her during those summers. I could have been with my mom or studying more, hell, maybe even learning a fucking sport. Either way, my *time* is the one thing she won't be able to waste again.

Staring back down at my journal, I shift my shoulders away from her. Maybe if I ignore her long enough, she'll get the hint. Might even get lucky, and she'll go away.

A moment of silence passes before Lily dips her head low, tilting it to read my scribbles. I move my body, so I can't even see her in my periphery. I hope she feels the heat radiating from me and backs off, but she either doesn't notice or doesn't care.

"So, what are we working on, Spence?"

I'm not sure which word pisses me off more. The way she holds the last syllable of my name and sounds like a fucking snake or the fact she said we, as if I would *actually* consider letting her help me with my project.

Damn Maurice for moving.

I don't look at her, but hiss my words to match her reptilian tone. "Don't think I'm letting you lay a finger on this project."

Her chair scrapes across the tile, forcing me to glance over my shoulder at her. Her small nose is scrunched as if she's smelled something grotesque, and I have to bite back a laugh of satisfaction. I'm sure she's not used to being talked back to by any of her minions. Or anyone in the school, for that matter. I've only been back for two months, but it doesn't take long to learn what the school thinks of Lily Conley.

Captain of an elite cheer squad, sure, but what they talk about most is how she has the aura of a fucking goddess and is every guy's wet dream. They say she doesn't talk too much —rather not get her hands dirty, and instead, lets her team carry out any trash she needs to dispose of. Nothing like the Liliana, I know. *Knew*.

Others say she's the female version of her best friend, Blaze. He's the star running back of the school, and like dear Liliana here; he runs this place. I've only run into him once, and that was enough. He has multi-colored eyes, one a metal gray, the other a piercing dark blue. It's unsettling when he looks at you, almost as if he can read your thoughts.

It makes sense that they're friends, though. Both seem void of any feelings and reek of entitlement.

"You don't have a choice, fuckwad." Lily snatches my journal from under me, and when I snap my head to her, my damn glasses fall off.

I ignore her snickers as my hands find the frame and shove them back on. My pulse becomes erratic, ticking in my veins so violently, I can feel my heartbeat in my toes. "If you think I'm going to let you have any input whatsoever, you've lost what little fucking brain you got up there."

She giggles, and it's so full of fake sweetness and corn syrup, I wonder if I can get secondhand diabetes. "Was that meant to insult me? Come on, Spencer, you're smarter than that. Well, *used* to be, at least..." She tilts her chin and looks to the ceiling as if thinking about something. "I don't remember."

I grind my molars, anger flushing through my body as she stands and sashays to the front. She whispers to Mr. Jones, whose face blooms a light pink before he nods and hands her a slip.

When she walks out, the rage doesn't leave with her—it intensifies. I have one fear in life. One. Last I checked, we shared the same sentiments. We go about them in different ways, but the roots are the same.

Being forgotten.

It's easy to lose yourself—to an addiction, an obsession, society, or illness. It's even easier for the world to forget you.

My mother, once a renowned photographer, made it her life's mission to capture people in unforgettable ways. She says everyone should leave a mark, or else there's no point in enduring all the torture this life will throw at you.

It's always felt like a silly fear—worrying if people would

remember you, but when I told Lily, she understood. That's when she told me about her parents. A father that was never home and a mother that never left her room. It's something she didn't want to experience ever again—being invisible to the people that are supposed to love you the most.

I sit back and sigh as my phone vibrates in my pocket. Staring at my notes, I decide I'm done with school for the day and begin shoving my things in my bag.

Fuck her and fuck me for even caring.

"Ar-are you okay?" Remy appears at the side of my table. Huge hexagon glasses amplify the small almond shape of her *natural* hazel eyes.

Remy is a classmate and my co-worker at Jenny's Smoothies and probably the only one at Emerald High that's smarter than me. I found myself kind of bummed when we didn't get paired up for the fair project. It would have been epic.

I nod, tossing a pencil behind my ear. "Yeah, I'm going to go home. My head hurts." I rub at my temple for good measure.

Her lips thin into a straight line, but she doesn't push it. "See you at work?"

"Of course."

Slinking past her, I slip from class. Mr. Jones doesn't even notice. It usually wouldn't bother me, but today... it does.

I make it to the parking lot before I remember my phone and slide it from my pocket.

Liliana: Come over tomorrow at ten, so we can work on OUR project.

"SO YOU GUYS used to be best friends?" Remy leans against the counter, a thin finger tracing the edge of her latest romance read.

I filled her in on my little encounter with Lily while working the slow-ass counter at the smoothie shop. Like most weeknights, it's been a proverbial ghost town, leaving us to our nightly vent sessions—mostly revolving around the insane workload from school. But tonight, I needed to tell someone what happened and calling my old friend William is not a good idea. Not right now, at least.

Even though I've only known Remy a couple of months, it feels like much longer. She's easy to talk to, a fantastic study partner, and it doesn't hurt she's nice to look at. Remy's short, only about five-two if I had to guess, and her curves are dangerously sexy. She hides them under oversized clothes, claiming to be fat in comparison to others in her family. I try to tell her that they have genetics on their side, but she always has a retort about hard work and discipline in the Asian community. She says it extends to their body just as much as their mind.

Disregarding the silly notion that she's overweight, Remy's got everything going for herself. Thinking about it now, her only downfall is the misfortune of having bad taste in men. She has a very misplaced crush on Blaze. I blame the romance novels she reads—they give her false hope and make her think she can tame the beast that lives within him.

No matter how much I try to convince her that's a bad idea, she blows me off. *"It's not like he'll ever notice me anyway. It's just a harmless crush."*

"Yep," I finally answer, wiping down the counter for the third time. The trickle of customers has left me too much time to think about the blonde-headed vixen, Lily.

I didn't want to spill my guts, so I told Remy surface details. Old friend, turned bitch partner, who's probably going to do more harm than good on my project. Even still, Remy narrows her eyes and sighs. "I'm sorry. I know you've worked hard on the outline. Have you thought about whether you're going to her house?"

I shrug, ignoring the pounding in my chest.

It's *all* I've thought about. It's frustrating that Lily can somehow stir up dormant feelings inside of me. That my body seems to have forgotten the pain she inflicted in my heart, or that the logical side of my brain can't remember the hours I spent in the dark searching for her light.

I run a hand down my face, taking a deep breath. As much as I want to pretend I don't give a fuck, I do. Even if it is minute.

"Don't let her know she gets to you, Spencer. People like her feed off that energy, and it will only make things worse. Focus on your part and try to give her busy work. Make her feel like she's really doing something."

Remy chews absentmindedly on her bottom lip as she returns her focus to the open book.

She has a point. I can see Lily making my life a living hell and derailing my project to spite me for the fun of it.

Maybe I will go.

Show Lily that I care just as little about her as she does me. Even if it is a lie.

FOUR

Playing with Spencer's fear—*our* fear was a low blow, but I can't find it in me to care.

I rub at my nose, a failed attempt to rid my nostrils of his lingering smell—an alluring combination of fresh air and cedar wood. It's a deep musk that calms me, reminding me of a time when nothing mattered but spending all night in a treehouse, surrounded by scattered popcorn and open manga. We would laugh until we fell asleep, always finding each other's hand in the middle of our dreams.

He never knew that part, though. I always woke up before him and would slip my hand out of his so he wouldn't see. See how much he meant to me. See that when I looked at him, I was envisioning all the seeds I'd planted over the last seven years beginning to bloom into something magnificent.

What I *didn't* want him to see, was how terrified I was he would forget me like the people who were supposed to cherish me. Mom, Dad, and my aunt Mina, who I loved more than my parents combined. All of them disappeared without a trace, leaving me to wonder what the hell was wrong with me.

For a while, everything was fine. But of course, Spencer decided to ruin it, burning my fragile garden to ashes with just a few words.

I won't let that happen again. I can't. Not after all the work it took to rebuild it.

Amora clears her throat, and I realize she's waiting. Her thin blonde eyebrows arched in anticipation. "So?"

We're meeting at my house to discuss everything I have planned, but I'm becoming easily distracted. Already his return is messing with me.

I shrug, half hoping she repeats herself while also wishing she would just read my mind so I don't have to talk anymore. She's been a friend since eighth-grade cheer camp, and it became apparent immediately she wasn't going anywhere. I'm not big on conversation, while she yelps like a damn chihuahua, continually droning on about guys, drama, and more guys. None of which I'm interested in. My goals override all the foolishness that comes with high school. Perhaps that's why my skin crawls when I think of my plan.

"What happens when you get him upstairs?" she repeats.

Part of me can't believe I've resorted to something so juvenile, but I need to make sure Spencer stays far away from me while ensuring my childhood secrets remain locked up. Nothing could tear up my future faster than Spencer Hanes and the map of where they're hidden.

Blaze grabs a fry from my plate, his dark eyes dim with boredom as he pops it in his mouth. His strong jaw clenches as he returns his gaze to the TV he's been brooding over, raking a hand through his dark strands.

Like Amora, we met in the eighth grade at his football game. Something about the mask he wore matched mine, and we gravitated toward each other. It's been nice having someone who understands me at my core. Understands when pain becomes a second nature emotion.

I snatch the second fry he tries to steal from his hand. "You think it's stupid?"

His lips pull down, and he shrugs, his black shirt tugging against his thick biceps. "Do what you got to do. You've come too far now." He grabs the fry from my lips. "Besides, you know I've done worse for less."

Blaze continues his assault of stealing my french fries as he scrutinizes the players running back and forth across the screen. He sucks his teeth when the referee calls a foul and leans forward, grabbing his phone from the counter. He makes quick work, tapping out only a few words before sliding from his barstool, and snatches up his leather jacket.

"Leaving?" Amora asks, her blue eyes sparkling under the kitchen lights.

It's incredible to watch the way girls drool over Blaze, and even more so when they know how he's incapable of feelings. He makes it clear, both with his general *fuck off* aura and the actual 'fuck off' that spills from his mouth. They never seem to mind, though, overlooking anything that guarantees one night under him.

"Stacy wants to swallow my cock. Care to join?" he asks her before he shoves an arm through his jacket.

"Only if you lick this cunt while she does it," Amora sneers, the twinkle now replaced with a borderline challenge.

He ignores her and leans in, leaving a whisper of a kiss on my cheek.

"Drive safe, Blaze. It's wet. Let me know when you make it," I call after him, stating the obvious. It rains almost every day. But I still worry about him on that damn motorcycle.

"Of course."

He waves me off, grabbing his helmet from the couch, and spares the game one last look before disappearing out the front door, leaving an empty void in the room.

Amora sighs, pushing her food around the crinkled yellow paper before turning back to me, her piercing blue eyes narrowing. "Why are you doing this again? I mean, don't get me wrong, this is going to be funny as hell, but why him?"

I roll my eyes, the lie slipping from my tongue as effortlessly as breathing. "I don't want to do the project. My plate is full already. A little blackmail, and I think he'll have no problem doing the whole thing."

Any sane, rational person would know how full of shit I am, but not Amora. She's so hell-bent on being a classic mean girl that she'll look past any reasoning just for the fun of it.

Blaze, on the other hand, saw through me the second I told them. I think it's those damn eyes of his. I swear they give him X-ray powers. Thankfully though, he didn't berate me with questions. Either because he doesn't care or knows the pain of hiding secrets through any means necessary.

She scrolls on her phone a few more minutes, flipping her bright yellow strands over her tan shoulder. "Alright, everything's a go. I'm going to go change, grab some liquor, and be back in an hour."

I nod but don't look at her. Instead, I focus my gaze on

the house behind mine. The lights in the far right room flicker to life and something inside me darkens. It crawls around my heart, squeezing the organ, making it harder to breathe.

After tonight, those lights will haunt me, and rightfully so.

A few hours later and music hums through my body, coating each nerve with its infectious melody, forcing my hips to move. I've had a few drinks, but Blaze made them, so they weren't too strong. Even still, liquid courage courses through me with the quick beat, matching my heart's pulse.

About a dozen people are here already, but most of them are in my living room, engrossed with the football game playing on the television. I look at the clock. Five till ten. He should be here any minute.

I adjust the tight black dress stuck to my clammy skin. I'm not sure why my stomach is in knots. I'm not nervous, at least I don't think. Maybe it's guilt, creeping into the small sober part of my consciousness, begging me to rethink my plan.

Grabbing the red Solo cup from Blaze that I know is water, I suck the cool liquid from the ice, reveling in the shiver that reverberates down my spine. I hand it back just as the doorbell rings.

Everyone else knows that when I have my parties, you walk in, so it must be him.

My stomach hollows out, making way for the hundreds of tiny butterflies swirling around inside, colliding with the Hennessy sprinkling down on them. The closer I get to the door, the more frantic they become, and my heart picks up speed, hammering into my chest.

Don't do this.

I ignore the thought—I don't have a choice.

Taking a deep breath, I reach for the cold metal knob, twisting it too slow before opening the door.

Spencer stands on the other side of the threshold—his white shirt clinging to the body I knew he was hiding under his flannel. His corded arms grip a journal at his side, while the gray sweatpants he's wearing leave nothing to the imagination.

My core tenses involuntarily, and I force my eyes back up to his. His face is unreadable as his chocolate orbs scan the scene behind me. "Busy?"

His voice is deep, husky, and travels straight to my pussy, my thighs clenching around the ache.

What the fuck is wrong with me? Focus, bitch.

I clear my throat, opening the door a little wider. "It's fine. We're going to be working upstairs anyway."

He hesitates, his eyes narrowing as unasked questions flit across them. I don't want to make it obvious I need him inside, so I wait, leaning against the doorframe. After a few more seconds, I raise an eyebrow as if annoyed and check an invisible watch on my wrist.

"I don't have all night, Einstein. Are we working or not?" I try to keep my voice light, playful even, in hopes he doesn't decide to go home. My heart accelerates, and I wonder for a second if he can hear it crashing into my sternum.

Finally, he sighs and steps inside.

I turn around, hurrying for the stairs on the right, but my pulse doesn't calm.

His agreement to come in is his signature to our end. The last formality needed to sever our lingering ties.

This is supposed to be a good thing—what I need—the quick death of something that shouldn't be alive. But the weight in my steps plant the seeds of doubt—the what-ifs and the maybes.

I shake my head, straightening my spine, as I rid the wayward thoughts and lead Spencer to the banister. Luckily, only Amora notices us drift up the stairs. She shoots me a wink, turning back to her latest boy-toy she's entertaining with her tongue.

Spencer follows behind me, and I can feel his eyes searing into my skin, lighting my back on fire. I shouldn't, but I like it. The combination of excitement, fear, arousal, and my plan circulate in the thick air around me, settling in my lungs. I suck in the sweet air and open my bedroom door, careful to leave the lights off.

He walks over to my empty desk, tossing down his journal. "What's going on? We're supposed to be working on the project, Lily."

I know it's my preferred name, but hearing it from his lips feels foreign. Like he's talking to someone else entirely. But his dark gaze is locked on me, his eyebrows knitting together in a delicious scowl.

My lips part and my tongue peeks out to sweep across my suddenly parched mouth. The dull ache in my belly flares when I see Spencer's throat bob. The muscles in his jaw tighten as his eyes begin trailing down my body. It's almost as if he's fighting the very act, and it turns me on. The thought that my old friend might see me, with just a fraction of the desire I've held for him, lights a match between my thighs.

I take large strides toward him, eating up the space in seconds. He stiffens, and I can't help but drink him in under the moonlight spilling in from the window.

He runs a hand through his dark locks, pausing at the

base of his neck. A muscle in his bicep twitches as he massages it before repeating himself. "What are you doing?"

I'm so close to him now, I can taste the mint on his breath. It mingles with mine, sending shivers down my spine. He closes his eyes, letting out a quiet, controlled sigh, and when they open, the passion darkening them swirls with the caramel.

In just those few seconds, I can feel my mask slip. The one that keeps me safe and guarded against all the things I'm terrified of. His eyes pierce through it, forcing me to see him too.

He's beautiful.

He was supposed to be... mine.

I wrap my arms around his neck and rise on my tiptoes, my lips grazing the shell of his ear. "Do you want me, Spencer?"

He moves his head to look at me, his jaw tight as he examines my face. He blinks a few times before his gaze finds my lips. "Whatever this is... stop, Liliana."

There it is. Even if it's just for this moment, he sees me —*remembers* me, and I take full advantage.

My tongue sweeps across his earlobe before dipping down the curves of his neck. He stiffens, grabbing my hips to keep me from smothering him with my body, but he can't control the growl that erupts from the back of his throat.

"Liliana," he warns, his voice impossibly deeper.

It makes the fine hairs on my arms stand, every sense suddenly heightened. Strong fingers sink into me, but I can tell by the way his breath hitches that he's losing control. Losing the willpower to keep from giving in to something that's been brewing for way too long. I kiss his soft skin, trailing my lips down his collarbone. He grips me tighter the more I push into him.

"Spencer, just fucking *fuck* me already." My voice is too heady, too desperate, too real.

But it does the trick. He releases my hips, and our bodies collide. One arm wraps around my waist while the other snakes up my back, and he tangles his hand in my hair, gripping it by the root. He tugs my head to the side, exposing my neck.

I hiss as the sharp pain subsides and turns into jolts of pleasure when his mouth connects with my jaw. His warm tongue slips across my pulse point, and my head tilts further, urging him to continue.

My sex throbs as he continues his descent and my knees begin to shake, forcing me to shift my weight onto him.

I yank on the hem of his white shirt, pulling enough that he lifts his hands, letting me tug it over his head—the dips and ripples of his muscles on full display. His glasses fall from his face, and he laughs. It's low, and the vibration against my chest heats my core.

He hooks his finger beneath my chin, tilting it gently to look in his eyes. The golden flakes in his eyes shine in the moonlight. In this moment, I forget everything, too transfixed, utter putty in his hands to bend as he pleases. It's as if the smolder has been waiting ten years to ignite.

His hand moves to cup my cheek, and I lean into it, my eyes closing under his warmth. I feel it before I open them—the heat of his lips closing in on mine.

No.

I promised myself I would do anything but that. The connection of our mouths would reveal the truth I won't admit, not even to myself, and ruin all the things I have planned.

Pushing him onto the bed, he huffs, not seeming to notice my deflection. I climb on top of him, digging both knees into the soft mattress on either side of his thighs. His sculpted body lays beneath my heated core, a definite bulge pressing into my ass.

I hook a finger in the waistband of his sweats, and he lifts his hips, allowing me better access to rip them from his body. His erection slaps against his stomach. It's even bigger than it felt, rock-solid, and glistening at the tip. I have an indescribable urge to lick it but instead chew the inside of my cheek to distract me.

Spencer grabs my forearm, pulling me flush on top of him, a primitive growl escaping his throat at our connection. His thumb frees my lips from my teeth before stroking the length of my jaw. "You are so incredibly infuriating."

"And it turns you on," I counter, gesturing toward his massive erection.

His eyes narrow, but before he can respond, I take out handcuffs hidden beneath the pillow. I clamp them on his wrist, which is in the perfect spot above his head, just under the metal headboard. He's attached to the bed faster than he can blink, and I have to laugh at the way his thick vein pulses in his neck.

His mouth drops open, and I have to stop myself from kissing it closed. Instead, I slip the key into his hand. "Just trust me."

His face hardens, and his head falls back. "That was always my biggest problem."

I swallow around the cotton suddenly caught in my throat. An odd combination of guilt and anger swirl in my chest, and I rub at the phantom pain. All I ever wanted was him. No. All I fucking wished for was to be wanted *by* him.

But he never did. Even after spending every day in the summers together, I was left to be forgotten the other ten months.

The rage in my gut bubbles, bile rising in the back of my throat. He doesn't get to make me feel bad for what's happened between us. This is his fault.

Two knocks on my door yank me from my thoughts, and Amora's voice rings through the hallway, signaling it's time.

Spencer's hands pause, but he doesn't release me. Instead, his dark eyes search mine. As if he wants me to stay. Here. With him. It's a quick lapse in judgment, but my gaze lingers at his lips. I want to kiss and bite them off at the same damn time.

Don't.

I clear my throat, forcing myself from his iron hold. "Let me get rid of her. Stay here. Please, Spencer."

He hesitates but doesn't argue and instead nods. A soft smile splits across his face, causing the dimples in his cheeks to deepen as he lets my hand slip from his.

It's strange how bad I would rather ignore the knocks and just hash it out with him. Settle things once and for all and find out why I wasn't enough. Or maybe just curl into him and let the worries of my life fizzle in his flames. And right now, it's almost as if I can feel him pull toward me as much as I gravitate to him. Which both pisses me off and excites me beyond comprehension.

That's impossible, though. Just like them, he never really cared. And now that I'm someone, his desire for me is only skin deep.

I stand, leaving the warmth of him, instantly wrapped in

the cool air whirling around the room. Every step feels heavy, weighted under a bag of bricks. It's as if my body knows that if I do this, that's it. There is no going back.

He'll hate me.

I look at him over my shoulder one last time, my heart stuttering at the beautiful sight laid out before me. For a second, I decide I won't do it. Maybe things can be different, he might feel something for me this time. But doubt—or perhaps reason, rears its head.

He'll forget you, just like he has before. Your parents couldn't love you. Why do you think he will?

The thought settles in my stomach, a pit of realization burning the fragment of hope to dust.

And at that, I open the door, just enough to slip out, leaving my heart in the room with him.

I don't need it anymore.

FIVE

I'm ass naked, handcuffed to Liliana's fucking bed.

Whatever dream I'm having, I need to wake up from it. My entire body both hums and burns with the aftereffects of her touch. Everything hurts and feels euphoric at the same time. It's a contradiction I no longer want to be a part of.

I pull against the cold metal, an attempt to feel anything other than the heat coursing through my veins. My free hand kneads at my chest, rubbing away the odd heavy sensation burrowing in.

Something isn't right.

No. *Nothing* is right.

How could I be such a dumbass and end up like this? Hell, she wouldn't even kiss me. If that's not the biggest red flag, I don't know what is. Not to mention, I've waited for this moment longer than I care to admit, and this... was too easy.

It sounded like my Liliana—felt like her. But when I looked at her, she was someone else, from those dumbass contacts to her stringy blonde hair. Even her normal light lavender smell was drowning in some expensive rose perfume.

I fucking hate the smell of roses, especially fake ones.

Muffled voices seep through the walls, and my eyes dart around the room for my clothes.

I need to leave. Now.

Clenching the key in one hand, I search with my fingers to find the hole and unlock the cuffs. Just as I slip the key inside, light from the hallway blinds me when the door opens, thrusting me into a temporary daze. I sit up as far as I can, shielding my eyes with my forearm. The silver glint of a phone is the first thing to come into focus before Lily flips on the light.

No. My heart bottoms out, landing in my stomach with a dull thud. My limbs scream for me to move, run, and never fucking look back. But my dumbass stays, confusion begging to find reason.

"What the hell are you doing in my room?" Her voice slices through the air, severing whatever piece of me still held on to the possibility of this being a misunderstanding.

The *reason* is she's a horrible, miserable bitch, who I've let waste my time. *Again*. But now, with the added perk of a full hard-on.

"Oh my God! Fucking perv was waiting in your room, naked!" The screeching of her friend, Amora, slices down my spine, lighting my back on fire.

My eyes stay trained on Lily's, whose face is twisted in disgust, a rose tint paints her cheek, and her ears burn a siren red. No part of her demeanor says she's surprised or ashamed...

My throat closes, nearly suffocating me, while anger boils in the pit of my gut. The room spins, and the only thing I can focus on is Lily's hand on her necklace as she pulls it back and forth. Something hot spikes in my chest, but I ignore it while I finish unlocking the handcuffs and bend to grab my clothes.

Maybe I should feel more embarrassed, but the rage rolling through my extremities leaves a dark substance floating around me, numbing my reaction.

I jerk on my sweatpants, balling my shirt in my fist as I push past the blonde twinkies standing in the doorframe.

"That's fucking disgusting. You need to file a restraining order, Lily!"

I think I hear a laugh, the same fictitious one from class on Friday, and it hammers the final nail in the coffin of what we were.

Amora's shouts are soon drowned in the music downstairs, and thankfully I'm able to slip out without a second glance.

I pull my shirt over my head and round the corner to my house. There's a bite to the air that wasn't there before sending jolts of goose bumps down my arms. At least that's what I tell myself until my phone vibrates in my pocket.

It's a video from Lily. I don't have to play it to know what it is.

Liliana: Keep your mouth shut, or everyone will know what a twisted, depraved freak you are.

I pinch my eyes closed against the burn that's suddenly crept into the sockets and take in a large gulp of air.

For two minutes, I could breathe.

For two minutes, I could see the girl that was my everything.

For two minutes, I didn't hate her.

But now, I remember just who Lily Conley is, and I can't wait to forget her.

"FUCKING BITCH SET ME UP." My fists curl around the edge of Remy's footboard, my knuckles blooming white.

After Lily sent me the video, I couldn't go home. I would have called William and done something stupid, something I would have regretted. Hitting up Remy was an impulse, but I'm glad I did. She told me to calm down and come over, so here I am. Standing at the edge of a princess bed, surrounded by hues of pink and piles of books.

I clench the railing impossibly tighter, ignoring the stabs of pain in my palm. My pulse continues to ravage through my head, the pounding in my ears making me dizzy.

For half a fucking second, I almost *trusted* her—thought maybe she actually wanted me the way I want her. How can I still be in denial after all this time? I'm so goddamn stupid. And that text... keep my mouth shut. I have no fucking clue what she's even talking about, and that pisses me off more.

"Fuck."

Remy's eyes widen as she slinks back into her fluffy pink futon, pulling a cream blanket to her chest. Her head shakes slightly as she searches for words. "I-I don't understand. Why would she do that? I mean, she's not the nicest person, but I've never heard of her targeting someone l-like this."

There's no way I'm going to tell her the truth. The sad fucking fact that I'm pathetic and still harbor some feelings for the damn devil herself. So instead, I lie, thinking of the only thing that might make any sense. "So she doesn't have to do any of the project."

Remy's small head jerks back, her eyebrows knitting together. "That seems...juvenile. Not to mention idiotic. You would have done the project alone anyway. Are you sure that's it?"

I sigh, scrubbing my hands down my face. Maybe I do regret coming over. Remy's smart enough to see through the bullshit I'm spewing, and I have no intentions of rehashing the dirty details of my past. "I'm sorry for coming here. And being so loud."

Remy flicks a hand around the room. "Don't apologize, Spencer. We're friends. Heck, I think you're my only friend. You can come here anytime. And don't worry about being loud. My dad works at the hospital overnight."

She lifts her blanket, patting the empty space next to her. I nod and flop down, surprised by how good the plush fabric feels. "Thank you."

Her bright teeth peek through her pillowy lips as she smiles and pushes back her glasses. "I'm here when you wanna talk."

She grabs the oversized tub of popcorn from her side table and sits it in her lap. Pushing play on the Hallmark movie I interrupted, she nudges me with her elbow.

I lean my head against her shoulder, accepting a handful of popcorn, and something in the air shifts, suddenly making me nauseous. This aura—I've felt it once before. It was when Liliana stopped being just the girl in the backyard and became the girl I needed. When she became my fresh air after a suffocating day at the hospital with my mom.

I told myself I would never let this happen again—needing someone to get through the dark. But then Remy glances down, her jet black waves brushing against my ear, and rests her head on mine.

A rush of calm floods through my core, my body relaxing at the connection. I don't think Remy will be someone I need to get me through the dark. No.

I think she'll sit in it with me until I find my own way out.

SIX

Spencer hasn't been to school the whole week. Five damn days.

I knew he would be pissed, maybe a little embarrassed—I mean, that was the intended goal, but this is ridiculous. We still have a project to get done and today is the deadline for our submission.

Not to mention my nerves have been wound up tight as hell, waiting to see how he would respond. I didn't really think about the aftereffects of the plan. I just knew I needed him to keep quiet, and this was my best chance at getting some leverage.

My pulse spikes, a sudden thought drowning out all the others.

What if he moved away?

Went back to his mom's and said fuck this project...fuck *me.*

The air in the room seems thinner—like it did every last day of summer all those years. He came and consumed my life in ways I couldn't describe, but when he left, he took that with him, leaving everything a little less colorful. Less beautiful. It's as though I was tolerating the bleak life I had, biding my time until he came back.

Leaning back in my chair, I huff and stare daggers into my phone. My fingers itch to text him and find out. Put me out of this disturbing misery. But I can't. I've put myself in such a stupid conundrum, my head throbs against the internal struggle.

I rub the ache in my temples, still staring at the phone. Every time the screen dims, I tap it, bringing it back to life, and hope a notification will pop up.

Why would he reach out to you after what you did?

The nerve in my molar sends a spike of pain down my jaw as I grind my teeth. I don't want him to reach out about us, but I do need the grade for this class. And if he did move away, the teacher would have told me.

Failing would be just as bad as Spencer disclosing all my secrets. I need to get an A in this damn class, and I have no clue how I can do that without him.

"He's already turned in the submission to Mr. Jones."

My attention snaps to the voice, it's soft, but there's a bite in her tone.

It's the girl with the hexagon glasses. Her inky hair brushes against her jaw as she straightens her spine, and I almost think she means to be intimidating. Her oval-shaped face mocks me with its symmetry. Even her lips have the perfect cupid's bow.

Irritation licks at my nerves. Partially because she's a natural beauty that doesn't seem to appreciate it, hiding her tiny body in hideous oversized T-shirts. And also, I can begrudgingly admit because she's spoken with Spencer about our project.

I prop my elbow on the lab table, feigning boredom, and blink slow. "Is that so?"

The small girl scoffs, folding thin arms across her chest. "It is. Not that you even *need* to know. As if you really planned to help."

It's a struggle to keep my face indifferent against the flare of anger coiling deep in my belly. This girl is a friend. A good one, I'm guessing, since she knows about my text to Spencer from that night. It makes me wonder what else she knows.

I flip my hair over my shoulder and drum my fingers on the dingy table. I wait a few seconds before letting my eyes flit back to her. "Was there something else?"

Her eyes narrow, but she shuffles her feet before she answers. "I think what you did was pretty horrible."

My eyes flutter closed before I sigh, turning back to my phone. A good friend indeed. To call me out, even privately, tells me I may need to look into their *relationship* a little more. "Okay, hun."

"Remy," she clips, needing to correct me.

Instead of talking, already having used too many words, I roll my neck and lean back. Thankfully, she gets the hint, turning on her heels and sauntering to the front, leaving an odd energy in her wake. It's unsettling that she knows, but the way her voice wavered just now says she's at least unnerved by me. That's something—means she can be frightened into silence if need be.

But the whole encounter goes to show, Spencer can't keep a secret. Rule two from a contract we once made. The penalty was a punch to the gut, if I recall.

I run my tongue over my top teeth, tugging on my neck-lace until it pinches the skin. My stomach is hollow, and instead of a flutter, it feels like a snake is swirling around the organs, making me nauseous.

I wonder what else he's told her.

Finally, I grab my phone with one hand and massage the knot in my neck with the other. I swallow down the bile and type.

Me: I need a stress reliever.

I don't have to wait long for a response.

Blaze: Say less.

"AGAIN!" I screech across the field, throwing my water bottle on the ground.

We've been at practice too damn long for the counts to still be *this* off. We only have a few minutes before we need to clear out and get ready for the game, and these girls are nowhere near ready. This is exactly why we've already started practicing for regionals. They're fumbling on top of one another, missing beats, and pissing me off with their lack of determination. And if there's one thing I hate more than a clumsy cheerleader, it's a lazy one.

I've lost countless amounts of sleep in order to perfect a routine before. I would eat, sleep, and breathe the damn counts until Blaze forced me to rest, and even then, I was watching videos of practice. I've worked hard, still do. I am proof that no matter what anyone tells you, you can do anything you set your mind to. Not only that, but excel, and be the best there ever was.

Make them envy you. Remember you.

Amora's blue eyes narrow in on me, her chest heaving as

she rallies the girls. "Let's go bitches! Pull your head out of your ass and do it right so we can fucking go!"

There's a chance I may also just be projecting, but I don't really care. The sickness from earlier has yet to subside, and I can't focus. My insides are rolling, and every few minutes, I have to swallow down the bitter bile.

That girl, Remy, could serve as an entirely different issue. First, I'm irritated that I don't know the nature of their relationship. I mean, considering he was about to be balls deep inside of me last week, it can't be too serious. But her knowing what happened means they're close enough that he *trusts* her.

And that bothers me. It grates on my nerves, forcing me to be a little more sensitive than I should.

What makes her so visible when I was anything but?

"Tuck your fucking knees!" I instruct Stacy, tugging my ponytail down for the fifteenth time.

I need to figure out how much she knows about me. Find out just what mini Katherine Johnson might say to the wrong people, given a chance. My wheels begin to turn, just as Amora nails her landing.

"About fucking time!" I ignore the sighs of relief that echo through the girls. "Shower and be ready by six-thirty."

I leave the field, not waiting for them to follow, and barrel into the locker room. I exhale a long breath when I see Blaze leaning against my locker, a white towel dangling from his index finger. His white T-shirt pulls across his chest then pools at his waist, where his own towel is tied. What kind of a guy showers before a game?

My broken little knight, that's who.

Blaze has always had the weirdest quirks, most of which are tied to things he doesn't even let me see. I may get the privilege to read more of him than others, but even I'm limited to specific chapters.

He tilts his head, brows raised. "Coming?"

Nodding, I accept the cotton towel and follow him to the showers—the private one at the end is already steaming. I throw Blaze a grin before stripping down and slipping inside, closing the curtain behind me.

"The party is set." His smooth voice sounds over the crash of water in my ears.

The temperature is perfect, a few degrees before scalding, and it pounds into my muscles, relieving some of the tension from earlier. "I need another favor, B."

I'm met with silence, so I continue. "There's a girl I need to be there. I have a feeling she may know a little too much, and I can't invite her myself."

"Name."

"Remy."

More silence. Only this one feels like a pause, a shift perhaps. I bite the inside of my cheek as I wait. Maybe there're lots of Remys. "I don't know her las—"

"Solace."

My eyebrows shoot into my hairline. "Like Solace University, Solace?"

"The one and only."

Shit. Solace University is a private institution damn near hidden in Emerald Falls Forest on the edge of the city. It's elite and only for the rich and genius. It was my dream school before I realized the magnitude of money you need to go there.

And money is something I don't have. Not anymore. It's tied to my father in Texas, who would love a chance to feel like a father by throwing some at me. Which was reason number one, I dropped the idea of going to Solace and decided to pave my own way.

I sigh, popping open my lavender body wash. If she has ties to Solace University, I definitely can't fuck with her. I'll need another tactic. "Play nice, and make sure she comes."

He lets out a yawn, pulling back the curtain, and dips his head to kiss my cheek. "Anything else?"

"No, thank you, Blaze. Good luck tonight."

"You, too." He pushes his now damp black hair out of his face and replaces the curtain. I chuckle as shrieks and gasps echo through the showers as girls make their way inside.

Closing my eyes, I lean against the cool tile.

The weight of everything is getting heavy, and I begin to wonder what it would be like just to let it go.

I bet I would be able to breathe again.

SEVEN

I don't give a fuck about what happened. Not even a little bit.

Did I expect it? No. Though, in retrospect, I should have felt it somewhere in between her moments of slight hesitation. But with Lily's body melded to mine, and her arms wrapped around me, it was like she *wanted* me, and I let that stupid ass moment melt my guard. It liquified from the heat of her touch, and I fell for it.

Hook.

Line.

And sinker.

Still, I didn't want to risk the slight chance of her getting the best of me in class. So I took a day off. Then it turned into two days, and soon it was a week. I don't regret it. Not seeing her for six days has given me time—to think, plan, and spend it with my mother.

I've been able to take her to a couple of therapy sessions, which is where I am now. Sitting in the hard plastic chair next to her, I scroll on my computer, searching for more ways to test my experiment's hypothesis.

How can different gradient colors affect human behavior and conversation?

My old partner, Maurice, and I already had a plan—script included, though I'm not sure how I'm going to pull it off now. I could ask Remy, I know she would help, but that would be selfish. She has her own project to worry about—even if she won't benefit from the prize.

Solace Scholarship.

Still, the idea of working with my foul blonde partner swirls what little contents are in my guts, making me nauseous.

I huff, closing my laptop with a snap.

"What's wrong, honey?" My mother's voice is the softest I've ever heard. It's like she's in a perpetual confessional and everything needs to be handled delicately. She tugs the pink shawl around her thin shoulders, leaning into me, letting her long gray locks brush over my bicep. "You can tell me."

I spare her a gentle smile and shake my head. Even if my mother wasn't suffering from the onset of dementia, I still wouldn't worry her with such petty drama. She's always had a fragile heart when it came to my happiness. I'm not sure if it's because I'm the miracle baby after fifteen years of infertility or the fact that being a mother at her age makes women a little more sensitive. Either way, I try to wear the mask of contentment well.

Even if it's only for her.

"You can't hide it from me, love. I can see it in the little lines on your sweet face." She closes her big amber eyes and rests into me. "These waves you're fighting against, hold steady, and hold fast. It will pass, my love."

Her words warm my body, swelling my heart, and for a second, I forget about everything else. She is all that matters to me. I don't have *time* to waste with her. Every moment needs to be filled with her love, advice, or even just her presence. Because soon... she won't rememb—

"Mrs. Hanes." A woman in scrubs stands at the door, clasping her clipboard to her chest.

My mother sighs before patting me on the knee twice and stands. I watch her dandelion dress sway at her ankles as she follows the nurse through the hall, leaving me alone in the waiting room.

The door closes behind her, and minutes pass before my eyes slowly drift back to my computer. I have my list of materials for the project, and the only thing left to do is talk to the head custodian about using an old room. The morning custodian says she works the later shift, so I'll need to stay after school sometime next week. Other than that and a few tweaks to the script, all that's left is the research part.

Reopening my computer, I flit through a few more websites, scribbling notes as I go. The color spectrum... how humans perceive light. Color... how our brain transfers data.

Every color affects different living species in multiple ways, each one dependent on other things such as mental health, empathy capacity, and processing abilities. At some point, I even start to make connections with colors and Alzheimer's patients.

My brain sketch with labeled parts is almost complete when my phone vibrates in my pocket. The irrational hope it's Lily sets off a hundred butterflies in my gut, but I instantly stamp them out.

Why the fuck would I want to hear from that horrendous bitch?

Remy: Come to the game with me tonight. Pleaseeeeee.

My eyebrows furrow as I ignore my shoulders' slight deflation and focus on the real surprise here. Remy has *never* gone to a football game.

Me: Why?

I tap the edge of my phone, tempted to call her and see if she's sick. I've seen her almost every day, but knowing her, she's read herself into sleep-deprived ramblings.

Remy: Just come. It would help if you got out.

Does she consider going to the game 'getting out'? Memories of William and I flash through my mind, and I wince at a few. Looking back, more than a few of them are cringe-worthy.

Me: I can't Remy, I have to work on this project. I'm behind as it is.

It's not a complete lie, but I'm definitely using it as a scapegoat. I glance at the time. My mom should almost be done, leaving me enough time to stop by the home improvement store for the LED lights.

My phone vibrates again.

Remy: You can't even work on your project alone. It takes two people. If you come, I'll help with the script.

I squeeze the phone tighter, the light flutter of hope dancing through me. Her offering does relieve some of the guilt I would have had asking. Still, Lily is a cheerleader, so she'll be there, and I don't want to see her if I can help it. *No*, it's not worth it.

Just as I open my messages to text her back, my mother reenters the lobby. Her mouth stretches in a smile as she walks toward me, arms open for a hug. I dutifully oblige, engulfing her in my embrace.

"Good session?" I ask, releasing her.

My mother's eyes sparkle under the fluorescent lighting, instantly rekindling the warmth in my heart. "It was amazing, honey. Now let's get Spencer from school early and get him some ice cream. You know he loves ice cream."

Bile hits the back of my throat, and I struggle to keep it down as my lips stretch into a dull smile. Not only does she think I'm Dad, she thinks I'm Dad from a time they were still together... when everything in my life was perfect.

When I didn't know Lily.

I swallow the burn and nod, my voice barely a whisper as I lead her out of the office doors. "Sounds great."

When these moments happen—the times she forgets who I am... it never gets easier. I thought it would. Maybe I would get used to it and learn to cope. But that's the furthest thing from the truth. It gets harder. It feels impossible to understand how your own mother can look at the son she spent eighteen years raising and not recognize him. No part of me is ingrained deep enough in her mind to help her remember my existence.

It's like losing someone who's still here—mourning their loss, just for them to return from the afterlife before fading away again. Then it happens over and over until you're not sure you can do it another day. But you do. Because the days she remembers... those days are everything.

I feel stuck—lodged in quicksand. I've struggled against it for so long, and now I'm waist-deep. Alone...forgotten. The endgame is clear. Now I just have to decide how fast I want to get there.

After securing her in the passenger seat of her smart coupe, I slip my phone from my pocket.

Maybe just this once; I need to forget for a little while too.

Me: See you at 6.

REMY ROTATES IN THE MIRROR, inspecting her outfit of choice. Jeans I didn't even know she owned hug her wide hips, lifting her ass to a perfect perk. Her small waist is on full display under the tight AC/DC shirt that's slightly ripped and hanging from one shoulder.

Her eyes catch mine in the reflection, and she twists around, a rose blush tinting her cheeks. "I look stupid, don't I?"

I decide not to lie since it's apparent she's stepping out of her comfort zone. The real question, though, is for who?

"Honestly, Remy, you look hot as fuck." I smile, leaning back on her fluffy futon, propping my arm across the back.

Her smile widens, and her cheeks push up, nearly causing her eyes to close. "Thanks, Spence."

My heart stutters. Only one person has ever called me that. Hearing it now from Remy feels... unfamiliar. I clear my throat, shoving the feeling back into the hole it belongs in.

Remy puts her school ID around her neck and shoves on a thin jacket. She tilts her head while looking at me, eyebrows raised, and I notice she's all but bouncing. I stand and move toward the door at a snail's pace.

She purses her lips and narrows her eyes. "Come on already!"

I yawn, stretching as I put my arm around her shoulder. "Let's go. Get this over with."

Remy socks me in the bicep, forcing a laugh from my throat. She threads a hand through her dark hair, her eyes softening.

Being around Remy is easy. It's carefree and smooth sailing, with no drama or secrets lurking in every corner. I once played with the idea of what it would feel like to be with her. Be with someone so unproblematic. But my body doesn't hum with the same high it does with...

No. I shake the disturbing thought away. Fuck her.

We load into my truck and make our way toward the game. The ride is refreshingly pleasant as Remy flips on the radio and immerses me into a full-on private concert. Her infectious laugh fills up the cabin as she struggles to hit the high notes. It melts away the tension of my morning, and for the first time in a week, happiness floats through my body.

We pull up to the stadium, and when I pull into a spot, I pause, turning toward Remy. "So, who's the guy? Am I allowed to know or?"

That same pink tint from earlier paints her face. She shifts, tucking a stray hair behind her ear, and bites into her bottom lip.

"It's fine. You don't have to tell me...now," I joke, turning the ignition off and opening the door. I whip around and open her side, holding my elbow out to support her as she hops out.

We join the large crowd swarming into the stadium. Tonight's game is against our rivals on the east side of the city, and it seems as if all thirty-five hundred students are here.

Remy agrees to find seats while I grab us some hot

chocolate from the concession stand. Luckily, everyone hasn't made it down yet, so the line isn't too long. I pull my hoodie up and scroll on my phone while I wait, reading another article on color, when I hear her name.

"Have you seen Lily?" The frail redhead in front of me huddles close to her friend. Her cheeks are rosy, matching her Rudolf nose.

The friend nods. "Yes, that bitch is so freaking pretty it's sickening. I can't wait till the halftime show. You know it's going to be epic."

My chest tightens, and an ache spreads from the pounding organ.

I don't care about her. Not anymore.

Repeating the short mantra, I bury my attention in my phone, doing the best I can to ignore the girls and the throbbing between my temples. After about fifteen minutes, with our hot chocolate in tow, I find Remy seated next to the band—far from where the cheerleaders are stationed.

The game actually turns out to be a nail-biter. Defense on both sides keeps either from scoring, and the offense can't seem to push through. I notice the way Remy sits up a little straighter when Blaze gets the ball or how she gasps when he gets rocked by the opposing team, but I keep my mouth shut.

When halftime comes, the score is still a big goose egg on both sides.

"I'm going to grab us some nachos." Remy stands and disappears in the flow of people probably doing the same.

I unlock my phone and finish the article I was on. Tonight isn't so bad. The cool fresh air is nice, and the game is pretty entertaining, to say the least. I spread my legs, leaning an elbow on my knee as I open my text thread with

William. He wants to take a road trip to visit, and I know I can't keep putting him off.

His ass misses me, and I'm not sure our FaceTime tutoring sessions are doing much good. The boy has it made with money and doesn't think he needs a fucking brain to run his family's potato distribution company in Idaho.

An announcement echoes through the stadium, and I realize the band is on the field. "And for your halftime entertainment, the Emerald Falls very own reigning Regional Champions, EFH cheer squad."

Everyone in the stands erupts in a furious cheer, rising to their feet as the girls walk across the field.

My heart picks up pace, but I force my eyes back on my phone, staring at the text when the drums begin their percussion. I do well for a few minutes, but then I *feel* her. My nerves light up, and a string of goose bumps trail down my arm even though I'm wearing a damn hoodie.

When I look up, Lily's the first thing I see.

She illuminates the space around her, and everyone else seems to disappear. Her hair whips around in the wind, twirling around her neck and falling between the valley of her breasts. Her hips move to the beat of the band, her arms whirling around, curling around her body, accentuating her curves.

She's half goddess, half hell, and she lights my fucking heart on fire.

Lily's eyes lock with mine, and just like that, every thought I've had, and the resilience I've built over the last six days, disintegrates in her flames.

The air thickens, leaving me struggling to swallow. The knot in my throat grows and soon breathing becomes harder. She keeps my gaze, rolling slower and jutting her ass out more, while like a dipshit, I greedily eat it up. My dick struggles against the zipper of my jeans, and I think if I clench my teeth any tighter, I may crack my molars.

It feels like ripping two strong-ass magnets apart, but I finally break eye contact and head for Remy. A new revelation washes over me, heating my face to a painful temperature.

Why deny it? Whether I want to or not, I do care. Too goddamn much.

And it pisses me the fuck off.

EIGHT

So he can't come to school, but he can come to a football game? Something he's never been interested in before?

The audacity. His ass knew I would be here tonight.

Irritation rolls in my stomach, and I chew the inside of my lip a little too hard, tasting the bitter blood on my tongue.

Tonight's game is packed, and while I have our routine on repeat in my head, it all comes to a stop when I *feel* him set foot in the stands. The fine hairs on my neck stand at attention, and the air blows a little warmer, despite the string of clouds moving in. When I look back, I find him without much effort, sitting next to that Remy girl.

I suck my teeth. Fine, since he wants to come to my turf and ignore my presence entirely, I'll put on a show. It's half-time, and the announcer summons us to the field.

We saunter onto the grass, and I ignore the hundreds of eyes on me, focusing on just one. And the second those amber orbs lock on mine; it's on.

My hips flit to the sound of the drums, soaking up every

ounce of attention he gives me. The attention I should have had over the past five days. I find it intoxicating that despite what I did, he can't seem to break away from me. Maybe that's why he couldn't come to school. Because even though he doesn't want to, he's attracted to me now, and it eats him up that he won't get me.

I'm not sure if it's satisfaction, rage, lust, or a combination of the three, but a tingle radiates through my body before nestling in my pussy, driving my body to pick up the pace. My hands slide down my curves and up again, showing him everything he almost had. Everything that was at the tips of his fingers.

A shiver descends my spine, and even though it's strange how euphoric it feels, I live in the moment. Reveling in the way he lights my body up without even knowing.

Until suddenly, he snaps his eyes closed and walks away. As if he's bored with the view.

The act hits me in the chest, leaving a hole in the dead center, allowing the nip in the air to flush the desire out like being dumped in a cold bath. There's nothing I hate more than becoming invisible and being left behind.

I bite back the burn in my throat and jump into the counts.

Screw him.

AFTER WHAT FEELS like the longest game of the season, I drive home, Lo-Fi flowing through the speakers. It's well past ten, but even in the dark, the low-hanging clouds loom over, ready to spill their belly on the earth below.

I hurry home, parking in the driveway, and run to the

front door, hopeful I make it inside before the downpour starts. But the light pouring out from the front window stops me in my tracks. My heart bottoms out, hitting my hollow stomach, instantly making me nauseous.

She's home. She's never home.

I stare at my keys, considering where I might go. Blaze is probably buried balls deep in somebody, and Amora is most likely just as busy. My eyes flash to the dark house behind mine, but I don't let them linger too long.

Letting out a slow breath, I meander to the front door. Maybe I left the light on while rushing out this morning. It's true my mind hasn't been able to focus in the past couple of weeks.

A violent tremor takes hold of my hand, causing me to drop my keys twice. Finally, I'm able to unlock the door, pushing it open as quietly as possible. If she is here, I might be lucky enough she's passed out, and I can slip into my room.

My face jerks to the right, a sting radiating across my jaw. My hand snaps to the tender spot before I spot her, standing in front of me in a deep red robe. Her dark hair is mussed, and streaks of mascara decorate her flushed cheeks.

"You dumb bitch. Where the fuck have you been?" My mom's voice slices through the air, hitting me square in the chest.

I close the door and push past her. If I can get up to my room and just shut the door, I'll be fine. Two feet is how far I make it before I'm yanked back by my ponytail. Her slurred words ring in my ear. "I asked you a question, you fat little slut."

Maybe if she was ever sober, or better yet even came home, at all, she would remember I cheer. It's like she only remembers the fact when she's telling me I won't make it into Kentucky.

"I was at the game," I say through clenched teeth. My body struggles against the need to slam my fist in her stomach, but I don't want to clean up the vomit she'll inevitably hurl after.

"Yeah, I'm sure you were, pinche puta." She releases me, shoving me against the banister. My hands reach out immediately, grabbing on and using it to propel me up, taking the steps three at a time, ignoring the sloppy slurs she yells behind me.

Running inside my room, I slam the door closed and lock it before pushing my back against it, sliding to the floor. Every part of my body shakes, a dangerous mix of anger and frustration sloshing through my veins like sludge.

I count my breaths, forcing my brain to slow its erratic thoughts. I haven't seen her in over a week—I guess my luck was bound to run out.

Luck. Luck was when I was young, and she stayed cooped up in her room, only coming out to eat. Luck was when we *did* interact, and I only had to endure pops to the back of the head or a belt across the leg. Or when my dad was here to make sure she didn't hit me too hard. I ran out of that luck about five years ago...

Wiping my brow with the back of my hand, I laugh; it's humorless and trickling with the sadness I wish I could let go of but never do. Instead, I always let it fester in my gut until I throw up and wonder when I'll ever be good enough for her.

At last, my tremors start to ease when a flicker of a light grasps my attention.

It's *him.* A sudden wave of calm washes over me, soaking

up the anxiousness and steadying my breath. Pushing to my feet, I move to the window, careful to stand in the shadows of my room so he can't see me.

Spencer's curtains are open, giving me a full view of him pacing his room. He's on the phone, and from the looks of it, thoroughly pissed off. He grabs the hem of his hideous pea-colored sweater before dropping it and threading his hand through dark locks. As he massages the nape of his neck, his eyes suddenly snap to my window, and my heart stops.

I hold my breath, inching closer to the middle of the window. For some reason, I want him to see me—*need* him to. An idea sparks in my mind, and I act fast, scared I may think better of it before I actually do it.

Sliding open the pane, I peek my head through. The air is moist and smells like it's only seconds away from filling with rain.

Slipping onto the sloped roof, I ease myself down on the ledge. The drop isn't but about ten feet—an easy stunt to a frequent flyer. I fall, bending my knees slightly when my feet make contact with the soft ground.

A few quick steps and I am at the large maple tree nestled in the corner of my backyard. It's just to the right of his window, only about five yards away, and I know he can see inside of it. One time when he had the flu, I sat inside and talked through the open window.

I hoist myself up the ladder, nailed to the trunk, my heart thumping against my chest with every step.

A year ago, Amora helped me clean it out and give it a new look. She griped the whole time but ended up loving it. Sometimes we come out here, escape from the day-to-day shit, and just relax. She didn't know it also served as an escape from my mother's occasional...outbursts. The inside is now painted a soft white, with a black abstract poster on one wall. A dark plush rug rests in the middle, and two gray poufs sit near the only window.

Positioning myself in the middle of the rug, I gaze out the glass at Spencer's window. He's still there, leaning against the frame, his arms folded across his chest.

Heat flares low in my belly as I keep my eyes trained on him, leaning back on the furry floor. My pulse races, and my breathing becomes labored, but I don't dare look down. Not yet. I want *him* to be the one to break away like he did at the game. I need to see if he's capable of doing that now.

I pull my tank over my head, exposing my breasts to the chilly air. My nipples pebble instantly, and I move one hand to roll them between my fingers. Spencer shifts and his jaw clenches, the thick vein on his neck makes an appearance, but he doesn't stop staring. In fact, his eyes darken, a forbidden desire rolling in them, turning me on more.

My thighs clench together, the sudden warmth deep in my core igniting a fire in my pussy. I want to plunge my finger inside and put my throbbing clit out of its misery, but I need to put on a show. See how far I can push Spencer Hanes before he cracks.

Trailing my other hand down my bare waist, I stop at the edge of my shorts, my head naturally lulling to the side with the small shocks of pleasure. Curling my finger around the string, I pull it slowly until the bow flops open, allowing my hand to slip inside.

A crash of thunder jolts my body upright as my index finger makes contact with the sensitive bud. I rest on my elbow, watching Spencer's chest rise and fall faster. Biting into my lower lip, I drag my pinky through the slippery folds, moaning at the sensation. I imagine it's his tongue, licking up and down, exploring every crevice, lapping up all the wetness that's just for him.

I slip the shorts from my hips, giving him a full view before sliding my hand back up my thigh. I roll my swollen clit, and a flutter descends in my core, heating my body up just as a string of lightning illuminates the dark sky. Finally, my eyes shut, unable to keep up the charade, and I give in to the burning ache.

My fingers massage the knot, moving faster with each rumble of thunder, hungry for release. An electric surge ransacks my nerves, pulling me deeper into the abyss. Breathing becomes impossible as my body tips over the edge. All I need is one last glimpse...

I gaze at the window and see him leaning against his arm that's resting above his head on the window frame. His hands curl into fists clenched so tight his knuckles are a bright white. He is so incredibly sexy when he's angry.

A burst of stars steals my vision, and my toes curl in, pulling every tendon in my foot. My head snaps back as the orgasm rips through my body, threatening to kill me with it. Every muscle clenches in unison, squeezing and releasing until finally, they relax entirely.

I fall back onto the rug, my eyes finding Spencer's window as I catch my breath. He's still standing in the same spot, his hooded eyes burning into me with a fury that lights my body up all over again.

My lips curl into a smirk, and as if on cue, he turns, disappearing into his room. Moments later, darkness swallows it, leaving me alone as rain breaks open the sky.

I won. But what, I'm not quite sure.

And for a moment, I wonder what I may have just started.

NINE

"Fuck her!" My voice echoes in the empty alley, bouncing off the brick and punching me in the gut. I bare my teeth and hurl the trash bag inside the bin, kicking the metal dumpster as the lid falls. "Fuck. Her!"

It's been incredibly slow at the smoothie shop, leaving me too much time to think about last night. To think about Lily's arched back, open mouth, completely lost in pleasure. Her body moved to a tempo only she could hear, but fuck me if I didn't try to find it. She had me on a leash, forcing me to watch all the things I wanted to do to her myself.

I couldn't stop staring. As much as I wanted to claw my fucking eyeballs out, I couldn't stop. It felt like I was a passenger in my own body, banging against the door, trying to get out, but no matter how hard I fought, I couldn't look away.

In retrospect, I bet that was her exact intention—make me pay for leaving our staring contest at the game. But really, what did she expect after what she'd done?

Handcuffing me to a bed, making me out to be some perverted sicko.

Even now, her endgame is unclear. This new Lily is uncharted territory, and I'm at a loss of how to navigate around her. The only apparent thing is that she wants my attention and sealed lips.

She wants *control.*

Something neither of us had as kids. Something I damn sure *still* don't have.

Whatever her fucked-up reason, I'm done being a pawn in this dumbass game of hers. My hand twitches at my side, eager to text William and tell him to pay me a visit. It would be so easy to revert back to the Spencer that got everything he wanted with just a smile. Then I could show Lily how the game is *really* played.

Hold fast, hold steady.

My mother's soft voice appears from nowhere, settling into my raging blood, cooling it instantly. It's a gentle reminder that getting caught up in this game will just cost more of my time. And that's something I don't have.

Lily will soon get bored, just like most juvenile bullies, and things will go back to normal. I only need to wait it out.

I trudge back inside to Remy. Only about an hour left, and I can go home, crawl in bed, and pretend like that shit didn't happen. Well, I can try, at least, while staying as far away from my window as possible. Maybe see if my mom is down to watch a movie.

Remy leans against the opposite side of the counter, tracing a line in her book as she reads. I've thought about telling her what happened, but she'd more than likely give me an earful I don't need. Tell me it's my fault for even letting her fool me—that I should have known better, which I *should* have.

Irritation swirls in my sternum, and I scrub my hands over my face, huffing through my nose. I take off my glasses for the third time to clean them. The cooling effect of my mother's mantra wears off as images of Lily flit through my head.

Every muscle I have tightens, knotting up as I replay Lily's orgasm. She was biting into her bottom lip as if it felt good, but her eyebrows were pinched as if she was in pain. Like something was ripping her in two. I held my breath with her, watching her unravel at the seams. She was so fucking beautiful in that moment. And as much as I hate to admit it, I was starving, and I enjoyed eating up everything she gave me. Even craved more after the fact.

I loathe how she can make me want her.

Fuck. *Her*.

Squeezing my eyes closed, I pinch the bridge of my nose, repeating my new motto. When I peer down my nose at Remy, I realize she's still tracing the same line. Like she's reading it, but her mind is somewhere else entirely, forcing her to reread it. "You good over there?"

I'm hopeful she can occupy my thoughts for the rest of our shift. Hell, I'll even listen to her drone on about her romance story if I have to—anything to feel something other than the conflict curling in my blood.

"Let's go to the Halloween party this weekend."

"What?" My face contorts. "Since when do you want to go out?"

I've only known Remy the past few months, but sharing the majority of our classes, as well as working with each other, has given me a pretty good look at her habits. She's an introvert through and through. A good girl, wrapped in a book, cuddled on the couch night after night. She prefers the fictional characters to her classmates and daydreams about them more than she'll admit.

Her face blooms pink, and she twists a loose hair back into her low ponytail. "I just want to enjoy senior year a little bit. Is that such a crime, Spencer?"

I scoff, misplaced frustration seeping from my pores before I can stop it. "It is when you're doing it for someone else and not yourself. Be real, Remy. Who's the guy? Are they worth losing yourself over?" Because no one is worth losing who you are.

Stop.

She opens and clamps her mouth shut twice, her eyebrows knitting together so tight they almost touch. "Okay, you inept jerk. I'm not changing for anybody. I just want to have some fun. What crawled up your butt and died?"

I can't stop the irritation from boiling over in my stomach. Why does everyone feel the need to change? And not only that, but lie about it, when it can't be any more obvious?

"Remy, I've known you long enough and seen the shit in your closet to know better than to believe the lie you're pushing. What's next? Dye your hair blonde? Start wearing heels to school?"

You're being a fucking asshole. Stop.

But I can't. The words ooze from my mouth like a toxin, ready to claim any victim in the vicinity. Then I remember a brief moment at school when Blaze said something to her as he passed by. I didn't think enough of it to ask, but now, things are making more sense. "Let me guess. Blaze? Is that who it is?"

Her sad eyes widen, confirming my accusation and a

wave of anger I've never felt before surges through, consuming me in its power. *Blaze*. He's Lily's right hand—has been since eighth grade, I hear. He's probably the reason Lily is the way she is. And now he wants to take Remy away too?

Fuck that.

"He doesn't like you. Whatever shit he's spitting, it's because he wants to dive in your pussy and claim another notch on his belt. Not because he actually wants something with you. Are you really that stupid?"

Remy's eyes shine under a wall of tears, and I immediately deflate. She rips the apron off her waist and throws it at me, twisting on her heels. "Close up by yourself tonight. And when you're ready to apologize for projecting your anger, you know where to find me."

I stumble around the corner, her name caught in my throat. A panic ensues, trapping me from saying what I need to.

Fuck.

I didn't mean to. *I'm sorry.*

Don't leave me too.

The door slams behind her, halting my pursuit, leaving me with the void of her absence. It wraps around me, whispering just what I am.

A fucking dick.

I HAVE to ring the bell twice with my foot before I hear a rustling behind the door. Steadying the pile of books in my arms, I peer to the side when Remy opens it. It's noon on a Sunday, but from the looks of it, I woke her up. Her dark hair is in disarray, matted to one side and flat on the other. Bags highlight both eyes she is currently rubbing, adjusting to the outside light.

Pajamas hang loosely on her tiny frame, and I breathe easy for the first time since last night before our fight.

There's my Remy.

She finally takes in the massive pile I'm balancing and gasps. "You bought everything on my to-be-read list? That's like two dozen books!"

"Twenty-eight," I correct.

"Oh my gosh, Spencer. I would have accepted just a verbal apology."

I twist my hips, pretending I'm going to walk off. "So you don't want them?"

Her hands jerk out, grabbing half the stack before I even have a chance to move a muscle. "I didn't say that. Come in."

A smile takes up my entire face, relief washing over me.

Trailing behind her, I notice the house is darker than usual. The entryway curtains are drawn, drowning the bright foyer in shadows. The open kitchen and living room are the same.

She reads my face and juts her chin out toward the back of the living room. "My dad's home. Don't worry. He can sleep through a freight train, but not light."

I nod, and follow her up the stairs, still consciously making an effort to keep my steps quiet. We enter her pink room, and she immediately starts sorting the books on her bed, humming to herself as she reads the backs. She bounces on her heels, and for a second, I wish I could pilfer some of that happiness. Bottle it up and take it with me.

"Not going to brush your teeth first?" I joke, falling into my usual place on the bubblegum futon.

Remy turns, narrowing her eyes. Lifting my hands in

surrender, I chuckle. I'm just glad she's receptive. I lean forward on my knees, tilting my head, and leveling my voice. "I really am sorry about last night."

She rotates back to her book, grabbing a few and placing them on the shelf. "I know. And whenever you're ready to tell me what happened—what *really* happened, I'm here."

I sigh, nodding as I rest my head back, relaxing for the first time in what feels like forever.

Remy finishes sorting a few minutes later and goes to grab us popcorn. She puts on Sleepy Hollow and curls up next to me, a happy glow radiating from her body. Little does she know it, but in the few months since I've met her, she's saved me.

It wouldn't hurt to return the favor. "So this Halloween party. You really wanna go?"

She nods, hugging a pillow to her chest. Her eyes peer up at me from her long lashes, and she smiles.

"Are you going to dress, you know slu—" The pillow she was holding connects with my face. "Alright, alright, we'll go."

She giggles, snatching the pillow and falling back into it. "I mean, even though you basically have to at this point, thank you, Spencer."

I grin, leaning into the futon. Even though my entire life is upside down, and danger literally lives in my backyard, I'm content. I feel at peace. I just hope it carries over tomorrow.

THE NEXT DAY, Lily doesn't show up to class, even though, according to Remy, she was at school.

It doesn't bother me. In fact, it's the perfect break. I'm not sure I'd be able to be in the same room with her after all the shit that's happened over the past few weeks.

But when she doesn't come the next day, annoyance pricks at my skin. I know I can do the project on my own; hell, I prefer it. But it's inconsiderate of her, especially since she supposedly needs the grade.

Wednesday comes and passes, and still, she doesn't come. I find myself getting irritable at the slightest inconvenience. *Why am I letting her get under my skin?* It shouldn't even matter.

This is ridiculous. It's Thursday, and I'm damn near done with the research part. I have a lot of things to draw out and label, but I need to start collecting data. Tomorrow I meet with the head custodian after school, and after that, I have to start the actual experiment.

I guess I may have to ask Remy after all.

Friday. Five days. It makes sense now. She's pulling the same shit I did last week. How fucking childish. Even so, I find it in me to tamp down the anger brewing under my skin and make it through the day. She can't *not* come forever after all.

When the dismissal bell rings, the campus clears out pretty fast. I assume everyone left to get ready for the game tonight or pregame. Maybe both. That is one part of Idaho I miss. William and I, drunk, out in a field with a flock of other people. There was no light pollution, so the stars scattered across the black sky were incredibly bright. We didn't have a care in the world.

In those rare moments, I didn't have to think. I could just surrender to the intoxicating bliss and beauty of the world. And for two seconds, it didn't feel like it was out to crush me.

I pass by an open window on my way to the second floor.

The field is full of football players running drills and the band marking time. I avert my eyes when I see the cheerleaders emerging from the locker room. No point in making my day worse by accidentally seeing *her.*

After walking all the way to the back, near the access elevator, I find the custodial manager's office and knock on the door. After a few moments, an older woman opens it. Her chestnut hair lays back in a tight bun, and though her amber eyes are sunken slightly, they have a familiarity I place in a matter of seconds.

"Mrs. Conley?"

I remember meeting her once, by pure accident. It was sixth-grade summer, a couple of years after her dad bolted, and we basically lived in the treehouse when I came to visit. We had run out of popcorn, and I went back inside to get some. I almost pissed myself when I saw her poking around the pantry because I thought someone had broken into the kitchen, until she turned around, a warm smile on her face. She introduced herself, and we briefly talked while I waited on the microwave to finish our snack. The last thing I recall was how sad I was walking back outside. How I had just talked to Lily's mom longer than Lily probably had her whole life. Even worse was she was really fucking nice.

"Spencer! Look at you! Oh, dios mío, look at how much you've grown." Lily's mother swings her brittle arms around my neck, and I haphazardly hug her back, surprised she even remembers me. "Mi hija didn't tell me you were back."

That statement confused me. *Why would she?* Not because Lily and I are estranged, but because Lily never talked to her mom. Then it hits me. I bet the woman doesn't even realize I know that. It strikes a feeling of pity for Lily that I quickly blow out. Fuck her.

Releasing her, I run a hand through my hair, and stop to massage the base of my neck. I shift on my feet, not sure what to say, and instead ask what I'm really curious about. "I didn't know you worked here. I would have come and said hi before."

She waves a brittle hand around. "Honestly, querido, I try to keep it a secret just as much as Liliana. Only working while the kids are gone, staying to myself. This life," she pauses, and I'm surprised by her forwardness. She shakes her head as if recollecting her thoughts, a brown tendril falling from her bun. Looking at her now, it's crazy how much she looks like the Liliana I knew...

"Anyway, you wanted to see me about a room?"

TEN

Sitting on the barstool, I stroke the half-empty green bottle in front of me. My black stiletto nail trails down the long skinny neck, stopping at the label before it drifts up again. It's almost as if the shape is purposeful—warning those of its contents, reminding them to drink it in small doses.

My mom doesn't know I saw her pour it in her coffee cup. But I did.

I always do.

Just because she fails to see me doesn't mean I don't notice every little part about her. I observe her any chance I get—which isn't often considering she *lives* full time with her boyfriend downtown. She only comes back periodically, and even that is too often.

Lucky for me, though, it is her morning drink of choice. I couldn't find it in the stash of good alcohol she hides here, and I didn't want to dish out fifty bucks for it.

The truth serum I need for Remy tonight.

Absinthe.

My mom staggers through the kitchen, her long sundress struggling to keep up behind her. For a brief moment, I wonder how she stays warm in the frigid October air, but then she turns, and the hint of pink on her cheeks reminds me. Her veins bleed liquor.

"House looks good, mija."

My face shifts, wincing at the phrase. I hate when she talks about the house, and even more so when she uses that term of endearment like she *actually* cares about me.

Mom hasn't given two shits about me since she took her first drink of hard vodka—probably ever, if I'm honest. And every single time she got wasted, she tore up this house, leaving me to clean it until it shined, hence her shitty comment. But by my eighth-grade year, she met a guy and moved out, leaving less to clean.

At first, it hurt to be left by both parents—forgotten, and thrown to the side as a mistake of their past. But eventually, that hurt turned into something else. Something tragic and twisted, coiling in the dark part of my soul, marring it with its ugliness.

I can guarantee that's exactly what my mom wanted. It's like she has some vendetta, and for the life of me, I can't figure out why. All I know is that she wants me to fail at life, just like she has.

But I've worked too hard to let that happen.

She stumbles over her sandals before holding on to the doorframe and opening the pantry. Her ugly brown eyes widen, probably at all the extra food for the party tonight.

My dad has bills and grocery money sent to an account for me. I never touch anything outside of what I need—

partially because I don't want to give him the satisfaction of thinking money can replace him being present. And also because every now and then, my *sweet* mother blackmails me when her funds get a little low. Says if I want her to stay out of sight of the school body, I need to make it worthwhile.

Which is total bullshit. She doesn't want anyone to see her just as much as I don't, but I entertain her for now. Only a few more months and my whole childhood will become a bad memory. And memories can be forgotten.

"Your father sent extra this time around, huh? How is he anyway?"

"Thriving," I lie. Honestly, I don't know. My dad hasn't called in a couple of months. He lives somewhere in Texas, flipping houses like hotcakes. After my mom's affair during my fourth-grade year, he left and only visits every now and then. Really, I think it's to check on his property more than it is to see me.

I swallow around the cotton ball lodged in my throat. Fortunately, I've been so busy I haven't allowed myself much time to think about him. Trying to ignore the sudden tightness in my chest she's caused, I fold my hands together and glare at my mother.

She grimaces, tucking her peppered gray hair behind an ear.

Guess the custodial position and blackmail money only pays for her habit and shitty apartment.

Leaning against the island, I prop my head in my hand, staring out the open window into my backyard. My eyes flash to *his* window, and my stomach flips, filling with an anxiousness similar to a couple of weeks ago.

Spencer will probably come with the girl tonight. Or

maybe not considering what happened last time he came over. Still, I can't tamp down the few butterflies that take flight at the chance he might.

"He still hasn't sent you money? What about cheer? Don't you need funds for that?" My mom's grating words slice down my spine.

I shouldn't be surprised, but it still stings. It's always about the money. She thinks he sends it sparingly, or else I'd be paying her rent. So anytime she comes home, she wants to know if my arrangement with my dad is any different.

Blinking back the burn in the corner of my eyelids, I return to tracing the liquor bottle's shape. "He has everything on autopay. I never see a cent."

It's hard to keep my voice steady, and I hate the way her mouth pulls into a lopsided grin. It's like she knows she's getting under my skin.

"Why are you here?" I'm careful not to snap since I'm not quite sure how drunk she is.

My mom tilts her face. "I can't swing by and make sure you're okay? I am your mother, and this is my house."

"Used to be," I counter. "Dad's name is on the deed, and after high school, it's mine."

I cross my arms and frown. *Just a few months left.*

Her eyes cut into me, darkening with a storm surging through them. "Aren't you trying to go to some cheer school? What do you need with a house?"

After a beat, she throws her head back and cackles. It bounces against the walls, echoing in the open living room before carving into my eardrums. I open my mouth to respond, but she cuts me off, downing the rest of her drink as she comes around the island. "Oh, you couldn't make the cut could you, chica estupida. Not so different from your mother, after all."

My lips pull back in a snarl, jaw ticking as I grind my teeth together. "I am *nothing* like you."

The cup she's holding connects with my face, the cheap glass shattering on impact. I grab my cheek, pain radiating across the spot as a warm liquid seeps between my fingers.

"You can act big and bad like you have cojones, *mija*, but the truth is, you're weak. And soon enough, when all these people see you for what you *really* are—what you bury deep inside, they won't want you either." She pauses, letting her words burrow in my skin like poison. "Soon, you won't be shit, and everyone will forget you. That boy included."

Her silhouette is fuzzy under the haze of my blurry vision, but I hear her keys jingle and the door slam behind her.

I crumple to the bright linoleum tile, gripping around my waist as a sob rips through my chest, shredding what little strength I had left. My heart thunks violently in my sternum, and even my hand pressed against it doesn't feel like enough to keep it inside.

Checking my reflection in the sliding back door, I make out a short, vivid crimson line just below my eye. My leg jerks out, kicking a barstool into the glass. The muscles in my body quiver as heat and realization wash through me.

She's right, after all.

I was weak the night my father left and agreed when he asked me if I could stay with my mother, knowing how much I didn't want to.

I was weak the day I told Spencer not to move to Emerald Falls.

I *am* weak because I'm letting his return threaten everything I've worked for.

My mother's poison is so deeply embedded that even with all my credentials, it's not enough. *I'm* not enough. It's making my mask of strength weak, and the edges are becoming fragile.

And the person that can crack it completely is thirty yards away.

"WHAT THE HELL DID YOU DO?"

Shit.

After my mother left, I sat in the glass too long, throwing myself a little pity party, and now Amora's in my foyer, watching me wipe up blood.

Being the child of an abuser, you pick up the natural ability to lie and cover it up rather quickly. So when I look up at Amora, with paper towels clutched in my hands, the lie comes out as easy as breathing.

"Trying to get this damn liquor from the top shelf, and the step stool slipped from under me."

She grimaces, bending down to help me with the rest. "I swear, for the best damn *tumbler* on this side of Washington, you sure are clumsy."

I laugh from my nose, using the counter to balance me. When I told Amora about the counselor, she almost had an aneurysm.

"You know that bitch is just mad because she couldn't make the squad back in her day. I don't need a damn guidance counselor, so just say the word. I will march in her raggedy office, and I will herkie jump her face."

"Thank you, Amora. Think you could help with the cut?"

I'm used to covering up bruises, but my experiences with cuts is still pretty limited. Usually, Blaze helps me, but it's too late since Amora is already here. Luckily though, it's superficial, and the only reason it bled so heavily was from the location—under my right eye where the skin is thin. The hour of ice while I sat on the floor helped but it's tender as hell and partially swollen.

"Duh, bitch. Let me grab my stuff. Meet me in your bathroom."

A few hours later and I feel much better about my appearance. It's still a little noticeable, but only if you're right next to me and looking directly at the spot.

Amora grabs the last bit of gel she needs and combs it through my ends. The tips of her pink and blue pigtails swing back and forth as she shakes her head. "Broke up with John."

I lift my eyebrows, a silent 'oh yeah?'

"Yep. Maybe I'll try Blaze this time," she suggests, watching me in the mirror as I smear lipstick on the side of my mouth.

There's no need for a response. I've told the girl too many times that even her nonchalant attitude won't work on Blaze. His tastes are preferred. But still, she can't help herself.

I check my reflection one last time. The green dye sticking my hair back, and the yellow bralette doing wonders for my boobs should serve as a distraction from any lingering facial puffiness.

My muscles relax as I straighten my spine, smoothing the lapels on my glittery purple jacket. I turn on my heels and leave without a second glance.

Amora follows me out of the bathroom, and we emerge

from the stairs to Blaze resting against the kitchen island. His school jersey hugs him in all the right places, and I see Amora stiffen in my periphery.

I can convince Blaze to do lots of things, but committing to a Halloween costume isn't one of them—a football player is as good as it gets. He tips his chin slightly, raking a hand through his dark locks, before returning his steel gaze to the TV.

Behind him, everything is set up. Kegs, red Solo cups, at least five varieties of liquor and juice, some nachos for those that dare to eat—all lined up and ready to start the night. Amora even had some girls on the squad hang up Halloween lights on the back patio.

The doorbell rings before I get a chance to ask him if our cocktail for our special guest is finished. My eyes trail behind Amora as she prances to the door, her pigtails and tiny skirt bouncing in tune to her step.

It's the football team in attire like Blaze's, followed closely behind by my cheerleaders donning Sailor Moon outfits. Soon after that, bodies fill the entire downstairs and trickle into the backyard.

Music hums through the house, and for a moment, I find myself enjoying it. This afternoon's incident long forgotten and the words of my mother drowning in its melody. My pulse hums in my veins, and I grab on to Amora's hand, leading her to an open spot in the living room. Our bodies melt together as we move, hips rolling in tempo.

Warmth spreads across my chest, and the growing crowd of onlookers fills me with deep-seated satisfaction. My eyes flutter closed, lost to the beat thrumming through my veins, but when they open, everything stops. Everyone in the room seems to blur as one person comes into focus.

My breath catches in my throat.

He's here.

I knew he would be, but to see him, to *feel* him sets my once calm pulse into a frenzy. Even with the muddled conflict that surrounds him and me, every part of my body trembles, aching to go toward him. The fine hairs on my arm stand as I take him in.

An emerald green shirt pulls across his broad chest, and a pair of dark khakis hang from his hips. The tee has short sleeves, leaving his corded arms exposed and my stomach clenching. If it wasn't for Remy, I almost wouldn't know what his costume is.

Next to him is the literal real-life version of Velma. Her knee-length skirt is pleated to perfection, matching the hideous Mary Jane shoes. Surprisingly, her orange turtle neck hugs curves I wasn't aware she had, making her a tad sexier than the cartoon character. Still, she's bumped her short black hair and attached a red ribbon for good measure, sending her sex-odometer to a solid two.

My eyes flit to Blaze, standing in the kitchen. His eyes are trained on the poor girl, and I don't miss the way his chest heaves a little deeper. I vaguely wonder if he feels bad about our plan but quickly dismiss it.

Blaze has no conscience. Well, maybe he's not entirely void of one, but it sure isn't as prevalent as the average person.

As if he can feel me, his gaze finds mine, and he nods, sending a tingle through my hands.

Tonight, I find out what the girl knows, while also freeing myself from the outlandish tie my body still seems to have to Spencer.

Tonight, I set the course to once and for all forget the boy that's been the root of my torment.

Of all my deepest fantasies.

Of my existence.

It's time to finally dig up the weeds in my garden and see if there's anything left behind.

ELEVEN

The air is thick and moist, which is fucking disgusting. Even taking a breath requires effort with the hoard of bodies stuffed in Lily's house.

Lily.

Agreeing to come was hard enough, but if I'd known it was at her house, I would have said no. Yet here I am, wearing the last-minute outfit Remy was able to put together, squeezing between a half-naked siren and her victim of choice. It may not be too bad, and hopefully, I make it through without running into *trouble*.

The sounds coming from the speakers reverberate around the house, coursing through my body, changing up the rhythm of my heart. Smiles, drunk laughter, and low eyes appear on every face in view.

We make it three feet before I see her.

Everything freezes on impact—the music, the people moving around, and her body. It's as if time slows to a complete stop, giving me time to *see* her. She's dressed—and I use that word loosely—as the joker. An insanely reflective purple jacket hangs off one of her tan shoulders while she moves to the beat. Her stomach is fully exposed as she only has on a lacey yellow bra that pushes up her breasts so high, they nearly kiss her collarbone.

And her shorts. Her fucking torn shorts stop right below her pussy, and my mind replays the moment I first saw it. Pink, swollen, and dripping between her fingers.

She's twisting around as if she's the only one in the room.

Moving her hips to the beat with the melody circling her, letting her hands drape above her head. It's sensual as fuck, and no matter how much I despise her ass, I can't stop looking.

My dick pushes against my pants, and I bite into my lip —eager to feel something other than the painful arousal ripping through my lower body. For two seconds I hold a firm grip, then her eyes collide with mine.

Fuck.

Heat radiates across my cheeks after I snap my face away, finally breaking the connection.

"Are you okay?" Remy tugs at my sleeve, forcing my attention to her.

I swallow around the lump in my throat and nod even though I hate lying. "Sure, but I'm going to head to the bathroom really quick."

She keeps my gaze, tilting her head as if to make sure I'm being honest. I ignore the drops of sweat beading at my temples and shrug. "Get us a drink?"

She huffs, but releases me, glancing toward the kitchen. "Fine, but hurry up."

Nodding again, I detach from her side, moving straight for the stairs on our right.

Lily's house, like all the others in our subdivision, is

pretty big. But even with the forty-five hundred square feet and dozens of bodies now between us, I can feel her as though she's right next to me. My nerves tingle, sending waves of frustration through my veins.

Not one piece of me should care. And yet, my body, more pointedly my dick, could give two shits what I think. Every fucking time I am in her vicinity, all I want to do is move closer. The constant disconnect between my mind and body feels as if they're literally going to rip me in half.

How fucked up is that?

I sigh and run a hand through my hair, tugging at the ends as I take the steps two at a time.

My heart slams against my chest when I make it to the top. The door to her bedroom sits to the left of the landing. Just a few weeks ago, it was the room I never thought I'd set foot in again, and now, looking at it, I feel sick.

I clamp down on my bottom lip again.

Fuck her.

Turning toward the bathroom, the hairs on the back of my neck stand. I don't even have to turn back to know she's there. "What?"

She giggles that same syrupy laugh that curdles my insides. "Well, that's kinda rude. Considering you're in *my* house and all."

Don't turn around.

Trying my best to ignore her, I take a few long strides to the restroom door. Lily swings in front of me, pressing her back into it, cutting my quick escape. In one hand, she has a red cup, while the other curls around the doorknob. "Here, let me open this for you."

My eyes automatically flash down, unable to look at her this close up. I clench my jaw, failing miserably at not grinding my molars. She doesn't smell like roses tonight. Instead, it's the scent I remember from when we grew up. A special lavender cream she uses for a light patch of eczema on her ankles. It made her skin so soft, she used it everywhere.

It makes my heart flutter a little faster, pissing me off.

She waits, not moving for a solid minute before finally opening the door, and stepping aside.

I slide past her, careful not to connect with her body, and walk to the toilet. When I glance up, she's still standing on the threshold, watching me with her head resting against the doorframe.

"Did you want to hold it?" I snap.

She scoffs, "Sorry, I don't have any tweezers with me."

My eyes roll back so far they hurt. "Can you just get out?"

The reason I came up here in the first place was to get a break from her, yet here she is, suffocating me with her presence.

Lily thrusts herself off the frame, stepping inside, and closes the door with her black boot. "I'm pretty comfortable, actually."

Running my teeth along the inside of my lower lip, I consider my next move. I could play this stupid ass fucking game or just ignore her. Hope she goes away. But curiosity gets the best of me.

"What do you want, Lily?"

She pauses, her eyes narrowing. "For you to keep your mouth shut."

She says it simply, almost matter-of-factly, like I should know this already. Irritation flickers in my veins, making my right eye twitch twice. "About what? What the fuck do you think I know?"

"Everything." It's a whisper.

I sigh, running a hand through my hair.

What happened to her?

The question sticks to the underside of my tongue, unable to push it up and spill out.

"Okay, I won't say anything. I'll keep your pretty little name out of my mouth. It tastes like shit, anyway."

She grins, but there isn't any humor in it. Taking two more steps, she's right next to me—if I take a deep enough breath, my chest will touch hers.

My breath falters, and hers stops completely.

Heat swirls between us, and I'm not even sure at this point if it's from disdain or something else... something impossible.

"There's another thing," she utters, quieter than before.

"Enlighten me, so I can fucking pee in peace."

Her gaze flits to my lips, and my dick twitches in response. After a second, she blinks twice, and lets her eyes slowly come back up to mine. For a moment, she almost looks like Liliana. "I want you to stay away from me."

My brows draw together, a little surprised. "I don't think I follow."

"I don't want us to have any contact besides the project."

She pauses, closing her eyes. When they open, and the contacts settle back over the irises, whatever I thought I saw, is gone. She grips my chin and almost snarls. "Or I'll let the school know you like to sneak into girls' rooms and handcuff yourself to their bed naked like some sick pervert."

I recoil, jerking my head to the side.

Even though I want to grab her by the fucking throat and rail her against the sink—force her to watch herself unravel around my dick and see how *sick* I can be, I don't. Instead, I ball my fists and shove them into my pocket. She doesn't deserve the orgasm, and I sure as fuck don't deserve the heartache that would inevitably follow.

She's silent, and though I'm not looking at her, I can feel her eyes search my face, scorching a path as they go. A second more, and she backs away, scoffing. "Don't worry, Spencer. I don't plan to ever touch you again. The first time was enough. It made me so ill, I couldn't eat for days."

I ignore the rock that caves in my chest with her words and snatch the cup from her hands. In two gulps, the hot, sweet licorice substance burns my insides on the way down. "I thought you looked a little hotter."

It's a subtle jab, but I know it hits its mark when a light gasp escapes her mouth.

Satisfaction rolls down my back, relieving a little tension as I leave her in the bathroom, returning to Remy downstairs.

The music is a little louder than before, and the light feeling from just seconds ago dies with the sight of Remy. She has her back to me, facing a pair of monochromatic eyes.

My spine stiffens when he hands her two drinks, jutting his chin toward the patio. I don't know Blaze, but with a best friend like Lily, he can't be good news.

I move through the small crowd, avoiding any chance encounters with as many sweaty bodies as possible. But by the time I reach her, Blaze is gone, and Remy's face is the color of a fresh tomato.

"What did he want?" I gesture toward the backyard.

Remy shakes her head and somehow flushes a darker shade of red.

"Just said it was n-nice to see-ee me."

My brows knit together at her slurred speech. I open my mouth to ask her what the hell that's about, but instead of words, laughter seeps out. It's a chuckle at first, bouncing my chest, but then it deepens, lowering into my gut. I laugh so hard my shoulders begin to shake.

What the fuck? *Stop laughing.*

But I can't. And now, neither can Remy. Her hand shoots to my chest, gripping it to stabilize herself against her dry heaves. We must look like complete psychos, but we keep laughing until our voices crack and cheeks start to hurt.

I smack my lips together, suddenly aware of the cotton-mouth I have. "We got to get a drink, Rem."

Her mouth drops open, handing me two red cups she manifests out of the air. "Ha! I like that."

We cheer to her new name and take our drinks in a few large gulps. The same sweet licorice taste from earlier flows down my throat. Remy lowers her voice to a whisper, letting her eyes dart around frantically. "Like a rem job."

Another laugh erupts from deep in my core. "It's call—"

A pair of nails rake up my back, searing the skin beneath as if there's no fabric to protect me.

Do I have a shirt on?

"For someone so smart, you're dumb as fuck. It's a r-i-m job, you idiot." Amora's voice cuts through the air, but it misses Remy completely.

Instead, we both look at each other and crack up into more chortling. I think Remy even snorts, which only pushes us further into our hysterics. Finally, under a little control, Remy's eyes widen, her hands curling around her stomach. "I ha-have to p-pee."

Amora steps into view, and I jerk back, bumping into a squealing sexy mail woman. I hadn't even realized she was still standing there, and seeing her now in her Harley Quinn outfit is kind of...sexy?

She's a pretty girl—tall, and slightly curvy in all the right places, with the clearest set of light blue eyes I've ever seen. But she's also a raging sarcastic bitch, who has fucked half the student body from what I hear.

"Bathroom downstairs has a line. Take the stairs. First door on the left."

On the left? That's not where it's at. *Is it?*

I'm not sure. *What was I doing before this? Oh shit. My shirt.*

Placing my cup on the counter, my hands rove over my upper body. I feel the soft cotton under my fingertips and sigh. *How weird would that have been*?

It is hot, though. Like, make-sense-why-a-guy-would-take-off-his-shirt-in-the-middle-of-a-party hot. I lift the bottom and wipe my forehead.

Why is it so fucking hot? Where is Remy again?

I can't seem to focus on a singular thought, and the giggle bug that bit me left when Remy did. So I concentrate on that. I just saw her. She said she needed something.

Was it a drink?

No.

Something about the patio, maybe... my arm tingles. It almost reminds me of that time William had me try Molly....

"Lily wants to know if you still want to fuck her."

My face snaps to the sound, shredding my concentration. Amora is still standing near me, leaning against the island, twirling a blue-tinted pigtail around her finger.

Lily.

I don't like her. She's not the same as she used to be. I miss Liliana.

A strange pain stretches across my chest, and I clutch at it, suddenly finding it harder to breathe.

Why is it so fucking hot?

"She wants to know."

"Do I want to have sex with her? I doubt that," I bite out. "Why?"

Amora laughs, pushing off the counter and moving into my personal bubble. She's too close, uncomfortably so, but I can't move. My feet feel like they weigh a thousand damn pounds. Her lips graze against the shell of my ear.

"She wants you to fuck her until she can't remember who she is."

I recoil, and my body tenses. All my blood courses south, leaving little for my head, which now feels incredibly light. Dizzy, even.

As if on cue, Lily appears, a red cup in one hand, and the sexiest fucking grin on her mouth. She hops on top of the counter, crossing her legs, and dangles a foot toward me. "Hey, Spence. How you feeling?"

Her voice is soft, smooth, and drives right into my core. Images of her laid out on the black rug, lost in the abyss, pass through my muddled thoughts. I wanted to jump through my fucking window and climb into that tree so goddamn bad. Every inch of me burned under the fire she started. And I liked it.

Why do I feel like I'm not supposed to like it?

"I'm hot," I manage to utter.

Her smile grows, somehow warming me more. It's not the sneer I'm used to. It reminds me of when she was my Liliana, making the second time I've seen it tonight. It's almost like she's still in there—somewhere under all the makeup, fake lashes, and contacts.

"Just take your shirt off, Spencer. Half of everyone here is naked." Lily waves a hand around before gripping her necklace, pulling it back and forth. "Nobody will care."

My eyes find themselves wandering, detached from what I'm telling them to do, and exploring the sight before them. They survey her exposed tan skin. It looks so smooth, like when you take the lid off a fresh carton of ice cream. *Velvety.*

I want to lick the dip between her breasts. See if they taste how I always imagined.

Then maybe after that—my eyes slip farther down her waist—see what her pussy tastes like.

There's a little bell going off somewhere. It's the smallest chime I've ever heard, but it sounds closer to me than Liliana.

I do want to fuck her.

I am going to fuck her.

As if she can see the revelation cross my face, she giggles. It's so light, infectious...real.

It's been so long since I've heard it, and suddenly I find myself wondering what I need to do to hear it again.

As her laugh subsides, she tilts her head down, her eyes barely visible through narrow slits.

"Kiss her boot." My head moves toward Amora's voice, but my eyes belong to Lily. I can't look away.

Fuck, it's so hot in here.

"Kiss it, and you can have her," she finishes.

I clench my jaw, and I vaguely hear something crack. Part of me thinks I must have misheard her, but then Lily juts out her foot, shaking the loose black boot at me.

I squeeze my eyes closed. *Focus.*

There is no way in hell I'm putting my mouth on this girl's goddamn boot.

Shaking my head and taking a few more rattled breaths, I open my eyes. They connect with brown ones I haven't seen in over five years, stealing my words from me before I can think twice.

"Okay."

TWELVE

It's funny how predictable people are. How they naturally crave things, and once you figure out what it is, they're putty in your hands. They'll do anything to get it, and by whatever means.

For Spencer, it's the new and improved Lily.

Back then, I was *boring, just something to do, nothing.* At least, that's what I recall him saying about me. But now, he sees I'm not that weak little girl anymore, fawning after him anytime he spoke. Or maybe it's because I'm hot, and the temptation of having something you can't is too strong to ignore. Either way, I don't care.

He's going to do it. He's going to kiss my boot. And maybe with a little luck, the strong-ass alcohol, plus the sprinkle of something extra Blaze added, will coax him to do more than just put his lips on it.

He tugs at the hem of his shirt, his caramel eyes never leaving mine. He's still thinking about it, weighing the pros and cons, but never once does he look at the people around him. It's like he doesn't know anyone else is here.

A strange combination of guilt and satisfaction swirl in my stomach. It's like baking the sweetest cake in the world and then devouring it in one sitting.

Two small drops of sweat roll down his temples, and no matter the number of times he wipes them away, they reappear. Finally, he yanks his shirt off, and my core clenches.

His entire chest is glistening like he ran two miles. All eight of his abs are on full display, and even a few passing girls stop and admire what I'm sure is an equally impressive back. I have to stop my eyes from rolling.

Spencer may look good, but inside he's just as ugly as me.

I lift my foot, leveling it with his chest, and he grabs it accordingly, wrapping his fingers around my calf. My skin burns under his touch, searing it like a hot poker. It feels foreboding. Like if I let this happen, there's no coming back. I'll be left with a scar.

But I think I crossed that line a long time ago.

Ignoring the searing pain, I tip my toe out, watching as his eyes darken and flit to my boot. His chest rises higher and falls deeper, and I imagine him standing at the edge of a cliff, weighing what the fall might do. He edges closer, and if I move an inch, it will happen.

Amora clears her throat, and when I snap my gaze to hers, those big blue eyes widen—waiting for the cue. I simply nod and cast my attention back to Spencer.

Out of my periphery, Amora signals the cheer squad. Within seconds, the football team and others crowd around, watching. Hoots and hollers break through the crowd—some egging him on, others saying how disgusting he is. But still, he doesn't seem to notice them. Spencer looks at me one last time sending a wave of nausea rolling through my stomach.

I shouldn't do this.

"Will, just shut up. She's nothing—no one to me. Just a summer friend that makes my summer suck a little less. Now lay off."

I blink the memory away and smile at Spencer, the same smile I use to get whatever I want, and it works. His lips touch my boot, and the herd behind him goes wild.

Different slurs ring through the air, but he doesn't regard them. Instead, his grip around my calf tightens, like the smooth patent leather is the sweetest thing he's ever tasted. His tongue sweeps out, licking the sides in a way that burns my cheeks. It's not like he's licking a spoon. No, this is different.

It's carnivorous, and for a second, I wonder what he's seeing. What he *thinks* he is actually doing.

His tongue swirls around, and he even sucks up the loose string, pulling it through his teeth with a growl. As sick as it is, my pussy quivers at the sight, lighting my nerves up in that region.

I clench my thighs together and snatch my foot away. "That's enough, you revolting dog, I think you cleaned all the shit off. Now get out of my house."

I press the tip of my boot right above his collarbone and shove him back, laughing when his ass hits the wood floor and his glasses clatter beside him.

The surrounding people jump back, screaming with laughter that finally wakes him up. His eyes flash to me, brows knit together, and then... he smiles.

A wide grin, that makes his dimples deepen profoundly.

It sets off a chain reaction in my stomach and if it weren't for the dozens of spectators, would have caused me to blush, maybe even smile back.

Spencer grabs his glasses, placing them on his face as though nothing out of the ordinary happened, and stands. His muscles flex with the movement, and even with the disgusting comments thrown his way, every girl I can see stops and ogles his frame.

I fist my necklace, pulling it so hard, I know it will leave marks if it doesn't cut through the delicate skin first, and watch him.

He slips his thumb across his bottom lip before turning, leaving through the door without saying a word.

I suck in air and realize I've been holding my breath. Everyone is still standing near me, crowding my space as though waiting for me to say something—announce something.

But I don't. That's not the MO I'm known for. Instead, I hop off the counter and find Blaze's steel eyes in the crowd. I tug on his jersey, and he follows.

We take the stairs at my pace, which is slow—the weight of everything finally pushing down on my shoulders, making it taxing even to move. My plan was to make him keep childhood secrets.

But truthfully, it was something else.

Something I can't admit. Not even to myself in the privacy of my own thoughts.

My phone jolts in my bra, vibrating across my chest.

I pull it out, wondering if it's him, but instead I frown. It's an unknown number that's called me almost every day this week. They don't leave a message or text me back when I ask who it is, so I assume it's spam.

We reach the landing just as I press ignore, shoving my phone in my jacket. Turning toward Blaze, I try to read his face. His beautiful eyes are low as if he's tired, and his lips are clamped together in a thin line. But nothing out of the ordinary suggesting he disapproves of my prior and current actions.

Suddenly those eyes narrow and I freeze.

Shit.

He moves in closer, grabbing my chin with his finger and thumb, adjusting my head to look at the wounded side. After a beat, the nerve in his jaw tics. "When did this happen?"

"Today."

"And you didn't call me because?"

I sigh, more guilt piling on what's already pulling me down. "Amora walked in when I was cleaning up."

He clenches his teeth. "Where is the woman now?"

Blaze is the only one that knows the truth behind my scars. Not too long after I met him in eighth grade, I lied about one my mother left on my arm. Told him the same thing I tell everyone else—a mark from a cheer incident when it was really a bruise from the end of a broom. But that's the thing about abused children. They can spot the lie in a heartbeat.

He came over later unannounced, barging into my house as though it was his, with a metal bat in tow. That's when he found out I live alone, and that same night, he learned my mother lives almost an hour away. Ever since then, he's taken care of the aftermath of her random visits.

"She's gone," I answer, softly moving my face from his grasp.

His chest heaves with his sigh before he nods. "Well, Amora didn't clean it well. I'll do it after the party, so it doesn't get infected."

My lips turn up just slightly, and I nod to the door. "Ready?"

"When you are."

I swallow around the lump in my throat. Even if Remy doesn't know anything about my secrets today doesn't mean Spencer won't decide to spill his guts tomorrow, and I'll be back to square one. The thought makes me realize the real reason I want to talk to her so badly. The whisper in the back of my head, I want to shut up once and for all. Shit, how far the mighty have fallen.

Hopefully she's too drunk to even remember this.

Running a hand through my green ends, I yank, forcing myself to calm down, and open the door.

Remy stands near my desk, in almost the exact spot Spencer stood a few weeks ago. Her face is buried in a psychology book about managing the effects of childhood traumas. When she notices us, her eyes widen. "I-I'm sorry. I came up here for the b-bathroom, but came in the wrong room. Then I saw this b-book."

I nod, walking over to my night table and flip on the lamp. "Got some daddy issues you need help with?"

Remy ignores my comment, her gaze stays on Blaze, who's still standing at the door. He's leaning against the frame, his large arms folded across his chest, but he's looking at me.

There's something floating in the air. Something tingling, yet suffocating, and I can't quite put my finger on it. He may be uncomfortable because of who she is, and considering he's going to Solace after graduation, this is a delicate situation.

Even so, I need to know if Spencer has told her anything.

"I'm sorry I'm in your room-m. I can leave now." She puts the book back on my desk and wraps her arms around her middle. Remy's face blooms a bright pink, and finally, her hazel eyes find me.

I grin, waving my hand as though dismissing her comment and flop down at the end of my bed. "That's not a problem at all, Remy. I'm actually glad we ran into you. Stay."

She stiffens, wiping her nose as her eyes bounce between Blaze and me. "I don't-t want to i-interrupt."

My brows draw together. "You're not. I don't recall you having a," I pause, not wanting to offend her.

"A stutter-r?" Her hands wrap around her core tighter. "It only manifests when I'm extremely stress-ed. Or—"

"Drunk," Blaze cuts in. He's observing her intently now, almost as if he's watching her mannerisms to commit to memory. Remy's blush deepens, and I almost worry it's from lack of air.

"So you and Spencer?" I cut to the chase. I'm mentally exhausted now and want to get this over with.

I massage the muscles in my right shoulder, tilting my head when I hit the worst knot. I don't want her to feel like it's an interrogation, so I try to keep my face neutral, focusing on the ache radiating across the blade.

"N-no no. Nothing like that. We're f-friends. Co-workers too."

Hmm. Spencer works?

I vaguely wonder why either of them needs jobs with their parents' financial status. Spencer's dad is a doctor, and Remy's owns a university.

"So you spend a lot of intimate time together?" I finally look at her directly in the eyes. I ignore the burn in my chest and the lack of moisture in my mouth. "Share a lot of things with each other?"

An odd sort of chortle shakes her body as she looks at Blaze again. She's fidgeting now, gripping the hem of her orange sweater and straightening her posture.

I huff inwardly. *Of course*. Who doesn't have a crush on Blaze?

Remy swallows hard, eyes fixed on a spot on my bedspread. "No. Not r-really. I mean, I tell him loads of things, and we talk about-t school stuff all the time. But we aren't intimate."

I grace her with a sympathetic smile. She doesn't know anything. The irrational jealousy I had dissipates but leaves an unwelcome warmth in my chest.

"Blaze is going to take you home now." I stand, walking toward my door. The girl doesn't respond and instead stares at him, eyes as big as golf balls.

I stop when I reach my friend, placing a hand on his still folded arms. "Take my car."

He nods, leaning forward to kiss my cheek. "I'll be back soon and fix your eye."

When I look back, it's not to look at the girl, but at the dark house in my backyard. The light in Spencer's room flickers to life, and I can't help but wonder.

Do I really want to win this game of chess?

Is it worth what I'll lose?

In the end, it is, because you can't lose what you never had.

THIRTEEN

I spend my entire Sunday in bed, with the worst hangover of my life. Back in Idaho, I drank my fair share with William, but this is fucking hell on steroids. Whatever I had was poison wrapped in a bow. My entire body aches, and every time I move, the tendons quiver as if they're about to tear. The headache pulsing between my temples has been going nonstop, making sleep damn near impossible. And the amount of times I've thrown up now is pretty concerning.

Leaning over the bed, I take the aspirin my dad so graciously left on my side table with a heaping dose of a lecture. Afterward, he told me not to bother my mother and let her rest. And while I feel like shit, a hole expands in my chest at not being able to see the one person who can make me feel better. Mom makes the best fucking soup, and I know talking to her would ease some of this pain echoing in my sternum. She'd tell me that everyone does dumb shit when they're fucked up and then make me wash my mouth out again for licking a boot.

I don't remember it at all, but that didn't stop the videos and pictures that found their way back to me. Remy has a social media presence to keep up with all the popular authors she likes to read, but on her feed this morning, there I was.

Half-naked, damn near on my knees, licking Lily's boot like it was a fucking ice cream cone.

When I squeeze my eyes closed, I see it. When I look at my hands or my chest, I see it. She's somehow ingrained herself into everything, and I begin to wonder if I'll ever get rid of her.

If I'll ever be able to forget her.

My head squeezes around the thought, and I groan, pulling a pillow over my face.

What the fuck am I going to do?

I could always expose her, embarrass her the way she's hell-bent on doing to me. But I don't want to start more shit or stoop that low. Whatever fucking tantrum she's having will pass, and soon enough, she'll find someone else to bother.

A vibration grabs my attention. It's Remy, calling for the seventh time. I sigh and answer, tapping the speakerphone button and putting it a foot away from my face.

"What's up, Remy?"

"I'm pretty sure this is what death is. This is what it feels like when he's at your door, fiddling with your strings, wondering which one to cut." Her voice is low, hoarse, and I can feel her sickness in my stomach.

I pinch the bridge of my nose and close my eyes. "Yeah. I think that's exactly what this is. At least you're not the school's new mascot."

Emerald High's bootlicking bulldog. That's the hashtag circulating with the evidence I'm a dumbass.

She huffs. "I'm really sorry for asking you to go. I kinda feel like some of this is my fault. I led you right to her."

"No, don't even worry about it. She was going to do something like this sooner or later. I'm sure of it. She's the fucking worst."

We sit on the phone quietly for a minute. And when I think she may have fallen asleep, she yawns. "Is this going to last all day?"

I smile. "Probably."

She groans, and I can hear her shifting in her bed. The noise makes me suddenly nauseous, and I burp. It tastes like rancid fire.

Fucking hell.

"I have an idea about how to deal with Lily. I need to take a nap, though, and I'll call you later tonight."

A soft knock at my door causes me to jolt upright. My head spins, and the room follows suit, already blurry without my glasses. I clench the sheets, steadying my breath before I hear another knock and Remy's faraway voice. "You there?"

"Yeah," I huff out. "Call me later."

She hangs up, and my gaze stays trained on the door. Dad's at the office, so it must be Mom. I wanted to see her, but I also feel like shit. If she sees me like this, she may think I've reverted back to my ways in Idaho. I don't think I can stomach her disappointment today. Still, I call her in.

"Come in," I mutter, and it's only after I say it that I realize how soft my words are.

Even so, the door opens slowly, and my mother stands in

the frame. The hall light behind her illuminates her head in a beautiful glow, making her look like the angel she truly is. She's dressed in a delicate cream sweater and green forest trousers. Her neck is decorated in a string of pearls, which is always a good sign—it means she had the energy to get dressed.

Relief courses through me, even in my hazy state. "Good morning, Mom."

My mother smiles and moves inside, carefully sitting at the edge of my bed. She crosses her legs, and her hand finds my shin. Back and forth, she rubs, quietly waiting for me to lay back down.

The sensation makes my eyes heavy—something about a mother's touch that soothes even the worst pain and lets you relax.

I fall back on my pillow and rest my head to the side so I can still see her.

"Rough night, honey?" Her voice is the sweetest thing I've ever heard, like in the movies where a princess sings to wild animals.

She's taken care of William and me on more than one occasion, and each time never a hint of judgment in her actions. Only advice. Good as shit advice that I never want to listen to because it always circles back to her thinking I'm heartbroken.

"How are *you* feeling, Mom?"

My mother sighs, her soft eyes lighting up with her smile. "I didn't feel so hot this morning, but after some medicine and a good breakfast, I feel much better."

I close my eyes, embracing the lightness in my chest. I know her condition can't be reversed, but when she's able to turn her day around before an episode, it gives me hope.

Hope that maybe she'll hold on. Remember me a little longer.

Love me… a little longer.

"Honey, your heart. I can feel it from here. It's aching. I thought moving back here might help, but I have this dreadful feeling it's only made it worse."

I can hear the sadness in her voice, and it drives me fucking crazy. My already pulsing head quivers when I shake it, desperate for her to know that *nothing* that's happening is her fault.

"Don't move." She squeezes my leg briefly before standing, rounding the bed, and sitting behind me. Her soft hand connects with my back, and she begins rubbing in circles. "I just wanted to tell you that no matter what is going on, I need you to remember to hold fast and hold steady. You are all that is good in this world, and no matter what tries to deter you from that, don't forget you're mom's sweet boy. Always, *always*, stay true to who you are."

I swallow around the lump in my throat and don't try to blink away the burn radiating behind my eyes. Instead, I close them completely, leaning into her touch.

Within minutes my consciousness ebbs, giving way to a surprisingly peaceful sleep.

THE BELL RINGS, and there's still no sign of Lily. Part of me feels light, hopeful she's switched classes, and Saturday night was the end of my misery. But then a familiar tingle descends my spine, and the she-devil herself swings the door open.

I bite the inside of my lip to keep from smiling—she dressed the exact opposite of how I see her like she's *pure*. Her oversized white sweater drapes over one shoulder and hangs over incredibly tight bleached skinny jeans. Her nude heels are too fucking high for class, but nothing surprises me with her anymore.

When she sits down, I have to temper a gag from the overbearing rose perfume encroaching on my lungs. It feels like thick poison, flowing down my esophagus, tainting my airways so I'll never be able to breathe anything but her.

"Well, I'm glad you decided to show up today." She slams a notebook on the lab table and shifts her body to face me. In my periphery, she curls a long blonde strand around a finger as she waits.

It's hard to ignore the heat of her body—it's mixing with the rage that runs through mine, leaving the air stifling.

Instead of responding right away, I clench my teeth, knowing we still need to get the project done. I hope I can strike the deal Remy came up with. I may not know this new Lily, but I know what used to get my Liliana's interest. Maybe some of her is under the mask, deep inside, but somewhere that I can still reach.

Peering at her from the corner of my eye, I shoot my shot. "Can I offer you something?"

"Oh, he speaks?"

My face snaps to look at her fully. Her makeup is thick today—it flakes a little at the corner of her eyes, which seem impossibly darker under the contacts. For a moment, I forget my train of thought, how angry I am, and an unhealthy dose of curiosity takes control.

What made you this way?

"Are you picturing me naked?" It's only a whisper, but it

snaps the thin thread, releasing the anger to flush back through my veins—eradicating the rare moment.

I tilt my head, letting a lopsided grin bring out my right dimple. Her breath catches, and my smile widens, noting the tiniest increase in her breathing. "No, but are you picturing me licking that little cunt of yours the way I did your boot?"

Her lips twitch, and a beautiful sneer takes over. "You can't lie to me, Spence. You ate up every helping I gave you." She dips lower, her mouth a few inches from mine. Her eyes linger on my lips, and I hold my breath, scared if I breathe too deep, we'll touch. "Do you *want* to lick it like you did my boot?"

My body stiffens, and my dick swells in my sweatpants, allowing her to see that she can still fucking affect me.

She tips her head back, a hideous cackle erupting from her lips. Ignoring all the stares around her, she invades my space again, swallowing the air I breathe out. "I'm only kidding. I would let you die of thirst before I let you drink from this pussy, *dog*."

Heat coats my face, and my nostrils flare. I'm tired of her smart-ass mouth, and for a second, I picture myself wrapping my hand around her throat so she can't talk anymore.

Fuck. Her.

She sucks her teeth and leans back, twirling her hair as if this was just some ordinary conversation. Like she didn't just fucking rip my gonads off and squish them under her heel. "Now, what's the offer?"

I spit the words out quickly, rage coating each one with spikes. "Don't come back to class. Make up something about your cheer schedule, or whatever the fuck you want, but don't come back. You do that, and you'll only have to help me with the experiment part. We meet once a week for six weeks, read a simple script, and go our separate ways. Back to our lives where everything was great, and we didn't remember the other was even alive."

Her eyes narrow, but it's the only change to her cocky demeanor. She examines her cuticles as if she can't be bothered anymore. "Fine."

My head jerks back, and a weird combo of relief and trepidation coil around my nerve endings, making my voice an octave higher. "Fine?"

Lily shifts, her gaze flashing to Remy before returning to her long-ass white nails. "Yeah. I have better things to do than waste time here, doing nothing. Just text me a time and location."

"Great," I respond, nodding to Remy, who's been looking back occasionally.

"Great."

FOURTEEN

"That's a pretty dope deal if you ask me. Free period to do whatever the hell you want and still get the grade?" Amora sits next to me on the bench in the locker room.

I'm not a thousand percent sure how I feel about this deal I've just agreed to. But I am pretty relieved he's still letting me work with him. I hadn't given the aftereffects much thought, and even though Spencer isn't the type to snitch, he could have pulled out on being my partner.

"Yep." I pop the p, braiding my hair to the side.

Amora stops fiddling with her socks and glances up at me. She's gotten a lot of sun lately, making the little brown freckles on her nose more apparent, and when she wiggles it, I bite back a laugh.

"Or maybe he doesn't give a shit." She shrugs.

This gives me pause.

All the horrid shit I've done thus far has been child's play because of the very tiny piece of me that still holds some regard to the guy he used to be. If he doesn't care, that means one of two things. One, he really does, and he's doing a good job suffering in silence. Or two, his replacement of me, Remy, is doing a good job helping him through it.

My stomach hardens, and my throat tightens—my mother's voice stabbing into my thoughts. Or perhaps, he really doesn't care because I mean nothing.

The revelation burrows into my heart like a poisonous barb, piercing through the soft muscle with ease. I clutch at the phantom pain, but it's too late. Each beat pushes the toxin further into my bloodstream until I see red.

I mean *nothing*?

Fine.

I can show him just how much *nothing* can mean to someone.

"Are you going to be late to practice again or what?" Stacy's grating voice draws my attention, but as always, I don't have to say a word. I'm glad for it because in my current state, I might shove the end of my heel through her eye.

"And if she is? You'll wait like the good little bitch you are." Amora snaps, standing up and sidestepping in front of me. "On your knees, ready to gobble up whatever scraps we feed you."

Stacy's a junior, and she's next in line to be captain after we graduate. I always tell myself that's the reason Amora has it out for her—make Stacy's skin thicker. But I have noticed Amora's snark is a little spicier after she found out Blaze has slept with her.

Stacy scoffs, tossing red hair over her shoulder. Her face flushes pink, but she keeps her voice impressively level. "I'm not rushing you. I was just wondering what to tell the gir—"

Amora's mouth pops open, a sarcastic cackle erupting from her throat. "I don't give a fuck what you tell them. You seem to be the only one that has a problem when we're two seconds late."

I massage my temples, the throb of annoyance slowly creeping in. Standing up, I grab my water and find Stacy's dim tawny eyes. Taking two steps, I stop right in front of her —my frame enclosing her space, reveling in the way she shivers, unable to look at me. "We'll be there when you see us."

She swallows and moves to the side.

Amora giggles, and I hear her steps bounce behind me. "Respect, bitch. Every mutt needs to know its place. If not, I can always teach you a new trick."

I roll my eyes and walk to my locker. Stuffing my clothes inside, I wait until Stacy has left the locker room. "New trick?"

Amora saddles up next to me, leaning on the locker. "Yeah. I got a few pictures of her I wouldn't mind posting around the school. Knock her off that horse she managed to find herself on."

My eyebrows draw together. "Pictures?"

"In some compromising positions, I might add. I think I'll blur her face out in each one, leaving just a piece of it clear. Let people put the puzzle together. Make it funnier."

I huff, turning to put the rest of my things inside the metal box, but my phone rings. It's that damn unknown number again.

"Who is it?"

"No idea. They never leave a message or respond to texts."

Amora holds a thin hand out. "Let me answer, tell them to fuck off."

Shaking my head, I push the green button and put it on speaker. "Hello?"

"L-na. I have tr-g t-ch its- y-ue." Every word is broken up by static and shitty service.

"I think they know you." Amora sighs.

"Maybe." I hit end and chuck the phone in with the rest of my clothes. "Let's go."

When we get to the field, only Stacy seems huffy that we are forty-five seconds late. And I can't lie, the majority of the afternoon is spent running the girls in the ground, since the one person I really want to is out of reach... for today.

It feels good to release some of the frustration. The more the girls fuck up, the tougher I get, and it works out in our favor. By the end, the routines are almost perfect, and a few tears of joy are even shed. We're close, and my chest swells when I think that in a few short months, we'll be reigning champs yet again—sealing my deal with Kentucky.

Almost.

After practice, I check my phone. Just a few social notifications and another missed call from the unknown number. Right as I begin to slip it into my bag, it buzzes.

Bulldog: Tomorrow, 3:20. There's a small door next to the service elevator by the upstairs art room. Don't be late.

A soft smile snakes across my face

Oh, I'll be late, and he'll wait.

I'll make sure of that.

FIFTEEN

It's 3:47.

Of course, she's fucking late. I mean, why wouldn't she be?

Annoyance licks my spine, making my nerves dance and my legs shake. I stroke a finger on the side of my phone, debating the best course of action.

There's always the option to leave and just ask Remy to help, or I could text Lily and ask where the fuck she is.

It's hard to admit—brutal if I'm being honest, but a piece of me didn't want to ask Remy in the first place because I actually *wanted* to work with Lily. I think some small, insane part thought that maybe I could get her alone and see what happened to my friend. My once *best* friend.

Closure. It's a hell of a thing. Without it, you keep it on your back, letting it weigh you down, making moving on to new things near impossible. And I want to move on. So, I'll wait. But only for three more minutes. After that, I'll bow out and just ask Remy.

Leaning back, my eyes drift around the small room. I

couldn't have picked a better space. It used to be a room to keep irate students who needed to blow off some steam or used as a holding cell until cops or parents showed up, but they haven't needed it in years. What's left is a six by six room, with one desk and two chairs. The walls were already white, so when I hooked up the LED rope lights, it lit the room with ease.

Today's color is blue.

It's meant to bring feelings of tranquility, peace, and productivity, but depending on the person's state, it can also invoke sadness or loneliness.

I'm tempted to turn it on now, see if it actually calms me down, but I want to stay true to the experiment. An experiment that looks like it's not even happening today.

3:50

Fuck her.

Giving up, I grab my backpack and swing it over my shoulder. But when I reach for the door handle, it turns, opening to Lily on the other side.

My heart jolts—fucking jolts, slamming into my chest. Her blonde hair is pulled into a messy bun, leaving her neck exposed, and my thoughts go the wrong damn way. Her black long sleeve dress has a little hole at the top, where a tiny button keeps everything together.

"Where are you going?" she bites. "I'm only a couple of minutes late."

"Thirty minutes late, Lily. I have shit to do." Rolling my eyes, I back up and let her walk in.

She sits down where I was, hanging her bag on the back of the chair, and props her elbows on the desk. "Okay, well, I also thought about locking you in here but decided to spare the custodian having to clean up the piss you'd leave in the corner."

A metallic taste hits my tongue before I realize I've bitten through my cheek. "While I'm happy you decided against it, I have places to go, so—"

"Ugh, I'm kidding. I got held up. Since you didn't see me today in class, that means I'm holding up my end of the deal. You need to do the same."

Mr. Jones is a strange man, who always seems to have his head glued to his computer, not to mention he's easy to get one over on, so I wasn't surprised when she didn't show. Lucky for her, when he takes attendance, he just asks if anyone is missing.

Lily tilts her head to the side, examining her nails like she always does when she won't make eye contact with me.

"Fine." I toss a piece of paper across the table and yank my chair out as far away from the desk as possible—which isn't enough in this small ass room.

She peers down at the table over her hands but doesn't move to touch it. Her eyes scan over the lines, and finally, she looks up. "A script? For what?"

It's hard to stop my eyes from rolling or the irritation that flutters through me, making my hands twitch. Of course, she doesn't know shit about the project. She's never even asked.

"I'm going to start the timer, and we sit in silence for three minutes, then we read. That's all you really need to know."

Her lips pull into a straight line, and just when I think she's going to be a smart-ass, she nods.

I take out the small remote from my backpack, turn the LED lights on to blue, and flip the room's switch off. When my eyes adjust to the new color, I pull out my script as well as a notepad and pencil.

3:55

"Okay, I'm starting the timer now." I keep my voice calm, trying to eradicate any form of emotion.

She doesn't respond, tempting me to steal a glance, but I don't. Instead, I focus on my phone, watching the numbers tick down.

The air around us thickens like it always does, and even forcing my breaths to become steady is hard. There's been some type of shift, a palpable change, and it permeates the air, pulsing between us. Lily repositions in her seat a few times, letting me know she feels it too.

After what feels like a fucking eternity, the timer sounds, and my eyes lift to her.

She's watching me—observing me as if *I'm* the fucking experiment. Looking back at the paper, I start the script. "Hey."

"Hey." Her voice is low, breathy, and my dick twitches defiantly.

"How was your day?" I continue reading.

This question is open-ended. If the person describes a shitty day without getting worked up, the blue is effectively altering how they perceived it. But it could also enhance feelings of sadness, cause them to be more emotional.

"Busy. Full of catching up on work and filling out college paperwork. How was your day?" Her tone remains impassive, and I bite back the need to veer off track, ask her what college she decided on.

When we were kids, there were no other options. We loved Washington and wanted to go to Solace. But I bet grown-up Lily has other plans now. I ignore the heavy weight on my chest and continue. "It was fine. Found out I have a shit ton of tests the rest of this week, so there's that. How are you feeling?"

She sighs deeply, and the little button keeping her chest covered nearly gives. I swallow around the memory of her in the treehouse, trying to sneak into my thoughts.

"Okay. How are you feeling?"

"Tired," I say truthfully. There's so much shit I'm tired of that it's hard to keep my eyes open anymore. The same stuff I used to tell Lily, and she would somehow make me a little *less* tired. She was the shot of espresso that kept me going. "If you could do anything right now, what would you do?"

Lily tilts her head, and her eyes narrow slightly. Her gaze slips from my face and drops down, slowly as though she's already telling me with her eyes. When she looks back up, she bites into her lip, letting her words become heady. "You."

My jaw clenches as every last drop of blood travels south.

I wasn't born yesterday, and I'm not stupid. Liliana used to want to be a psychologist, so what she's doing right now is pretty fucking obvious. She wants a response. There's a part of her that needs to know I still care.

But that's something she's not getting. She can take my little standing social status, reputation and even make my dick hard as hell. But she can't have the power of knowing my heart doesn't beat the same when she's not around.

As fucked as *that* shit sounds, there's too much history, too many memories that Lily owns for me to forget—even with her lashing out.

Still, every time I see Lily, I realize how that girl I loved—the one I was willing to leave my mother in Idaho for, isn't there anymore, and a piece of my heart returns to me.

My chest heaves. "I would sleep."

Lily grimaces, fiddling with her bun, before looking back down at the paper. The last part of the script instructs us to say anything extra we're feeling. It's an optional part but will give me insight if the colors compel us to say anything.

The room is still, quiet—not even our breaths are audible as I wait. Finally, she looks up. "I don't have anything else. Do you?"

"Not a thing." The words rush out.

She stands, yanking her purse from the chair, and walks toward the door. She stops when she opens it, turning slightly. "Nothing I've done bothers you?"

Yes. "No."

The tip of her smile is barely visible before she disappears, leaving the echo of her heels behind her.

THE REST of my week is jam-packed—so much so that the whispers, stares, and slurs that follow me go completely unnoticed. Remy is the one who points them out the next day at lunch.

"Are you okay, Spencer?" She's twirling her spaghetti with one hand and tracing the spine of her newest book with the other. The oversized sweater hangs down around her wrist, and every time I think it's going to dip into the sauce, she shifts.

"Great, why?"

"I mean..." She pauses and turns to look behind her.

Following her gaze, it's apparent people are staring at us. A group of football players are gawking the most obvious, and instead of looking away, they laugh, passing elbow jabs.

"Have you seen Lily's social?"

"You know I haven't." The response is a little sharper than I mean it to be, but she knows I don't look at that shit.

Remy stops swirling her pasta and digs out her phone. After pressing a couple of buttons, she turns her phone toward me, giving me a full view of Lily's Instagram. It's nothing I haven't seen before—the picture of me licking her boot, but it's the caption that curdles the lunch in my stomach.

I will be leasing Emerald Fall's favorite bootlicking bulldog and his services to a closet near you. Stay tuned for details on rates!

The response from the first time this went around wasn't so bad. Hell, Remy told me some of the girls even wanted me to lick their pussy like that, but now, Lily's labeling me nothing more than a piece of property to be loaned out.

A searing heat washes over me, scalding my skin. I scan the cafeteria for her, and like a fucking magnet, my eyes find her quick. She's perched on a barstool near the windows, a smirk painted on her face.

My Liliana is dead. Has been since our seventh grade summer. Whoever this is, is a fucking bitch I wouldn't even let suck my dick.

Whatever fucked-up game this is, she can have it. Nothing is worth losing who you are.

Fine. Lily wins.

I'm done.

"Pretty sure I lost my appetite, Remy."

She nods and pushes her glasses back, gathering up her items.

"You don't have to come with me." Dumping my tray, I turn to walk back to her before stumbling over something.

My face hits the linoleum with a loud pop, and a sharp

pain rings across my face, threatening to rip my eardrums open. A warm fluid drips on the hand I tried to use to catch my fall.

Everything is out of focus, but I can hear the jeers echoing just fine. A red splotched Nike kicks me to the side, and a vaguely familiar voice rings out. "Ay yo, Lily. Your bitch bled on my fresh ass Nikes. That should be a free service for him to lick it off."

I'm on my feet before she can respond, and my fist connects with the blurry figure in front of me. He staggers back, and I thrust forward, a left hook catching his jaw. The crack is audible, but I don't give a fuck.

Staying with him as he steps back, I land two more jabs into his soft muscle before three strong arms wrap around me. The more I struggle against the restraint, the tighter they hold, yanking my arms behind me.

"Mr. Tilman! Back away from Mr. Hanes right this second!" It's the assistant principal, but her voice is too far away. She won't make it before he gets a few licks in.

And fuck does he.

The first one hits the side of my stomach. My muscles clench just before impact, making the pain worse, letting it radiate across my core. The second one is an uppercut to the direct center, shoving all the contents to the back of my throat and spewing out of my mouth without a fight.

Whoever was holding me drops me immediately, letting me fall to the ground. A crowd of hazy faces backs away as well, screaming about the stench.

When the AP reaches me, an all too familiar tightness pulls across my chest. The same one I got every time I was in trouble at school. Every time I knew my mom would come and have to listen to the teacher tell them how utterly disappointing I was—a waste of a good brain.

Hold fast, hold steady. Don't let anyone make you forget who you are—my sweet boy.

Yeah... Lily won alright.

SIXTEEN

For the first time in forever, I stay home the entire weekend, confined to the four corners of my room, chugging coffee like it's water. Deadlines are approaching, and these essays won't write themselves.

Unfortunately, cheer is not recognized as a sport, and a full-ride isn't guaranteed. My GPA is going to help, along with winning regionals, but I still need to apply for more scholarships.

Dad refuses to pay for Kentucky, saying I have a spot waiting at Solace, but I don't want anything handed to me. When people give you something, they in turn hold power over you—the ability to either take it away on a whim or hold it over your head.

So instead, I've worked my ass off to get it paid for by myself—a big middle finger to the parents who probably won't even notice. But I'm proud of myself regardless. I may have started cheer for the wrong reasons—cover some bruises, become the hot chick Spencer wouldn't ignore, and maybe grab some of my mother's attention. But in the end, it gave me a reason to keep getting up every day. There were girls who needed me, and I couldn't let them down.

A flicker of white draws my attention to my window. Pulling my blanket around my shoulders a little tighter, I stand, edging toward the sight.

Snow.

The first of the season. Flurries of white dance in the sky on their way down, spinning around one another before breaking off and finding new partners to twirl with. A particularly big one plummets faster than the rest, and when it gets to my eye level, I realize I'm not the only one watching it.

Spencer.

He's leaning against his window frame, hands in his dark wash jeans and a snug black tee stretching across his chest. His glasses were broken in the fight in the cafeteria, which would explain the fresh raw line across his cheek.

He got off with a warning at school since, technically, he didn't initiate it and had no prior offenses. I've thought about the altercation a few times, remember him lost in the pure fury that shook his body. I was at the edge of my seat, stiletto nails sticking so hard in my palms I still have the marks. Watching him feel something in that moment, something at the hands of my doing was the hottest thing I have ever seen.

Spencer threads a hand through his dark locks and sighs. He doesn't notice I'm watching him. At least if he does, he doesn't seem to mind, and something about that sends a spike of heat through my chest.

I hate that.

I hate that after everything, his body still calls to me. Every ounce of my being wants nothing more than to be next to him—while to him, I am nothing. I hate him.

"William. How many times do I have to tell you? We've been friends forever, bro. There is nothing going on with me and her. She's not even my type—too plain, boring. She's nothing."

The voice on the phone is so loud I can hear it through his ear piece. It's deeper than it should be for a thirteen-year-old, and his laugh curls the hairs on my neck. "You're a dog, Hanes."

Squeezing my eyes against the burn of the memory, my chest heaves. The once dull pain, now alive, radiating through my body with a vengeance. It's hard to look at him without hearing his whispers from that day.

When I look back at him, his eyes are locked on mine. My breath hitches—no, it stops. Each nerve ending tingles as we stand, waiting, but for what I don't know.

Do something. Anything. Urging him with my thoughts, I take a quick breath. Just once, I want to see that same fire in him like from the cafeteria. I want to know I get under his skin the way he does me.

Instead, his gaze flits down before he thrusts himself off the window, turning and disappearing behind his curtains.

My shoulders deflate as I let the air fill my lungs. This is stupid. I'm stupid. Falling back on my bed, letting it curl in around me, sleep comes. The crushing weight of nearing midterms, scholarship deadlines, regionals, and all things Spencer finally taking its toll.

When I wake up, I have too many messages and notifications, but one makes my heart stutter.

Bulldog: Monday, 4:45

I'M EARLY TODAY, but only because I want to get this over with. The quicker we start, the faster we'll be done, and I don't have to see Spencer the entire week. Blaze took me out to eat for lunch, so I spared myself the nausea of having to see him while I ate.

Slipping into the worn chair, I sling my bag on the back and begin drumming my fingers on the desk. Waiting is still something that drives my nerves into overdrive, though I'm not sure if it's from irritation or anticipation.

The door opens a few minutes later, and Spencer appears in the frame. He doesn't notice me a first, flopping into the seat with a sigh, letting his backpack drop from his shoulder with a dull thud. His ugly confetti sweater hugs his biceps as he runs a hand through his hair, and that's when I notice he still doesn't have any glasses. The scratches on his face are starting to scab, and I ignore the twinge of guilt that wells in my throat.

I swallow it down and clear my throat. He deserved it. "Rough day?"

Spencer jerks back, his eyes narrowing, and I assume, trying to get me into focus. I wonder how he managed to get through the day like that.

"Between being barked at all day during the passing period, finding a bowl of dog food in my locker, and a new collar with a 'Lily's pet' tag, I'd say yes."

A hideous bark of laughter spills from my mouth before I can stop it. I knew when I posted it on social media, things would get a little rough, but this is gold. Part of me wonders if he's connected the dots. If he's figured out why being a dog is so significant.

Spencer shakes his head, and his body vibrates with the anger he won't let out, which makes the prior guilt fade. He still won't react. Why?

"I'm going to start the timer. Please don't talk until then."

My head snaps back. "The only reason I won't is because I don't have anything else to say, not to mention I don't speak bitch, so, ya know."

The nerve in his jaw tics as he clenches it, but other than that, he says nothing, grabbing the remote from his backpack. He clicks a button, and the room illuminates into a golden yellow, similar to when the sun first starts to set.

We wait in the requested silence, neither of us daring to look at the other. While normally I would feel happy surrounded by yellow, its brightness irritates me today. But maybe it's because I'm having to wait again. Either way, my pulse increases, and I can feel it in my wrists, tapping against the thin skin. It's annoying as hell. Clenching the charm on my necklace, I pull it back and forth, paying little attention to the sting of it digging into my fingertips.

Finally, the timer goes off, and he jumps right into it. "Hey."

Making my voice as bored as I can, my hand waves cheerfully. "Hey."

"How was your day?"

My eyes flash to his, and a smile creeps across my face, widening when he shifts in his seat. "Marvelous. How was your day?"

"Dumb as fuck. How are you feeling?" he continues, keeping his face impassive, but he can't stop the nerve thumping in his temple.

"Annoyed," I chirp, honestly. "How are you feeling?"

Spencer's eyebrows draw together slightly, and his head quirks, but he doesn't inquire further. All business. Cool, that's what I wanted anyway.

He clears his throat and mimics my response, "Annoyed. If you could do anything right now, what would you do?"

"Fuck your mouth," I reply, hoping to get some type of reaction.

I have no earthly idea why it matters so damn much. Why I can't just let it go and move on. Why after all this time, I still think about that day I climbed up the rose trestle outside his window to have my heart ripped out of my chest.

Because that's what he left me with—a mangled piece of meat that barely even beats anymore.

Coupled with the occasional beatings from my piece of shit mother and total neglect of my father, he made me the very thing that's sitting in front of him now. Losing him, the last person who was everything to me... that's what broke me. It made me realize that the only person that ever truly, really cares about you is yourself. Everyone else is just a good time or collateral damage.

"If you could do anything right now, what would you do?" The burn behind my eyes is strong now, but not enough for me to give in and let him know he still hurts me even when he isn't doing anything.

It's just been me, struggling with making him keep a secret and wanting to fuck his brains out, while he hasn't done anything this entire time. He's just sat there, taking it all without a word...

Biding his time...

Like he's just waiting for this thing between us to pass...

Then it hits me.

Spencer hasn't done anything. He was enrolled almost three months before I even knew he was here, and even that encounter was by chance. There was no way in hell he didn't know I was here.

Why haven't I realized this before?

He purposely avoided me.

An anger I haven't felt in years rears its head, soaking into my blood like a hot toxin, spewing through my body. My hands shake under the table, but I keep my face as calm as I can.

He doesn't get to win. Not anymore.

He mumbles something about doing research, and I realize it's now time for the extra part. I clamp my mouth closed, unable to verbally say anything else. The room is suffocating, full of his scent, and I don't want to breathe it anymore.

When he realizes I have nothing to add, he leans back. "Stop with the bully act, Lily. It looks like shit on you."

Bile hits the back of my throat. That's what he thinks I'm doing? Bullying him, and he's a victim? Like he's the one that didn't rip my heart out like a fucking coward.

I scoff, standing, and shoving the heel of my palms on the desk. Rage continues to flood my system, driving it into sensory overload, coating my words in a venom I hope knocks him on his ass.

"Fuck you, Spencer. Fuck you for thinking I care in the slightest about your meek existence. You are the shit beneath my heel that smells so foul, I just throw them away. You think I'm being a bully? I'll show you what a fucking bully I can be." I yank my purse up by the straps, whipping it around so it hits him square in the face and slam the door closed behind me.

Charging forward through my blurry vision, I don't stop or look back and let the tears coat my cheeks. They aren't tears of sadness or hurt. They are from the deepest, darkest part of my twisted soul. The last part that gave a fuck, which is now burning in the fire of my fury.

I hate him, and I want him to feel it. I want him to look

down at the shards of his life after I've demolished it, leaving it at his feet, and feel it all.

Then he will know what it is to have nothing or no one in your corner. He will know the same reality that I've known since I was twelve years old. And I think I'll start with the thing he does care about.

Remy.

SEVENTEEN

My phone buzzes for the fifteenth time, and I don't even bother looking anymore. My last test is coming up, and with the nonstop shit at school, focusing has been nearly impossible.

It's been a whole fucking week, and people still haven't let up. The constant gifts left for me have become so abundant, the local shelter knows me by name. I've dropped off donations every day. Dog bowls, food, leashes, toys, you name it. At first, it was easy to ignore, but it went from annoying to straight fucking harassment. The amount of little scabs running across my palm from clenching my fist is pitiful.

Hold fast, hold steady.

I played my mother's words on a loop to keep from bashing in every head that barked at me. She's forgotten about the fight already, but I haven't forgotten the face she made when I got home. It was the same one she gave me back in Idaho when all she saw in me was a bloody disappointment.

There isn't much time left before I'm just another stranger, and I'll be damned if that's the last look she ever gives me while remembering who I am.

I won't lie, though. Holding fast and steady this afternoon has proved fucking difficult. It's Friday afternoon, just a couple of hours since school's let out, and my phone won't stop ringing. I answered the first one, but after being barked at, I haven't bothered picking it up again. Somehow my number got out, that much is obvious, but then the emails started coming in. How the fuck they got that is beyond me.

Now, I'm waiting for Remy to finish up her book club meeting, so we can FaceTime study for this chemical compound test. Glancing at the clock, I consider texting her. Tell her I'll just come over tomorrow after work so that I can turn off my phone.

Right as my finger hovers over our text thread, a bright smile and hexagon glasses flash across the screen.

"Spencer!" Her voice is breathy like she's been running. "I've been calling you. Where are you?"

Guilt takes the place of annoyance, and I sigh, rubbing the nape of my neck. I must have missed it while ignoring others. "You and thirty other people. I'm sorry, I don't know what th—"

"I know! That's why I've been calling. Can you come over?"

My brows pull together. "Yeah, of course. Now?"

"Yes, hurry up, Spence."

I pause, feeling my face contort at the use of the nickname before responding. "Okay."

After hanging up, I turn my phone off, unable to take any more of the calls, and throw on a hoodie. Whatever the fuck is going on, there's no doubt in my mind who's the cause. The moment she swung herself out of the room, I knew.

Lily's pissed.

But I'm not sure why. She mentioned multiple times about keeping my mouth shut, which I've done. No one knows her mom's a custodian, and I damn sure haven't told them Lily's family abandoned her. So I don't know what her problem is. She seems to be pissed I don't react, but that's like Bully Survival 101. Don't engage, and they'll leave you alone. But it seems to have the opposite effect on her.

My eyes flash to the house behind mine. It's hidden under a fresh blanket of snow, the smoking chimney showing the only signs of life inside. The life that for some reason, is hell-bent on making mine miserable. An unwelcome ache radiates across my chest, but I force my gaze away, snatching my keys from the kitchen counter and leave.

The influx of snow we've had causes it to take a little longer than normal to get to Remy's, which lets my mind wander more. Frustration burrows in my head as I try to wrap my thoughts around what the fuck happened with Lily and me.

There's something I'm not seeing. Something I've *missed*, maybe.

By the time I arrive, the sun is setting, and a chill cuts through the air, threatening to bring a blizzard with it.

Remy must hear me pull up and opens the front door before I get out of my car. She's bundled up in fleece long johns, and a chunky knit blanket's wrapped around her. Her short nose is already blooming a pink that's spreading to the tops of her cheeks. Those big hazel eyes are wide beneath her oversized glasses as she watches me trek up the driveway.

I make a note to clear it before I leave in case she needs to go somewhere.

"What's up?"

She closes the door behind me but doesn't respond immediately. Instead, her eyes focus on the floor, and she chews on the corner of her lip. After a few seconds, she tilts her head toward a stack of crumpled paper on the entryway table.

Grabbing the one on top, I glance at Remy before opening it. Her voice is barely above a whisper. "I got as many as I could find."

The flyer is the printed photo from the party with a bold print, listing the appropriate time I can be reached for services, along with my phone number, email, and place of fucking employment.

It's not anger or rage that floods through my body, it's validation. It's knowing my suspicions were right, and every bad thing in my life stems from this new Lily. The one I loved isn't underneath some complicated layers, waiting to be saved.

This girl is damaged beyond recognition, leaving me mourning the loss.

"It could always be worse." Shrugging, I toss the paper back down and stride up her stairs two at a time.

There's a pain, one I don't want to acknowledge, stabbing into my heart. Each breath I take makes it worse, shoving whatever's poking it, further in. I flop down on her futon in my usual place, and my hand massages the ache.

Remy appears in the threshold, still bundled up. She peers over the rim of her glasses before pushing them back up the bridge of her nose. "You're not mad?"

"Nope."

It's not a lie, but it's not the truth. Honestly, I don't know what the fuck I'm feeling.

"Seems a little much for someone to do just because they want you to do their part of a project, Spencer." Remy sits next to me, folding her legs beneath her. She almost looks like a little kolache, and it makes me smile.

Her eyebrows knit together, and I realize she's waiting. When I merely shrug again, she clears her throat. "I've thought about things lately, and I noticed something. You know a lot about me. Like a lot an—"

"No, I don't," I interject. I know where this is going, and I'm not ready. Having a friend of the opposite sex is easy, but when they know too much, when they know *everything* and become a best friend, that's when you have to worry about losing them—about becoming strangers that know each other's secrets. I don't want to lose Remy.

"What's my favorite color?" She's not going to let this go.

"Pink. But come on, that's pretty easy." I gesture around the room. "Your favorite hobby is reading. You always have a book, most of the time your finger is tracing some part of it. You're smart as fuck, and low-key a little funny. You stutter when you get nervous and chew on your bottom lip so much, it explains why it's always swollen. Let's not forget your bad taste in guys. But those aren't intimate things, just simple observations of a scientist."

Remy huffs, leaning back a little. "I see. And are you always that observant?"

I nod. "Always."

"Okay. Well, it looks like we have a few things in common. Like our poor choices in who we like."

My head tilts. "You lost me."

"I mean, this thing with Lily. Crush gone wrong? Or mayb—"

"Crush? Remy, fuck that girl. She's a psychotic fucking train wreck, and the only kind of crushing I want to do, is my hand around her throat. I can't believe she's changed so damn mu— Fuck." Remy laid the trap in front of me, and I still fell in.

"Changed. The Lily I've known about has been the same since she was a freshman. Who's the Lily you knew?"

I sigh, scrubbing my hands over my face. She doesn't need to know every detail, but keeping up the vague lie is becoming exhausting. "Her name was Liliana when I knew her."

After that small admission, the words flow. I tell her everything. How Liliana and I met, our childhood, the time spent in the summers under the stars, and all the days we wasted in the treehouse. My mother's condition and her parents' absence. I tell Remy how much I loved Liliana.

I loved her.

The once annoying stabbing in my chest stops. Now, it's a twisting sensation, and everything inside my ribs seizes. My ribs cave under the pressure, and suddenly I can't breathe.

I need to leave.

"Remy, I got to go. Thank you for ripping the posters down. But really, don't worry about it. I don't want you becoming a target or anything." No matter how much I try, my voice cracks, strained under the lack of air.

Remy, being the amazing friend she is, just nods and stands, walking me to the door in silence. When we get to the front, the weight has lessened, and I turn on my heels.

"Where's your snow shovel?"

She shakes her head, "Oh no. You don't need to do that,

Spencer. My dad should be home in the next couple of days."

"Where?" I say again, though this time, I'm not asking.

A smirk lifts the right side of her mouth, and she juts her chin toward the side door. "Left side of the garage, in the tall bin."

Nodding, I head out. "See you tomorrow, Remy."

I find the shovel and tug my hoodie on, leaving her garage open a foot so I can roll it back under when I'm done. The frigid air wraps around me, tightening every muscle in my body. The wind has died down, leaving a new layer of snow on the ground. The crunch of it beneath my feet echoes into the night as I trudge to the side of the driveway behind her car.

Taking my time, I start, pushing all my weight into the handle. I force all my attention on the satisfying lines I make as I pile the snow on the side. Clouds of smoke come out in puffs as the thin air becomes harder to breathe.

For the next twenty minutes, my mind is nothing. It's barren of any thoughts besides the cold, and the stars shining ridiculously bright despite the amount of light pollution our city makes.

Finally, in my car, the vibrations of the engine purring as it warms settle my chatting teeth. With the thawing of my skin, comes the memory of the first and only time I ever saw snow with Lily.

"I can't believe you're here! How did you get your mom to agree?" Liliana's warm brown eyes are the only thing keeping me from freezing. Her smile is stretched from ear to ear, making the one-day trip all the more worth it.

"Oh, she didn't mind since it's just today."

Liliana's smile flips, and my stomach plummets with it. "Just today? I thought you'd be here all week."

"I know, I'm sorry. But hey, at least we get to build a snowman. Scratch it off our bucket list."

She pouts for a minute, pushing her lips out, and I wonder what it would be like to kiss her. Share our first kiss in the snow. Maybe after the hot chocolate, grinch movie, and some snowman building. Maybe.

I didn't kiss her. The chickenshit I was. And come to find out, she would kiss Johnny Macland at the city Christmas Yule a week later.

I was so mad, I almost caught the bus to go punch his ass in the face. He knew I liked her. William had to talk me off the ledge. Probably explains why I'm calling him now.

"Aye, man, what's up?" William's voice fills the car.

Hearing it does something. Almost as if it's a reminder and a realization all at the same time. He was there through it all. The beginning, middle, and end of Lily and I. He knows the way she burrowed into my fucking skin, tattooing herself into my chest. Will was also the one that had to put me back together when she ripped herself out, leaving a big-ass hole.

I slam my fist into the dashboard, and the tears that have been teetering on the edge finally go over, searing down my face. Anger boils in my gut. I'm pissed I still fucking care.

I still fucking care.

A shuffling on the speaker reminds me that William is still there. He clears his throat and sighs. "I'm on my way."

EIGHTEEN

His little friend has done a good job taking down all my posters, but my cheer team is better. They replace them faster than Remy can find them, all for the cost of twenty minutes off practice. The truth is, they would have gotten the time anyway because I need to make sure I look okay for my afternoon meeting with Spencer.

He hasn't said anything, and I can't lie, that bothers me. He still isn't fazed by anything I dish out, and it's starting to make my insides burn. *How is he so detached?*

The only thing he really cares about is maybe Remy, and after a talk with Blaze, I realize starting any drama with her will only cause me problems. So now, I'm left scraping the bottom of the barrel for ideas to piss him off.

A thought crosses my head from a week ago in the locker room. Amora threatened Stacy with a screenshot. Posting it as a puzzle around the school for people to piece together. Maybe that would do something to him. Pull him out of his shell once and for all. I would do anything to see him get angry.

I make it to the tiny room before he does, and lean back in my chair, inspecting my cuticles. Since we are the only ones ever occupying the space, the mixed smell of us still lingers in the air from last week. Its hues of lavender and lemon with deep cedar. It's intoxicating and incredibly frustrating.

The door handle jiggles, signaling his presence, forcing my spine to straighten. I brush a hand down my arm, smoothing the goose bumps before he walks in.

Spencer's head appears first, and a strange combination of satisfaction and hunger jumbles my nerves into a knot. Dark circles highlight the skin under his equally dim eyes. His brown locks are in disarray, falling onto his forehead and brushing the edge of his new square frames. The black hoodie he's wearing hugs only his biceps and hangs loosely over his core. He must have forgotten a belt, leaving light wash jeans clinging just below his waist.

He's tired—exhausted.

So the flyers are working.

I smile inwardly, loving the way my chest swells with a tinge of arrogance. He's not so invincible after all, and even if the inconvenience is slight, I'll take it as a victory.

He flops into his chair, not daring to look at me, and takes a small controller from his pocket. He sighs and clicks a button on it. The room instantly glows a dark crimson red. It's a dangerous color, and my pulse responds immediately, nearly doubling its resting pace.

My eyes lock on his hands as he sets a timer on his phone, still unwilling to gaze at me. Annoyance flickers through me, and I suck on my teeth. He winces but keeps his stupid stance.

The three-minute wait is unbelievably long, and the

number of emotions wracking through my mind leaves me almost panting for breath. I'm exasperated. Irritated, my heart still flutters when I see him, and he can't even be bothered to look at me.

Yet, I'm confident. Powerful in this moment that everything he's feeling is caused by me. Every insult, down to the small donations left at his locker. All of them, remind him of me, and sick satisfaction leads to my next conundrum.

I'm horny... as hell. My knees clench together to keep the heaviness from taking over. It's hard to ignore the slickness between my thighs.

Finally, his damn alarm goes off, and he doesn't wait. "Hey."

His voice is rough and deep, like he just woke up. It shoots straight to my core, making my own voice sultry. "Hey."

His eyebrows pinch together for a second before his face returns calm, bored, and he focuses on a stray spot on the desk between us. "How was your day?"

"Boring. How was your day?" I think I'm holding my breath as I wait for his response.

"Just grand. How are you feeling?"

"Vexed. How are you feeling?"

He shifts in his seat, nearly parallel with the table, and puts one arm on it. He scrapes at the corner, peeling a splinter of wood. "I'm fine. If you could do anything right now, what would you do?"

It's clear he wants to be done with this, but unfortunately for him, I don't. "I'd put a leash on my bitch and take him for a walk. Maybe get him a treat if he's good. What about you, Spencer? If you could do anything right now, what would you do?"

At last his eyes snap to me, blazing with the fury I've longed for. "Fuck you, Lily. I can—"

"I'm sorry, Spencer." I lean forward, both elbows on the table, a glorious grin spreading across my face. "I don't partake in bestiality. But you know, I have heard Remy might."

"Don't say her fucking name, Lily. Whatever sick obsession you have with me doesn't involve her." His body is shaking—so much anger vibrating through him it's almost tangible.

I ignore the pang in my chest at the way he defends her and huff. "I'll say whatever the hell I feel like. And until I get what I want, no one is safe."

Before I can blink, I'm against the wall with Spencer's hand wrapped around my throat. His body is flush against mine, the heat of his breath searing a path down my neck and spreading across my collarbone. The brown is nearly gone from his eyes, leaving black orbs with bits of gold. They glimmer under the light which now surrounds his head in a red glow. The God of War has nothing on Spencer Hanes at this moment.

"Is this what you *want*, Lily? A fucking reaction?" he snarls, his lips grazing the shell of my ear.

Heat swirls in the small space between us, leaving my head swimming and speech unfeasible. Instead, I nod and feel him smile against my neck. My skin burns everywhere his body is touching mine and yearning for it in the places he isn't.

"Why?" He runs his nose along the edge of my jaw, and I gasp. He grips tighter, tilting my head away. I can breathe, but swallowing is near impossible.

"Fucking answer me." His voice booms in my ear, jolting

me upright. His arousal presses into my thigh, and my core clenches. This isn't the sweet Spencer from my treehouse. This one is dark... mean.

"Because," I rasp. My mind is spinning, and for some reason, I can't lie. "I want to know I affect you."

"That much is obvious, but I want to know *why*." His nose continues its assault, trailing down the length of my neck, and I arch—*arch* into him, molding my body against the surprising hardness of his. Everything is on fire. It's a furious mix of anger and desire, and I... want this.

I want *him*.

Get control.

"Now," he hisses before nipping my eardrum, his grip tightening.

"Because I..." The words die in my throat. I can't say it. I won't. No matter how much my body wants him, he doesn't get to have my thoughts. I won't make that mistake again. "Get your dirty ass paws off me, or I'll—"

"You'll what? Get more of your sheep to leave me gifts? Bark at me till they're black and blue? Do you think I fucking care, *Lily*? Do I l*ook* like I care?" The way he draws out my name feels like a slur. When I clench my teeth in response, he laughs. It's low, deep in the back of his throat, and his grin is wide—like the cat that caught the canary.

No, he doesn't get to win this time.

"Spence, get your fuc—"

His mouth crashes into mine, stealing my words, my breath, my soul.

It's not tentative or soft, it's angry and possessive. He bites into my bottom lip, forcing my mouth open in a gasp, and takes full advantage, sliding his tongue inside to fight with mine. Though the word *fighting* is an understatement.

We wage war on each other.

He takes my breath and gives me his, but it isn't enough. Nothing is enough. My fists find his shirt, balling the fabric to pull him somehow closer than he already is. He threads his fingers in my hair, gripping it by the root and tugging our bodies flush. There is no way to tell where his ends and mine begins.

A groan vibrates his body, sending wild tremors down my nerves. My veins throb, threatening to burst at any second. To think I've been kissed before is the stupidest thing I've ever thought.

This is my first kiss. The one that makes me feel like I could combust at any second, but not care, because he would put me back together. Then do it all over again.

He breaks from my mouth, and before I have time to whimper a protest, his lips are on my neck, somehow licking and nipping at the same time. I feel my eyes roll to the back of my head, and I mewl, hoping he doesn't stop.

"I bet if I slid my hand down here, you would be fucking dripping." His fingers tickle around the waistband of my jeans, and my stomach tightens.

Everything clenches and screams, begging for him to just do it.

"Is this what you want from me, Lily?" His lips are back at my ear.

"Yes." I don't recognize my own voice. It's breathy, needy, and weak. But he hears it just fine.

"Remember this. Because now that you've had your fix, I will *never* fucking touch you again."

And then he rips his body from me in one fluid motion, letting a deep chill wrap around me in his absence. He played me like a damn violin, and I showed him how, singing as he did it. I blink the fire away, curling my hands around my stomach.

How did I let this happen?

"I hate you." It's a whisper, but I know he hears it when his eyes narrow.

"Believe me, baby, I hate you more." Spencer grabs the notebook on the table before sparing me one last glance. "You can parade around here like a queen all you want, but I know the truth. You're nothing but a fucking *peasant*."

With that, he slams the door behind him before I take my next breath.

My chest feels hollow yet heavy, and there's an insane burn inside my nose. But this time I don't ignore it. I embrace it. I let every old scab bust open and bleed out, committing this new pain to memory. Because I will remember this and let it remind me why I won't mess up again. My fingers find the charm on my necklace, clench it, and pull it back and forth until my neck burns from the friction.

Well, Spencer Hanes, welcome to the end. And believe me when I say, what I did before was child's play.

With my mind made up, I exit the small room, and what little air I have left flees my lungs. Stacy stands with her back against the wall, fingers playing with the hem of her cheer skirt. She peers up at me before smiling.

Shit.

Instead of walking toward her, I click the down button on the service elevator right next to me. If I were to talk to Stacy now, I'm liable to bash her poor head against the locker through no fault of her own. It's just because I can't do it to Spencer.

With a dull wave, a small wish she didn't hear anything, I clamber inside the elevator and glide down to the first floor.

The elevator doors open, and I swear someone is playing a goddamn trick on me. My mother sits at the entrance with her cleaning cart, drinking from a metal cup.

You've got to be fucking kidding me.

Her eyes connect with mine, and instantly I know—this bitch is drunk on the job. I'm quick to move around her, ignoring the sounds of the metal hitting the cart. I make it two feet before her cold fingers wrap around my arm, swinging me back to face her.

"You're just going to walk by your mother, you fucking puta?"

"Mother? Bitch, my dad was more of a mother to me. My aunt Mina was more of a mother. *I* am more of a mother to me!" I can't stop it. I try, I really do, but it's like trying to hold water in a strainer.

And the consequences are instant. The cool metal of her cup crashes into my jaw, spilling its contents all over my blouse. Whiskey burns the inside of my nostrils, and I'm pretty sure she cracked my tooth as the metallic liquid fills my mouth.

She pushes her cart onto the elevator, turning to look down her nose at me. "You are *nothing*. Don't forget that."

"Lily? What the fuck!" Amora's screeches echo down the hallway, squeezing my heart in half.

No, no, no, no, no, no, no.

She reaches the elevator as it closes, slamming her fist into the reflective doors. Amora whirls around to me, still crumpled on the floor. She crouches down, grabbing my face with surprising gentleness. "Your mom?"

Her baby blues search mine, her eyebrows furrowed and

curled upward. It's as if she's putting the pieces of a puzzle together, filling in gaps. Tears linger on the brim of her lid. And in this moment, I no longer care that my entire world can crumble if she knows. I need her to know because I can't hold back anymore.

And I don't.

I nod my head, letting the tears sear down my face, and sobs rip through my body. Everything is shaking so violently, I think Amora will call for help, but instead, her arms wrap around me. She pulls me into her chest, rocking me back and forth, smoothing her hand down my arms.

"Shhh, Lily. I'm here now. You don't have to carry this anymore."

NINTEEN

"You did what?" William leans back in my desk chair, throwing a blue stress ball in the air. His long black sleeves are rolled halfway up his forearm, just under where his tattoos start. Only one emerald butterfly is visible, vibrant against his smooth brown skin, and each time he extends his arm, it looks like the wings are flapping. I've been watching it, trying to distract myself from the ones in my stomach as I tell him about my royal fuckup with Lily earlier this week.

Turns out the red light can make you do stupid ass things, and now it's all I've thought about—replaying it in my head on a constant loop. If it's not my dick throbbing in my pants, it's the twitch behind my eyes, reminding me of my mistake.

And now that William's here, I have a feeling things are going to get more chaotic. He has a way of acting on impulse. Like now, being hours away from home, and I can bet my bank account his mom doesn't know. After my breakdown outside Remy's house, he practically forced me to let him come for the weekend, help me move on from the stress like he did three years ago. At the time, when I was wrapped in too many emotions, I said yes.

Because at the time, things weren't that bad. But then I kissed her.

I kissed Lily.

What the fuck was I thinking?

I brush my thumb across my lips and can still feel the warmth of her mouth. Her taste was sweet, but not like the fake sugar that spews from her daily. It was like honey—real... raw, unfiltered.

Everything about it was primal. Aching need fueled every movement I made. Well, that and her desperate whimpers. I almost lost control completely, caught up in everything I ever wanted at the tips of my fingers. But she opened her eyes, and when I saw the fake hazel instead of her chocolate brown, I remembered.

She's not the one I want...wanted.

"You've lost it, Hanes. You need a good fuck. That helped the first time." He tosses the ball at me, and I let it bounce off my arm.

I grimace, ignoring the horrendous flashbacks trying to flit through my mind. Fucking Lily out of my system didn't work, but I couldn't bring myself to tell William that. After sophomore year, he forced me to every party, wing-manning the shit out of each one. He was a good friend, doing what we thought would help. But when I found myself on top of someone later, she always had brown hair and chestnut eyes.

A means to an end. But the end never came. I was never satisfied or happy after, just numb. I was confused back then. I still cared about her. I still *wanted* her.

Now?

Now, the ache running through my body is nothing more than anger. Anger that I wasted so much time caught up in a girl wearing a mask. I had it backward—thinking Liliana was still underneath it when really that was the persona all along. The more I think about it, the more frustrated I get with myself.

When people show you who they truly are, believe them.

"So what are you going to do?" William's large frame hops from my chair, leaving it spinning behind him. He's only an inch or two taller than me and is bulky where I'm lean.

"Any parties happening this weekend?" He sinks into my bed, propping a hand behind his head, and pulls a thick curl out straight to examine it. "Let's grab a couple of girls, or maybe a few, and have a good time."

I scoff, falling into the empty chair. "Yeah, at Lily's. And there's no fucking way I'm going there."

"Yes the fuck we are." Will releases his dark coil and leans on his side. "It's perfect, actually. After all the shit she's done, bring out the Spencer I know. Show up, get a few girls, and let her see that bullying a guy doesn't matter. He can still get pussy."

"Dude, I need a break from seeing her."

"We're going."

"She'll probably have someone kick us out on sight."

He huffs, puffing up his chest. "And we beat their ass like old times."

"You know I can't." With William, I don't have to explain things when it comes to my mom. On too many occasions, he had to help me find her when she went on walks and didn't come back for hours. He was actually the one to call my dad and let him know what was going on. I was hardheaded. Thinking I could carry the weight of her, school, and my future. I think part of me didn't want to give up his real friendship and come back to the one that broke me in two.

"How is Ms. Hanes?"

I shrug, rubbing the spot above my shirt pocket. "Her and my dad are visiting some places this weekend. Where she might be more comfortable." That last part is a whisper.

Williams' lips form a thin line. "I'm sorry, man."

I shake my head. "It's just...one day, she won't remember me at all. And I don't want her last memory to be of me disappointing her. If that means I take Lily's shit a little longer, so be it."

William nods. "Yeah, man, I get it. Alright. Well, I promise to behave if you say we can go." He holds up two fingers pinched together. "Scout's honor."

"Says the same boy who went across to the Girl Scouts camp and got a blow job."

"Hey! Still to this day, the best blowie of my life."

We erupt in laughter. A genuine, deep, fuck-the-rest-of-the-world, laughter. And for two seconds, I forget the pain digging in my side.

"WE'RE OUTSIDE." I end the call and point to Remy's driveway. I told her I was being kidnapped and dragged to a party against my will. She threatened to call off work an entire week if we didn't pick her up too.

She appears in seconds, and William sucks in a sharp breath. Her curvy frame is on full display under a cream sweater hanging over leggings. Tan boots grip her calves and have a heel, boosting her small height a few inches. A woven beanie sits at the back of her head, leaving her face exposed. There's a blush overtaking her cheeks and button nose, somehow making her cuter.

I hit Will in the shoulder before he can get any ideas. "She's off-limits."

"Ugh." He rubs his bicep, scowling but not taking his eyes off Remy. "You don't like her, so why can't I have some fun?"

"Romance reader."

His annoyingly bright eyes flash to me. "Fuck. Yeah, hard pass."

Remy stops when she sees us, so I open my door, waving her over. "We took William's truck."

"Yeah, I can see that. It's huge. How in the world am I going to get in there?"

"I'll pull you up."

She walks closer, moving cautiously until she's at my side. She looks up and sees Williams' perfect smile next to me. I don't think I've ever seen Remy's eyes so big. "H-hi."

Holding out my hand, she grasps it, hoisting herself into the back seat of the truck, her gaze flicking to his too many times.

I sigh, close the door, and make the introductions quick. "William, Remy. Remy, William."

"Heya, sugar. Nice to meet you."

It's hard to keep my eyes from rolling. It's like he can't even help it—his promiscuous nature oozes from every part of him whether he wants it to or not.

We take the ride back to my neighborhood, and I can't seem to hear the conversation they start having. Each time we pass a stop sign that's closer to her house my pulse increases, leaving a whooshing sound in my ears that makes my head dizzy.

I haven't seen her since the kiss. And after William answered a few of my spam calls, even that's died, leaving me to think it all fucking happened in my head.

But when we pull up, and I feel the thud of my heart in my throat, I know it didn't. My body vibrates with the fucked-up combination of nerves, anger, and arousal. I'm beginning to think I'm going crazy. That's what Lily's done to me.

Always done to me.

Made me think things that weren't real. Feelings, who she was... the list goes on.

William decides to park at my house, and we walk around the end of the street, wrapping back around to Lily's. We fall behind a group of juniors giggling and rattling off about the football game from Friday. They are all huddled close, shivering with their laughter. For the ground to be covered in snow, it always surprises me the lack of clothes people wear to these things.

"So this is it, huh? The house of the famed Liliana." William looks around, letting his eyes linger on a few groups of girls.

I nod, unable to really speak. I don't see her, but I can feel her. The heat on the side of my face is scalding, but I can't force myself to look just yet.

No matter how much we can't stand each other, in that room, we both wanted each other. And that scares the fuck out of me.

"Well, well. I thought I told Blaze to take the trash out." Amora skirts in front of us, blocking our path to the living room. She turns to Remy first, letting her icy eyes trail down Remy's body.

"And who is she supposed to be? Someone we actually give a fuck about?" William looks at me, his thick brows raised.

"Oh, honey, I'm not sure who you are, but I'm all you should care about." Amora turns to William, a placid expression on her face, but the vein in her neck pulses.

"I'm anything but sweet, bunny. Now, hop along and bother someone else."

William twists and faces Amora. I don't miss the way her eyes widen slightly or the hitch in her breath. It's the normal reaction when girls meet him. Hell, guys too. But she doesn't back down. "Bunny. That's cute. Know what else would be cute? Watching your nose play peek-a-boo under my pussy."

He scoffs, but a playful smile curls the end of his lips. "Sorry, dove, I'm fasting. But even if I wasn't, I'd have to pass. You look a little clingy."

Amora tilts her head back and laughs so hard she snorts. She flips her blonde strands behind her exposed shoulder, and suddenly all humor has left her. "I only use you boys, for a little light amusement. And while you look like a fun time," her eyes drop the length of his body, stopping right at his groin before snapping back up. "I bet I'd be disappointed."

She disappears before William can respond, but even if she hadn't, he looks stumped. His mouth is open, and his eyebrows are furrowed. It's a face I have never seen on him before. "Who was that?"

"Lily's best friend."

He huffs, running an oversized hand through his hair. "Hmm. That explains a lot."

Remy grunts, leaning against the wall. "C-can we get some drinks?"

I wrap my hand around her wrist, rubbing the back of my burning neck with the other, and lead them toward the kitchen. "Say less."

TWENTY

the Party

Lily

That's him. *William*. I know it is.

Anyone that hot at Emerald Falls can't go unnoticed. Hell, I'm surprised Spencer made it that long without people talking.

When we were younger, there was only one guy he used to talk about. The one who had him ten months out of the year and still called him almost every damn day. Pissed me off that he even answered the calls. He was supposed to be *mine* for those seventy-four days. But I always felt like I was competing for his undivided attention.

It makes sense he would bring him here. Parade the very person that was our end.

I ignore the pang of jealousy that shoots through my

limbs when I see Spencer grab Remy's wrist. I know they aren't involved intimately, but it still bothers me to see him sensitive, soft with someone.

That's it.

I've done everything to get a reaction out of him. Embarrassed him, inconvenienced him, annoyed the fuck out of him, and probably given him blue balls a few times. But I've never tested his endurance to watch me with someone else. And I know just the person.

Amora bounces through the small crowd and up the stairs. She rubs the gaggle of goose bumps down her arm. "Who the fuck is he with?"

"A friend from where he used to live."

"Hmm." She chews the inside of her cheek. "I want to sit on his pretty face."

Chuckling through my nose, I watch over the railing as Remy and Spencer make it to the kitchen. They both motion to the juice, then their bodies shake in unison as they laugh and grab a beer. It always surprises me to see Remy out of her element, doing something I wouldn't imagine her doing. It makes me wonder vaguely who she is behind the person she shows the world.

"Let me have a little fun with him. Then he's all yours."

Amora giggles, rocking on her heels. "Ooooo. What are you going to do?"

Just then, William leans close, asking Remy something. She points to the hall behind my kitchen, shakes her head, and points to the stairs. He must have asked about the bathroom.

Perfect.

I tuck a stray hair behind my ear and fix my shirt before

waving my fingers at Amora. "Put on a little show before the big finale."

She grins, shaking her head before floating down the stairs. She stopped asking a long time ago why I put so much effort into messing with Spencer. Not sure if she thinks it's still about the project or if she knows better and is just having fun. Either way, she's more than willing to partake in my game.

William rounds the banister and saunters up the stairs. Depending on whether he's seen a picture of me will affect my plan, so I take the cautious approach, leaning against the wall and scrolling on my phone.

When he speaks, I have to force myself to keep my composure. It's deep—deeper than any eighteen-year-old I've ever heard, and husky. "Well, hello there, sugar."

I peer up from my phone and bite my tongue. He is hotter than sin up close. A set of four freckles decorate his prominent jaw under some light stubble. His lips are full, and I think any woman would kill for his eyelashes. And while his body looks to be carved out of marble, it's not the sexiest thing about him. It's his eyes. They are a dark forest green that you could happily get lost in.

Somehow I find my voice and make it as sultry as possible. "Hey. New around here?"

Spencer

THE HAIRS on the back of my neck stand up straight, tingling the nerves in my scalp. There's a coolness in the air that seeps into my fucking skin, setting my spine at full attention. Maybe it's because I'm back in this damn house or that every blonde that passes in my periphery makes my shoulders tense.

It's like waiting for the other shoe to drop, knowing that something is bound to happen because of what I did. I shouldn't have kissed her. I mean, that's fucking obvious, but I couldn't help it.

Now, my nerves are shot to hell as I mull over her possible responses.

After a few more minutes, I realize we're done with our second beer, and William still isn't back. "What is taking him so damn long?"

"Maybe he's found a girl to entertain himself." Remy shrugs, handing me a shot.

We agreed on no open drinks, but Remy has a good way of reading people, and I can tell she's trying to calm me down. "Or maybe Amora caught up to him."

I shake my head, gesturing to the large group around the fireplace. "She's over there. But you know who I haven't seen? At her own party, no less?"

The thought pierces through me, a hot flow of emotions boiling the contents of my stomach. There's no way.

"I'll be right back. Don't leave." She nods, but when her eyes drift to Blaze, sitting on the back of the couch, I can't help but groan inwardly. "Stay here, Remy."

"Yeah, yeah. Go get William." She shoos me off, tilting the beer bottle to her lips.

"Fine." I grimace but leave her, making a beeline for the stairs.

As soon as I touch the banister, I feel it. It's like an electric shock to my nerves, warning me to stop now. But like the dumbass I am, I keep going. Each step is heavy, weighted by something I can't seem to shake. The higher I climb, the faster my pulse thrums in my veins.

Then I hear it. The moans and cries I heard just this week. They're a little different now—high and strained, almost forced. But the same voice nonetheless.

I reach the top, knowing what I'm going to see, but it doesn't matter. My heart bottoms out, flopping into my stomach like a fish out of water.

William is mauling at her neck like a fucking animal, his hands twisted in her hair, pulling her neck back just enough to give him better access. One tan leg is wrapped around his waist, her heel digging into his jeans pocket. Her hands claw at his back, trying to pull him somehow closer than he already is.

My mouth is dry; a cotton ball lodged in the back. When I try to swallow around the knot, I almost choke from the pressure.

Of fucking course she would pull this shit. It's all she had left to do. She's engrained herself into every aspect of my fucking life, so I can't escape her. Everywhere I look, there she is. My project, my friend's tongue, my backyard.

The air thins out, and I decide this is it. I need to leave. Grab Remy and just fucking go. But just as I move to turn back downstairs, Lily's eyes open and find mine.

Lily

I did it. I finally got under his sturdy ass armor.

The look on Spencer's face is a pure mix of rage and agony. His lips are parted, and crimson red is flushing up his neck and spreading across his cheeks. His breaths are shallow, and I pity the flesh at his knuckles that's blossoming white from the tight clench.

He's battling what to do. I can see it in the tic of his jaw.

Should he yell? Throw this guy off me? Or instead, just watch?

There's no denying William knows what he's doing, but after being under Spencer and feeling the passion that hides under his nonchalant exterior, this pales in comparison. Everything begins to blur into the background as he works his way lower, unaware of Spencer a few feet away. My pussy clenches as he pushes into me, his erection flat against my entrance.

I groan, gripping his back, my eyes still planted on Spencer. After all this, I still wish it was him.

Maybe that's what's wrong. Maybe we need to just get it out of our system. Fuck the hatred out of each other and move on.

Forget.

Spencer finally sighs, letting the emotions slip from him as fast as they came, and I want to scream. He's going to walk off. Act like none of this bothers him and go right back to pretending nothing I do affects him.

My eyes widen. I feel them stretch open, almost begging him to do *something*. To *care*. But he doesn't. His throat bobs around a swallow, and he's gone, back down the stairs, like he never came.

I stop breathing. The burn in the back of my eyes are too strong to ignore. There's a heat covering my face, and I realize I'm ashamed. Ashamed that I'm resorting to being a petty toddler throwing a tantrum for attention. I should be used to it since the ones that are meant to care about me ignore me the most. But I'm not. Spencer is just a constant reminder that no matter how much I act out, it won't be enough.

I'm not enough.

Shifting my weight, I pull my heel from Williams' back pocket, pressing my hand against his chest. After a few seconds, he stops, peering at me from behind a forest of lashes.

His dark emerald eyes give me pause. There's something sparkling in the corner I can't quite read. He backs away, smoothing down his shirt, and pushes back thick locks that had fallen into his face. "You must be Liliana."

I suck in a deep breath through my nose. "Lily."

William nods, pursing his lips into a line. "Did he see?"

Suddenly, my mouth is dry, and I can't find my voice. He huffs, closing his eyes, and wipes a hand down his face. "Well, fuck. If this isn't the shittiest thing we could have done."

The temptation to read into that is strong. The way he implies Spencer gives a shit. But I know better now.

"I'm going to go to the restroom and get him the fuck out of here." He stalks behind me but turns before closing the door, swiping a calloused thumb over his lips. "You know, in a few months, none of this shit you're trying to do will matter. You'll be just a bad memory we laugh about until you're a name we can't remember."

Anger flares under my sternum when the door snaps closed. Gripping my necklace, I trek to the stairs, balancing myself on the banister. Even with everything in my control, I feel helpless. Like everything I'm doing is both working and backfiring all at the same time.

Screw it. Time for a show.

I mean, what else could I possibly mess up?

Spencer

Where is Remy?

My eyes flit to the kitchen, annoyance simmering in my already wrecked chest. I told her not to leave, yet she's gone. Hardheaded, just like every fucking woman in my life.

I find Blaze still in the same spot, his hand tracing the trim of lace down the back of some cheerleader's dress. Stacy, I think.

Grabbing my phone out of my pocket, I scroll to her name, and send a quick text. The faster I get out of here, the better. Maybe if I just stay right here, she'll come back looking for me and William.

William...

Fuck.

If I don't think about it, I'll be fine. I just need to get the fuck ou—

"Hmmm." I hear her purr behind me.

You got to be fucking kidding me.

I sigh, turning to see her propped against the counter, her little minion of a friend standing next to her.

"Oh, Spencer." She projects her voice and people within earshot turn to look. She glances down at her red heels, titlting one to the side for a little show. "My shoes seem to be pretty clean. What are you doing here, pup?"

A round of snickers echo through the kitchen. I roll my eyes and twist to leave, scared the lingering rage boiling under my skin will show. "You're right. I'll see myself out."

She knows I'm being curt, and even though she's done enough to last the rest of my life, it's clearly not enough. "Aw, don't tell me you're jealous of me and your little friend, Spencer."

I grit my teeth, turning just enough to look at her. "The only thing I'm jealous of is all the people who haven't met you."

Lily grins, biting the corner of her lip as if to keep from laughing.

"Maybe if I throw a stick, he'll leave faster," Amora chirps, arching an eyebrow.

I ignore her friend completely. "Do you ever get tired of being such a bitch, Lily?"

She doesn't miss a beat. "Call me what you want, but you can't say I'm *forgettable*."

Her words curl around my spine, snapping the last piece of me that gave a fuck, sending splinters through my heart. The liquor now rolling through my veins only intensifies the pain as it burrows into the muscle. Each beat pulling the splinter further inside until I'm sure I'll never get it out.

"I *fucking* hate you." My voice doesn't even sound like mine. It's raspy, deep...broken.

"Do I look like I give one fuck, Spencer?" she snaps.

Amora giggles, twirling a strand around her finger. "Nope, not one."

Lily leans against the island, a hand clenched around her necklace. "Exactly. Therefore your comment is irrelevant.

Now, unless you're here to clean someone else's shoe, you can go. Leave the hot guy though."

My mouth pops open, but a light tug on my elbow draws my attention. When I look down, I find Remy's glossy eyes. Her brows are furrowed, and her face is pinched as if she's in pain. "Let's go."

Suddenly there is no one else, the background fades into a blur of muted colors and voiceless music. All that's left is Remy.

She doesn't say anything else, leading me out the door and into the cold. I follow behind her obediently, not even realizing when we're walking through my front door and up to my room. It's as if she's switched on my autopilot somehow, and I'm merely going through the motions.

The bed sinks under her weight when she sits, waiting in silence as I turn on the bedside lamp, snapping back to reality.

The curtains are the first thing I notice. They're open, and the glow from Lily's room feels like a light to a bug. Before I close them, a shadow passes in front. No, two shadows.

Everything I held in finally crashes over the edge, pouring down my body, leaving it trembling. She kissed him on purpose. She knew he wouldn't fucking know who she was and she knew it would piss me off.

Fuck her.

My eyes squeeze closed against the burn.

I want to forget her.

Just for one fucking second.

I want to remember what it was like to not be so consumed by her.

To be able to breathe.

"Spence?"

The name pierces through my ears. But it's not Remy I hear. It's Liliana. The light, carefree Liliana. My heart thumps against my ribs violently, an ache radiating across the bone.

"Spencer?"

A hand touches my shoulder, forcing my eyes open.

Those eyes. They're so similar.

I move before I think, grabbing the sides of Remy's face and pressing my lips to hers. They're like soft pillows and taste like cotton candy. Everything about her is sweet, innocent. Even her hands lightly wrapped around my wrist are timid but welcoming. I deepen our kiss, groaning when I feel her hands squeeze me tighter.

My mouth moves of its own accord, kissing along her jaw, down her neck. Remy whimpers, her hands finding my chest, and pushing slightly. "Spencer..."

"Remy, please. Just..." I choke out. "I need to forget her. I *have* to. I can't...I can't..."

She grabs my face, pulling me to look at her. There's a shimmer on her cheeks and it only takes a second for me to realize it's from my face. I was crying. I *am* crying.

How fucking pathetic.

"It's okay, Spencer." Her small thumb runs along my temples. Her pupils are dilated, flicking back and forth as she tries to find the words.

I shake my head, "It's not."

She folds her arms around me, pulling my head to her shoulder. "Maybe not right now, but it will be."

TWENTY ONE

Nothing could have prepared me for school Monday. Despite the bundle of nerves I've been since the party, everything has been relatively quiet. But as soon as I walk through the doors, I feel the energy in the air. It's electric, clinging to my body like a second skin made of pure static. After striding another five feet, I hear the whispers streaming through the hall. They're all of the Spencer variety.

When the fuck did he get so hot?

Shoes? Girl, I need him to lick my entire body.

After the pleasure of not seeing my mother the entire weekend, I thought it was a sign of a good week to come.

Instead, it was an omen—the calm before the storm.

That storm is currently dressed in dark, torn jeans, a tight-fitting black shirt, and a pair of Steve Madden combat boots. Spencer's dark hair is pushed back, but stray brown locks sway on his smooth forehead.

There are no glasses on his face, leaving his caramel eyes fully exposed under the bright fluorescent lighting. He and

Remy are leaning against the lockers, both of their heads buried in a physics book. His right dimple sinks in when she points to a page.

Something's different about them. Their body language is off, perhaps less intimate than before. His shoulders are square, angled away from her, and he's making sure to keep a couple of feet between them.

A sick sort of satisfaction slides down my spine as I watch them, but Amora pops my happy bubble with her whines. "Girl, I can't with this damn algebra review packet. It's Monday, and he really wants to start our week like this? He was fucking passing them out to us in the hall! Teachers shouldn't be allowed to teach when they aren't getting any at home."

I grant her a half laugh, half huff, and nod to Spencer. "Have you seen this?"

She flips gold locks over her shoulder, letting her baby blues flash to him. "Yeah, that's all anyone is talking about. It's pretty fucking annoying. It's like Clark Kent took off his glasses, and everyone's losing their goddamn mind when just last week they were leaving dog food in his locker."

My sentiments exactly.

The high of his appearance will likely dwindle as the day goes on, so I decide not to think about it too much for now. Still doesn't stop my eyes from sliding to him a few times.

"See you at lunch." I give Amora a small wave and strut to math, making sure my path diverts right in front of him. I let my hips rock a little harder, and my hair sways near his arm when I pass. Even though I don't look, I can feel the heat of his stare on my back. It warms my core, and the brief sense of gratification boosts my mood to get me through the morning.

At least... I thought it would.

I heard Lindsey is gonna make a move. Ask him on a date.

Why were people such assholes to him? He's a total cinnamon roll.

Girl, Lauren is going with him to the movies this weekend.

No, I heard he's going with Tonya to a new restaurant downtown.

Bitch, if I don't have him eating my ass by this weekend, I'm-

By lunch, I'm not sure how much more my bleached roots can take. I can't breathe without hearing people pine over him, and the comments are getting dirtier by the second.

"He hasn't been in the lunchroom all week." Amora flops down across from me, pointing a Barbie pink nail across the table.

I don't bother looking up and continue twirling my pasta around my fork. It still pisses me off that he was the laughingstock this weekend, and now he's on everyone's to-be-fucked list just because he's wearing something decent. Meanwhile, I had to change everything about myself to be noticed.

The thumping between my temples accelerates, forcing me to try and rub the pain away. "Yeah, I know."

Amora sucks her teeth, leaning on her elbows. "What's up?"

I shake my head, averting my gaze. Amora may be a little bit of a lackey, and only speaks sarcasm, but she's proved to be a good friend. She's had to talk me off a ledge on too many occasions, yet when it comes to Spencer, I can't find it in me to tell her. As always, the words die in my throat, and I lean back, letting my fork clatter on the tray.

Amora leans in, lowering her voice where I have to strain to hear her. "Is it about her?"

She means my mother. After she found out everything in the hall, she started checking in on me a lot. I've had to stop her from waiting after school to prevent any possible 'run-ins.' But really, I'm happy she knows.

"I know you're eighteen, but we can still call CPS, can't we?"

Child Protective Services. There was only one time I thought about calling them. It was the first time my mom hit me hard enough to consider it—about three weeks after Dad left and two hours after her first drink. When I told her I was going to tell someone, she told me they would take me away from her and the boy in the backyard.

When she said that, my world stopped spinning. I would have done anything not to be separated from Spencer, and so I did. Endured years of the on again off again abuse only to find out the boy I did it for didn't even like me. Not to mention if I called CPS, I risk having the police involved. The last thing I need is to draw attention to the school's custodian getting arrested.

Shaking my head again, I inspect my nude tips.

"Girl, give me something. I can't just sit here and watch you shrivel up like this. It's pathetic." She waves a hand when she sees the anger flash across my face. "Which is something you're not. Now, put your fucking crown on and talk to me. What do I need to do?"

My eyebrows stay furrowed, but I clamp my mouth shut. Nothing I do works, so what's the point? This won't matter in a few months, anyway—regionals in March, Prom in April, Graduation first week of May.

Then I'm out of here.

Spencer will be just a bad memory, along with the rest of this screwed-up city.

I shift in my seat at the ache blooming in my chest. It doesn't matter that no one will miss me. That *he* won't miss me.

"Look at those freaking sluts." Amora's voice snaps me away from my wayward thoughts. "Flocking to him like vultures to roadkill. If only they knew what a freak he is."

"A freak?" Against my better judgment, I steal a glance at him. My heart stutters when our eyes meet, forcing a gasp from my mouth. One side of his lips draws up before he looks back at Stacy, whose leaning over his table, tits pressed to her chin.

"You did have him handcuffed to your fucking bed, Lil."

My core clenches involuntarily as the unwelcome image of a naked Spencer flits through my mind. Hooded eyes, sweaty brow, throbbing erection. A heaviness settles between my thighs, and I let my gaze flash to him one more time.

More cheerleaders have found their way to his table, fake laughter bouncing off the walls like we're in an amphitheater, and they're competing for his attention. Trepidation wiggles through my nerve endings, and the bitter taste of metallic hits my mouth when I realize I've bitten through my cheek.

Why do I care?

It doesn't matter why. I just do. And that notion alone is enough to formulate the idea. "I'm going to print the screenshot from the video."

Amora lifts a thin brow. "I mean, I can see the appeal, but his dick is big as fuck. Won't that just make the situation...less ideal?"

I appreciate her not pointing out the obvious. "Nothing a little Photoshop can't fix."

She shrugs and stabs her salad. "Send it to me, and I'll take care of it."

THIS AFTERNOON'S practice is probably the longest I've had in my life. Every muscle in my back is tense, straining against each move, threatening to tear at any second. Nothing I've done today has been able to get my mind off my plan for Spencer.

I've made my point—multiple times, and yet, I can't seem to satiate my desire for petty revenge.

It almost seems like more trouble than it's worth now. I'll let this be the last thing. After that, we'll be wrapping up the project, and I can finish the senior year strong. I need to refocus on the real prize. *Kentucky.*

Leaving the girls to run a few laps, I head into the locker room and gather my stuff for a shower. Right as my fingertips press the locker shut, my phone vibrates violently against the metal. I bite the inside of my lip, annoyance prickling behind my eyes, but I decide to see who it is.

Unknown.

It's been quite some time since the last call, and a prodding voice in the back of my head tells me to answer it.

"Hello?"

A shrill scream nearly blows my phone's speakers. "Sobrina. Ay, dios mio. I have been trying to get a hold of you for weeks! My damn phone had some damage, and anytime I tried to call you, it went to voicemail."

This voice. It's older, more panicked, but familiar. I haven't heard it in nearly ten years. *Holy shit.* "Aunt Mina?"

"Si! Who else would it be! Querida, please, tell me where you are. I have been looking for you."

Confusion and anger slither up my spine, working its way into my already tense neck. I haven't heard from my mom's sister in a long time, not since right after my mother's affair.

Before that, though, she was the best thing in my world, always checking in on me and FaceTiming every week. She lived halfway across the country, but she always made time to chat—about school, my parents, the boy in my backyard, everything. She was more of a mother to me than my biological one.

But when my life started falling apart, and I needed her the most, she followed up with my family's signature disappearing act. I figured she was just another person who forgot I existed.

Somehow I find my voice. "What do you mean you've been looking for me?"

"Pequena, I have been looking for you for thirteen years! Oh, we have so much to talk about. I will explain everything when I get there."

Thirteen years?

My parents and I moved to Washington when I was five, right after my grandmother died. I didn't know her since Mom never took me to see her, but I remember how worked up she was. It was the first time I saw my parents fight, and not two weeks later, we were on a flight to Emerald Falls.

Did my mother not tell Mina where we went?

Thankfully the lockers are near to hold me up as my knees nearly collapse. I scrub a hand down my face, my mind reeling, trying to put the pieces of an incomplete puzzle together.

"I'm in Emerald Falls. W-Washington." My voice cracks, and she sniffles in the receiver.

"I'm coming, Sobrina. Ay, dios mio, baby. I am on my fucking way. Text me your address." Muffles in the background indicate her rush. My mouth opens to respond, but the slam of a door and jiggling of keys gives me pause.

She's really coming?

"I love you, Liliana. See you soon."

The phone clicks and my screen dims. A sudden stream of tears breaks free and tumbles down my cheeks. Hearing her voice... those words break open a chasm in my chest, letting everything buried underneath bubble to the surface.

There's one emotion, in particular, I shouldn't be feeling, but it takes over all the rest. It blooms in my mind like a sunflower in a garden. Despite what may be around it, it's the only thing you notice.

Hope.

It's digging in deep, spreading its roots to the tips of my toes. I hope she comes. I hope she—

Muffled chatter echoes through the outside of the locker room, signaling the girls are coming. Using my discarded sweater, I wipe my face just as they walk inside. I slip into the shower hall before they notice and enter the last stall, sliding to the floor. My shoulders shake as silent sobs wrack through my body, coming from the depths of my shredded heart.

I grab the small charm on my neck and pull it back and forth, breathing through the swell of emotions.

Maybe, just maybe, I'm not alone, and I'm not completely forgotten.

TWENTY TWO

A small bell rings from my pocket, filling the tiny room with its soft tone. While I used to cringe at the sound, I haven't had to lately. Just last week, I was the laughingstock, the dirt beneath everyone's shoes. The stand-in joke when someone needed a good laugh.

Now?

Now I have three dates in one day, four on the next, and I plan to go on every single one.

Back in Idaho, when William pushed me on the dating train, it was a nuisance at first. Meaningless dates with knock-off Liliana's to fill the void she left. But after a while, I started appreciating them. They gave me the release I needed after studying day in and day out. They let me forget for a few hours that my mother was in the next room, literally *forgetting* me.

It forced me to stop thinking about the one person I couldn't have and the fifty others I could.

Maybe these new dates can provide some of the same therapy they did then. At least I can hope.

The metal doorknob rattles before Lily appears. Despite the weather, she's wearing a long sleeve off the shoulders sweater and a heathered pencil skirt. Soft blonde curls tumble around her, and my eyes find themselves attached to the silver necklace lying on her collarbone. The little charm is hidden beneath her top, but I vaguely try to make out the shape.

"Eyes up here, pup," she hisses, tossing her handbag across the chairback.

I roll my eyes, quickly tapping the remote on the table while simultaneously starting the timer. A royal purple floods the small room, making Lily's contacts reflect an iridescent glow.

For the remaining time, I don't bother looking at her. I can't. Every time I do, images of her wrapped around William flood my thoughts. My jaw will clench until I'm sure I've cracked a molar. Little spots will cloud my vision as the anger begins to consume me, and my breaths will come harder and faster like I'm trying not to drown.

Still, even without looking, it happens. Slowly at first, then all at once. My pulse begins to race, and soon I'm struggling to suck in air.

Fuck her for making me want to punch my best friend in the face. And honestly, fuck her for making me feel.

The timer buzzes, pulling me back up for air. I gulp it greedily before silencing the alarm, keeping my eyes on the table. "Hey."

"Hey."

"How are you?"

"Dandy. How are you?"

"Busy," I cut, glancing up.

She scoffs, rolling her eyes as she crosses her arms and mutters, "I'm sure."

"How are you feeling?" I ignore her comment. I'm sure she's referring to the influx of attention surrounding me, especially since a few of my dates are members of her little cult cheer squad. It must really fuck her up that after all she's done, girls still want me. Too bad I can't make her watch the way she made me.

"Dandy," she repeats, but the tips of her ears bloom a soft pink, forcing my lips to twitch and split into a grin. That makes the blush worse, and the heat spreads to her cheeks. She purses her pouty lips, and my gaze snaps to them.

I wonder if she purred under William the way she did with me. If she melted from the warmth and fell apart in his arms. From what I saw, it looked like it, but it didn't *sound* like it.

And if anyone knows how to fake something, it's Lily.

The memory of them together tries to weave through my chest, squeezing my heart in the process. I clear my throat, a failed attempt to dismiss it as I wait for her question.

"How are you feeling?" Her words come out slow and soft, almost as if she cares about my response. It's the perfect therapist's tone. I'm curious if she still practices it in the mirror like she used to.

"How long are you going to sit there and talk to yourself, Liliana?" I huff, tossing the big beach ball in the air.

She turns, her sun-kissed tan from our day in the ocean shimmers under the setting sun. We've been in the treehouse for a whole hour and haven't read one manga or ate one bucket of popcorn. Instead, she wanted to practice some psychologist lines in the mirror.

"You never let me practice with you, so I have to do it somewhere."

"Because you make me feel like some kind of lab rat," I spit, but quickly find myself regretting it. That's not the real reason, but I can't bring myself to tell her that. Tell her how good she sounds for a twelve-year-old kid and makes me want to scream on a white couch about all the bottled-up thoughts stuck in my head. And I don't want her to see me as a freak. As someone to fix, or pity.

No. I want her to see me the way I see her.

With love in her eyes.

I swallow down the knot forming in my throat and answer. "Hopeful." *Regretful.* "If you could do anything right now, what would you do?"

Her glistening eyes narrow, and after a minute, she sighs. "Eat popcorn. If you could do anything right now, what would you do?"

My breath catches in my throat. A fucking reaction. I know that's what she wants—what she always wants, yet I can't help but wish a piece of her really means it. Clearing my throat, I force myself to stay focused. Just one more question. "I'd be balls deep in someone."

Her jaw clenches and relaxes three times before she smirks and flicks a stray chip of paint off the desk. "I'd feel bad for the girl on the receiving end of that. Probably the smallest three inches she's ever seen and the worst two minutes of her life."

"Correct me if I'm wrong, but three inches is enough to reach the G-spot, isn't it?"

Her mouth pops open, but she clicks her tongue in annoyance to cover her surprise. "I don't have anything extra today. Are we done?"

The question slips out before I can stop it. "What are we doing here, Lily?"

Her small head tilts sideways, brows pulling together like she's genuinely confused. It's the face she used to make when we were younger. When she was caught doing something and couldn't lie to me about it because I know her tell —cherry red ears.

My heart feels heavy, and there's a slight hitch in my breath, but Lily doesn't seem to notice. She untenses her face and leans back, hands folded deftly on her knee. "We aren't doing anything."

"Don't play stupid. We're playing this little back and forth game like two pawns on a chessboard," I snap, ignoring the thrum of my pulse at the back of my throat.

She forces a laugh, a thick vein protruding from the side of her smooth neck. "Spence, please. I'm the queen in this *game*. I'm just biding my time before I wipe you off this board and claim checkmate."

The way she says it so simply, like it's as easy as saying the sky is blue, boils the blood coursing through me. "What the fuck happened to you?"

Lily jerks back, her eyes widening as she shoves a deep red stiletto nail into her sternum. "Me? Look at you. Mister, *I don't give a fuck what everyone thinks*." When her finger turns on me, a pink indent remains on her skin. "You come to school with your hair slicked back, a tight shirt on, and think you're suddenly the shit?"

"That's not what I'm talking about, Lil—"

"Then what are you talking about? Please, let me know."

"You're a bitch. And a fucking bully—"

Her sudden cackle surges across the table, thumping into

my ego with the force of a cannon. "Bully? Are you five? Can you really not take what I've dished out?"

I throw my hands up, defeat leaving a sour taste in my mouth, compelling me to spit it out. "It's not that I can't take it. It's that the person on the giving end used to be..."

The burn prickling the back of my eyes forces my mouth to clamp shut. The heat expands in my head, making me dizzy. I squeeze my eyes closed and pinch the bridge of my nose, willing the ache away. I can't fucking do this.

Hold fast, hold steady.

"Used to be what?" It's just a whisper, but something that sounds a lot like hurt lines her words.

"Be my best friend," I finish.

When I open my eyes, Lily's are on me. She blinks twice before gazing down. Her knotted fingers twist back and forth, palms digging into her thigh. I can tell she wants to say something. Tell me the thing I'm clearly fucking missing...

But she doesn't.

Two seconds pass, and the mask is back, guarding her while shielding me from *seeing* her. Her delicate features become impassive again, and she shifts in her chair, gripping the once tucked necklace in her hand. "Are we done?"

"Yes."

No.

She doesn't skip a beat, standing and throwing her bag over her shoulder. I want to yell, to grab her around the waist and beg her to talk to me. Tell me what happened. Explain why we are so content being just strangers that know each other's secrets.

Why we are okay with hating each other.

But like her, I don't. Instead, I watch Lily walk out the door like the coward I've always been when it comes to her.

Because no matter what I say, she'll still leave, and I'll still let her.

I STARE at the flyer clutched in my hands.

That's me. Naked and handcuffed to Lily's bed. My face is blurred out and my dick has been photoshopped, but the message at the bottom is clear enough for anyone to guess its owner.

The dog of Emerald Falls may be lacking, but he'll make up for it with his submissiveness.

Of course, she did this. Why not? There is no bar too low for her.

"Did you see the mascot they had tattooed on your thigh?" Remy's voice teems with irritation, her little face turning red as she nods to the paper.

At this point, Remy isn't surprised by anything Lily does anymore. But she says the pieces aren't adding up. She claims Lily is lashing out. Though from what, I can't care to guess because honestly, *she's* the one who hurt *me*. Lily is the person who changed, who shut *me* out, told *me* to stay in Idaho, and ended our friendship.

My head begins swimming, making me dizzy, forcing me to sink into her fluffy futon.

Remy pats me on the shoulder before collapsing next to me. "I mean, it's obvious the picture was doctored."

I huff, scrubbing my hands over my face. "Yeah, but I don't think that was the big turnoff. It must have been the fun little caption. Every date canceled."

Remy's bright eyes widen, and her mouth creates a

perfect O. "I mean, forget them, right? Obviously, they weren't worth your time."

"Remy, I could really use a distraction, someone to sink my dic—"

"I'm going to go wash my ears out, be right back." She shoves her shoulder into mine and stands, dramatically walking toward the door.

"Oh stop. That shit you read in the romance novels is ten times worse," I deadpan.

She flushes a deep fuchsia almost immediately, releasing the doorknob and wrapping her arms around herself. A tightness tugs across my chest. *Shit.*

"I'm not judging you, Remy. I was just saying it's not like you haven't heard it."

Her bashful gaze meets mine, and a smile spreads slowly across her face. The laughter she'd been holding in spills out, bouncing off the walls. It's a sweet sound, light and infectious, coercing a chuckle from me easily.

"You were messing with me?"

"Of course. I know what I read. It's called smut." She flops back down, grabbing the paper from my hand. "Not as entertaining as this, though. I just wanted you to smile a little."

I roll my eyes, letting my head fall back. "I'm not her enemy."

"But she doesn't seem to know that. For her, you are, and she's going to win if you don't figure out what game you're playing."

My hands curl into fists before I unclench them and dig the pads of my palms into my eyes. "It seems like chess, and according to her, I am just a pawn."

Remy's brows knit together, and she chews on the inside

of her bottom lip. After a few seconds, her hazel eyes narrow. "Okay, so your original lie of why she was bothering you may hold some truth."

"Huh?"

She grunts, waving a hand around. "I'm saying. She obviously got put in our class for a reason. Maybe something to look good on her transcript? So she could be using you for that."

"Yeah, but she said she was waiting to call a checkmate."

"*That's* the part about your past. You're missing something, Spencer. No eighteen-year-old girl is going to go out of her way to do all this." She points to the flyer. "Unless she's been hurt. Bad."

"Remy." I gaze back at the ceiling, following a path in the textured paint. The hollowness in my chest is back, expanding into my gut.

If I knew what I did, I wouldn't hesitate to fix it. Even though I despise who she is now and can't stand the feelings my fucking body goes through from just seeing her, I would try. Because Remy is right. This isn't Liliana. No one changes this drastically without a catalyst.

I shouldn't care. The logical side of my brain is screaming for me to let it go, not to look into things anymore. What's done is done, and there's no coming back from how far she and I have fallen.

But then there's my heart. As torn and broken as it is, its beats are strong, thrumming through my body with any thoughts of her. It consumes me with a raw passion I can feel from the shell of my ear to the tips of my toes.

So while I may hate the girl with damn near every fiber of my being, I want to set things right.

Maybe then, I can let her go.

TWENTY THREE

There's a horrendous flutter in my stomach, sloshing around the three cups of coffee I drank this morning to keep myself awake. I stayed up all night, nerves still in shambles from my meeting with Spencer, and anxiety whips through me as I clean the house again for the fifteenth time.

All I thought about were his eyes. The caramel swirling around his chocolate irises as he looked at me with a strange sort of curiosity. Like he doesn't know that everything we are now is a result of *him*.

I almost told him. Almost broke down and exposed how weak and messed up I am over it. Because I *am* hurt. I'm pissed and even worse, my heart still doesn't know whether to beat or stop when he's near me.

My eyes flicker across the backyard to the dark house behind mine, and a familiar tightness pulls across my chest before I rip my gaze away.

I can't allow myself to think too deeply for too long.

Sighing, I fluff the navy pillow one more time, double-checking to make sure everything is perfect.

My aunt Mina's flight is coming in today. Actually... I glance at the stove clock, and my pulse stutters. *Shit.*

Her flight's already landed, and since she refused to let me pick her up, her Uber could be here any damn second.

Taking the steps two at a time, I fly up the stairs and into the bathroom. When I look in the mirror, it's hard not to cringe at my appearance. The shiner my mom gave me last week is now a ghost of a bruise, leaving a tint of green that's easy enough to cover. A little dry shampoo and a messy bun take care of my hair problem. But the red rim surrounding my eyes will have to be blamed on my contacts if she asks.

But she might not. Why would she? My nerves start to tingle again. What if she does?

I remember when I was young, around seven, and we would video chat, she would ask me about anything and everything.

"You look so pretty. Did you put that yellow bow in your hair?" My aunt's face fills the small screen, her grin stretching from ear to ear.

I beam my biggest, proudest smile, not even worrying about my missing top tooth. "Yes! I even did the braid, Aunt Mina. I watched a video on it!"

"Ah, mija, you did so well. Muy buena. ¿Dónde está tu mamá?"

Peering over the iPad, I make sure Dad isn't anywhere near me. Shrugging, I wipe away the sudden gush of tears, burning my eyes. "Her room. Like always."

"Do you know where you are yet?"

I shake my head before my father calls from the kitchen that it's time for bed.

I never understood what she meant when she would ask that. When she first asked me about it, I would always tell her home. But then she would prod with more questions like street names or the name of my school. She even wanted me to describe my neighborhood.

I've been looking for you for thirteen years.

It still doesn't make complete sense, and I feel like I'm putting together a puzzle with only my sense of touch. I can't see the overall picture, but the pieces are beginning to lock into place.

Tugging the oversized sweater over my head, I turn to the bathroom door just as the bell rings.

She's here.

With shaking hands, I clutch the stair railing and descend as slowly as possible. The door feels so big in comparison to my hand as I grip the cold metal knob and turn. It swings open with the cold breeze, letting snow flurries dance inside the threshold.

My aunt Mina stands in the middle of the door, wrapped in so many layers, I can't make out her face, and she has a small suitcase by her side. A bubble of nervous laughter spills from my mouth as I take a step back. "Aunt Mina?"

The triple-wrapped figure shakes and moves sluggishly inside. Her voice is muffled, but I'd know it anywhere. "Si, now help your dear old aunt. I'm liable to get frostbite out here!"

I giggle again, wiping my slick hands on my jeans before moving to grab a padded arm. I help her through the foyer and shut the door, then pry the luggage from her frigid grasp. It's an odd meeting, but it's much less awkward, which eases my pulse a little.

"It's not that cold."

She huffs, using her marshmallow-puffed arms to unwrap her three scarfs. "I have never seen snow my entire life. All these jackets are from the airport store."

Laughing, the wound muscles in my neck seem to relax. She was always good at weird situations, had a way of taking them and inserting her charismatic charm to pacify even the worst circumstance.

I help her unzip the four types of jackets. Each one shed makes the rush of blood in my ears impossibly loud.

Down jacket.

Parka.

Fleece.

Body warmer.

When I finally reach the warm body of my aunt, a fire hits the back of my throat.

Her burnt honey eyes are the same as I remember, tucked behind small glasses that frame her heart-shaped face. Her beautiful olive skin is without one wrinkle, except the two little crow's feet at the corners of those stunning eyes. Her perfect ruby lips stretch into a smile, and when I look back up, I see a trail of tears making a path through the light dusting of her blush.

We both pause, but then, as if not a second of time has passed between us, she grabs me, embracing me in a type of hug I've long forgotten. I melt into her, wrapping my arms around her back and squeezing until the muscles in my fore-arms quiver. The combination of everything that's happened with Spencer and me, my shitty parents, and my lack of sleep overwhelm me, letting the walls I've built crumble on impact. The sobs rip through my body, and I grip her tighter, scared if I let go, she might disappear like everyone else.

Right now, I'm not Lily, nor the captain of the cheer squad, or even the Queen of Emerald Falls. I'm the five-year-old little girl, holding on to her aunt for dear life, so I don't have to move to the opposite side of the map with people that don't even love me.

"Shhh, mija. I'm here now." My aunt's hand strokes my hair, tucking a loose piece back into my bun.

I'm not sure how long we stand like this. Second, minutes, hours. But when I'm finally able to loosen my hold, my body and mind are spent. My shoulders fall as I back up, and I wrap my arms around my waist, partially embarrassed I've just slobber-sobbed on the woman.

She steps forward, closing the gap and placing two tender hands on my shoulders, anchoring me in place. A shiver reverberates down my spine, the intimate touch is something so unfamiliar to me now, my body doesn't know how to respond.

Mina's eyes soften, a small grin curling the edges of her lips. "Whatever is going on in that loca head of yours, stop it. I'm here now, and I am not going anywhere."

I swallow around the knot in my throat, blinking back the wall of tears now clouding my vision, and attempt a nod.

"How about some tea?"

"Sounds great," I croak, wiping my face raw with the back of my hand.

We move together, walking through the foyer to the open kitchen. She sets her jackets in a pile on the edge of the couch before strolling to the large back sliding door. Her eyes drift to the dark house, and she turns her face, calling over her shoulder. "That little boy still live back there?"

The knot I swallowed earlier plummets to my stomach,

making me nauseous. I'd told her about Spencer when I first met him. "Yeah, but he's not so little anymore."

She laughs out her nose, turning to climb onto one of the barstools. "I suppose he isn't."

The lightness in her tone suggests she thinks there was more to my comment, but going down that wormhole isn't on the menu today. Today, I want to find out what happened. Where the hell she's been and why I've been left alone.

"So, how was your flight?" I initiate the small talk, moving around the kitchen to make some tea.

"Mija, why are you nervous?" Her voice is soft and a little timid. It forces me to look over my shoulder at her while I fumble around with the kettle.

"I'm not." *Lie.*

Well, not a complete lie. My increased heart rate and trembling knees also prove something I don't want to admit —I'm scared. No, terrified, really. I have no idea what the hell is about to happen. If she'll answer all the questions I have. If it will change anything. If it can *heal* anything.

My aunt folds her hands on the bar, and I catch a glimpse of her fresh white tip manicure. Still no ring. I have no idea how a gem like her hasn't been whisked away by now. Even when I was young, I saw the way her soul illuminated the world around her, casting its light into every dark crevasse. And she had the personality of your favorite warm drink. One sip, and your whole body swells with happiness.

All this lost time.

An ache stretches across my chest, and the small talk I had planned evaporates.

We stay quiet as I prepare our drinks, and while the silence is welcome, it also shifts my stomach's little contents.

Finally, I give her a glass and lean against the opposite side of the counter.

She stirs her tea methodically before tapping it against the lip, casting rhythmic clinks in the air. When her warm honey eyes lift to me, she grins sympathetically, sighing as she sits back. "I suppose you have a lot of questions."

I nod, tracing my finger around the rim of my mug. It's warm in my hands, and I mentally anchor myself to the sensation.

"Ask me, but know I won't lie to you, mija. You're old enough now to know the truth. But first, can I ask *you* something?"

My eyebrows knit together, but I nod again.

"Where is everyone? Robert, your mom?"

My previously warm fingers start to tingle, and I lean into the counter deeper to keep myself steady. I should lie, but it burns on my tongue. "I don't know. They haven't lived here in months."

Her lips pull into a straight line, and her jaw clenches, but she doesn't say anything. Instead, her throat bobs with a swallow, and she clears her throat. "Ask whatever you need to know, mi amor."

And I do. I ask her everything.

"HOW ARE YOU?" Blaze grips the heel of my foot, squeezing and kneading it through the thin blanket.

I called him after the day with my aunt, and as always, he came. The perfect knight.

My mind is still reeling from the day, and thankfully since it's Thanksgiving break, I have time to shift through all the shit I'm still processing. I lean back into my pillow, letting my head thunk lightly against the wall, and stare down the bed at Blaze.

"I'm still not sure. Just a lot to take in."

"Summary?" His dark brow lifts, his gray eye shimmering under the soft light of my lamp.

I peer out the window and watch the snow tumble around, dancing with other flakes as they make their descent. It's so graceful, it's almost like watching an intricate ballet. The whole ensemble is peaceful, lulling me into a sleepy daze.

I'm so tired.

Blaze squeezes my foot lightly, drawing my attention back to him.

A summary. Where would I even start?

"My mom never wanted kids," I choke out the hardest part. Maybe then it will be easier to say the rest. "She never wanted me."

He sighs and stands, flipping off the side table light. He scootches me over and slides under the sheet beside me. The warmth of his body soothes the ache a little that's radiating across my chest.

Blaze leans in close, rubbing my cheek with a calloused finger, and I realize I'm crying. "You don't have to do this today."

I sniff, shaking my head. "Can we just lie here for a bit?"

Even in the dark, I feel his soft smile as he pushes me onto my side and curls up behind me, wrapping a strong arm around my waist. Blaze knows better than anyone the pain of having shitty parents. We share that commonality, and I think that's why we have such a special bond. Somewhere between best friends and siblings, sharing a connection no one our age should have to.

His deep hums vibrate my body, calming my mind, and thrusting me into a comfortable sleep, his words echoing as I fall.

"I'll sit with you in the dark until you're ready to find the light."

TWENTY FOUR

"Don't forget to get a list of all the emails and learning portals." My dad's voice booms through the speaker as I finish plating my mother's breakfast.

I nod even though he can't see me and make sure I have it all listed on my day's agenda. "Yeah, I got it, Dad. Anything else?"

He sighs, and I picture him scrubbing a hand down his face before scratching the stubble on his chin. He sounds as tired as I am. Thanksgiving break wasn't as relaxing as I'd hoped—most of it was spent finishing things I wouldn't be able to over the Christmas break. I uploaded the majority of my science data into the cloud so I could work on it anywhere and finished organizing some binders for next semester's classes.

"No, son. I just want to make sure you finish strong, even with our new circumstances."

A sting seeps from my heart, rolling around my chest and pinching the muscle. I rub at it absentmindedly, peering up as my mother meanders toward me. Her long gown is too big on her now, leaving the bone structure of her shoulders poking through the fabric. She moves slowly, and I don't miss the way her thin arms trail across the back of the couch as if to help steady her.

"It will be fine, Dad. Mom's up. I got to go." I turn back to my mother, setting her bowl down on the bar. "I'm running a little late today, but I have your alarms all set, and lunch and your sticky notes all done. Your favorite shows are programmed and all on timers so you don't have to worry about a thing. Nurse will be here any minute."

Her lips stretch into a smile and relief surges through me. She knows me today.

"My sweet boy. You always take such good care of your momma. You'll make some woman very happy someday."

I grant her a smirk and a small chuckle. "I don't know about all that, Mom."

"Hush child. You're perfect." She reaches out a frail hand and I take it, grimacing when the cold extremity nearly shocks me. Her soft eyes scan my face and I feel bare beneath her stare. She's always been good with reading me like a book, telling me things I didn't know I needed until she said them. "You're still sad about something."

I try to smile but realize I can't, and instead just nod.

She strokes the side of my hand with her soft thumb. "If you continue to focus on this hurt, you will continue to suffer, son. Try to remember, not all storms come to disrupt your life. Some come to tear everything down, so you can build something new."

This time I do smile and release her hand so I can round the bar to embrace her. Imagining life without her feels impossible yet inevitable. Creeping closer to reality and pulling me further in the dark.

I struggle to breathe over the pain, restricting my throat and ignore the prickling at the back of my eyes.

Hold fast, hold steady.

After a few minutes, I grab her breakfast and help her back to the room. I set her up for the day and kiss each temple.

"I'll be back soon. Please get some rest."

She smiles and turns to her soap opera, stirring the oatmeal I know she won't finish. "Be sweet, my precious son, and have a good day."

I clear my throat, and softly close the door, locking her inside.

Just three more weeks. *I can make it.*

THE DAY LASTS at least ten hours, and by the time I collapse in the chair of our experiment room, I'm two seconds away from falling asleep. Lucky, or unlucky, depending on how I look at it, Lily appears on time.

A long black dress clings to her curves, showcasing every dip and arc of her body. I try my best to ignore the surge of blood to my dick and remind myself what a fucking bitch she is. How everyone in the damn school has a real fucked image of said dick, and she's the reason I haven't gotten any. And while the meaningless sex isn't a huge deal, the distraction that comes with it is.

I flip on the light and set the timer, focusing on the time as the numbers tick by. Today's color is a soft shade of pink. It fills the room with a strange soft aura, and my pulse increases at the thought of the many ways today could go. The color is known to stimulate creativity and calmness, but once adjusted, can invoke feelings of agitation and passion.

The timer buzzes and I start. "Hey."

"Hey," she mirrors, and it becomes clear neither of us want to be here.

All the better for me, I'll make this quick.

"How was your day?"

She yawns, covering her mouth before examining her cuticles. "Long. How was your day?"

"Busy." Which is a lie. It was fucking overwhelming. Even though all the teachers and counselors were kind about my situation, getting set up to take on the load nearly caved my brain in. "How are you feeling?"

Her eyes flicker to my lips unexpectedly, and I shift in my chair. "Better. How are you feeling?"

Better? The phrase is loaded and I can't lie and say I'm not curious. While I want to cuss her out for the posters from before break, and ask her what her fucking problem is, there's something different about her too. She seems lighter maybe. Even her shoulders rest a little higher. Maybe she's happy she fucked up all my dates?

No, there's something else playing behind the shimmer in her eyes.

She clears her throat and I realize I've just been staring. "Anxious. If you could do anything right now, what would you do?"

"Leave. If you could do anything right now, what would you do?"

I sigh, sitting back and think of the millions of things I plan to do instead of working on this damn project. "Rest."

She scoffs, crossing her arms and purses her lips.

Yes, the busy queen bee of Emerald Falls has so much to do, so many people to command, she probably thinks rest is for the weary.

"What do you plan to do in the future?" I have no fucking clue why I ask her that.

Clearly neither does she. Her arched brows furrow and she taps a long nail impatiently on the desk. "Kentucky. I'll be cheering there."

"What happened to psychology?"

She huffs, inspecting a crack on the wall next to her chair. "Please spare me the lecture I know you have. Nothing is wrong with going to a school for cheer. What if I want to cheer for the NFL one day?"

Something close to anger bubbles underneath my skin, searing through my veins. "Football? You want these good ass grades to go shake your ass for a football team? Who the fuck has you wanting to do that? Blaze?"

Shit. As soon as I say it, I feel like an asshole, but I can't turn back now. And while I do think cheer is pretty badass, I can't stop the hateful words from spewing like a toxin.

Her chair screeches against the linoleum as she backs up, her teeth gritted as she hisses. "Don't you dare say shit about Blaze. You don't know him."

"Oh, I'm sorry. But really, did he fuck all the common sense out of you? You're going through all this trouble and giving up your dream for something you can only do while you're young and hot?" The once light pink hue in the room has now darkened to a red. Or maybe it's the blood rushing through my head.

She's let some dumbass fuck her and her head up, and the last bit of respect I had for her dwindles, burning in the flames of her ignorance.

Lily stands, her chest heaving from her own anger beginning to boil over. Her knuckles bloom white as she clenches her fists. "Fuck you, and at least Blaze didn't leave me to fucking rot here alone, Spencer!"

Her words cut through me, slicing me raw. "Leave you? *You're* the one who told me not to come!"

Rage spins through me, coating each nerve in pure fire. Beads of sweat roll down my temples. If she thinks she's going to turn this whole thing around and play the fucking victim, she's got another thing coming.

She did this.

She *keeps* doing this.

Lily's head whips back, a humorless laugh shaking her body. "Are you kidding me right now? For someone so damn smart, how can you be so dense?"

"What the fuck are you talking about, Lily? It's clear you hate my fucking existence. So please, enlighten me as to how any of this is because of me!" I'm standing now, irritation licking up my spine and tensing every muscle in my body.

"She's nothing—no one to me. Just a summer friend that makes my summer suck a little less." She spits the words like acid rain, and they hit their mark, searing into my chest.

The conversation is one I remember because I had it a million times. Every time I came here for the summers, William would give me shit about being pussy whipped over Liliana. When I was younger, he would call it sprung, but when we grew up and figured out that sexual desire was coursing through me, he changed the phrase. And he wasn't lying.

I was.

I was head over fucking heels for this short, sassy, smart, brown-head girl. The one that kept me up till two am in the treehouse reading cartoons and watching scary movies. The girl who took away the pain of watching my mother slowly deteriorate.

She was everything.

But like any fucking stupid ass kid, when William gave me a hard time about it, I lied. I didn't want him constantly calling me a pussy.

"This..." I pause, breathing slowly as I recall the time Liliana's mood shifted one afternoon. She must have heard me talking to him somehow. "Is all because of a conversation you weren't even supposed to hear?"

A bitter laugh echoes in the space between us. "No shit, Sherlock."

"Lily. Why the fuck didn't you ask me about it? I would have fucking explained!" I rake a hand through my hair, gripping it by the roots. "All this time."

All the lost time over a misunderstanding.

I want to punch my fucking face in. "We were best friends, for fuck's sake, Lily. I would have told you—"

"Told me what? Made up some lies so I would forgive you? Make—"

"That I loved you! And I didn't want to keep hearing shit from Will." I bark, unable to keep the confession locked away. It's the past, but it's the truth. A truth she needs to hear, even if it isn't the case anymore.

Her hazel eyes widen, and her mouth drops open but nothing comes out for a full minute. "What?"

"To which part? That I loved you?" I scoff, rolling my eyes. "Come on, Lily. Anyone with fucking eyes could tell I was crazy about you. Had been since the day I saw you climbing your trees with those yellow ribbons in your hair."

Even as a kid, when my soul saw hers, it smiled. I just didn't know what it meant back then.

She shakes her head, her gaze locked on the desk between us. When she speaks, I think it's more to herself than to me. "That's not possible."

I answer her anyway. "Yes, it is. I was, and if you would have just *talked* to me, all this could have been avoided."

A hollowness expands in my chest and my feet move of their own accord, carrying me around the desk. I reach up, grabbing both sides of her face, and force it so she's looking at me. Our breaths mingle, and my stomach clenches when I smell the sweet honey coasting off her lips, reminding me of their taste.

"Why didn't you just talk to me?" She tries to jerk away from me, but I hold her still. She doesn't get to run away this time. "Talk to me."

Lily's eyes fill with tears and finally, they spill over, running down her cheeks and dripping onto my wrists. "You left me."

My entire body tenses. The sight of her breaking down cracks open a piece of my chest, surging around my heart and squeezing. There is something so much deeper than I can see, and even with everything that's happened... I *still* want to see her. To fix whatever has made her feel like she has to wear this facade, because it can't be just from me.

I rub away one tear with my thumb and she closes her eyes, leaning into my palm. Whoever we were ten minutes ago slips away, leaving two best friends who've missed the fuck out of each other.

"Liliana?" I whisper, and immediately I regret it.

Her fake green eyes land on me, and I can see Lily's mask is back in place. She shoves my hands away and reaches for her bag. "Fuck you, Spence. You have no idea what I've been through. You don't get to just say it was all a big misunderstanding and think that will make everything okay."

My stomach bottoms out and bile hits the back of my throat. Without thinking, my hand lurches out, gripping her forearm and spinning her around. "And you don't get to sit here and act like you haven't made my life a living fucking hell these past couple months. Like you're the only one that has shit going on."

Lily's hand moves fast but I'm faster, catching it right before it connects with my face and yank her body into me, crashing my lips on hers.

A combination of anger and hurt swirl in my head, making me dizzy, but the sound of her moans in my mouth push it away, replacing it with hunger. Her hands tangle in my hair, tugging it with such force spikes of pain radiate through the roots.

I slam her against the wall, gripping a thigh that she wraps around my torso, bunching her skirt around her waist, and grasping the back of her neck with my free hand. We push into each other, forcing every part of our bodies to connect. My dick swells, pushing through my sweats and into her hot center that's pressed against my stomach. I can feel the heat through her thin panties and a growl rips from the back of my throat.

Her hands leave my hair and claw at the hem of my shirt, pulling it up until I disconnect from her sweet mouth and lift my arms so she can tear it over my head. I kiss along her jaw, nipping as I make my way down her neck, reveling in the way her leg tightens around me, drawing me somehow closer to her center. One of my hands roves over her breast, rolling over a pebbled nipple, while the other moves to her hips, my fingers digging into her soft side.

She tastes so fucking good.

Her smell, her perfect skin, everything about her in this moment as she's wrapped around me strips away every thought. My head is mush, only able to focus on her writhing under me, aching to feel how much I want her. Lily's whimpers are music to my ears as I work my way down, licking across her collarbone until my tongue finds her necklace. I follow it down until the charm scratches under my chin.

Then it happens. She rips herself from beneath me and is across the room before I can decipher what the fuck just happened. Her chest is still heaving as her hand clutches the necklace, pulling it back and forth.

I lift a hand, grabbing my shirt off the floor while keeping my eyes on her. I keep my voice steady and calm. "Lily, I'm sorry. I don't know—"

"Just leave me alone." She yanks her bag from the back of the chair, disappearing out the door and leaving me reeling.

And as always, I let her go.

Because nothing meant for you will run away from you.

TWENTY FIVE

The girls run through their fifth repeat of our routine, nailing every count. It's been a long time since I've been this proud of them, so I decide to reward them with an early finish. Having to move practice inside because of the weather seemed like torture enough as the gym AC sucks, and barely moving has us coated in sweat.

I stand from the basketball bleachers and commence a slow clap, strolling toward them. "Great job, ladies. I think we can call it."

"But Tonya has been off the entire time." Stacy pouts, crossing her pale arms over nonexistent breasts.

Everyone looks at Tonya, her tight coiled curls bouncing from a humorless laugh. She scoffs, flipping Stacy off, and I bite my lip to keep from laughing. "She was on point, just like everyone else."

Stacy rolls her eyes, huffing as she bends to grab a towel. Amora is on her before her fingers graze the cotton and snatch it away. "Listen, you little shriveled up cunt. Part of being a captain is knowing when to call the practice and when to push harder. Everyone has done pretty fucking amazing. So how about you show some gratitude and stop bitching about practice being cut a few minutes. It smells like you could use the extra time in the shower."

Amora flings the towel at Stacy's stunned face and laughs. Stacy looks at me as all the other girls file into the locker rooms, muttering under their breath.

I shrug, popping a fresh cherry in my mouth before I stand. "If you want to make captain next year, you better get your shit together."

Stacy's eyes bulge out from her face, spit narrowly missing me as she shrieks, "If I *want* to be? You said that spot was mine!"

"If everyone hates you, you won't have shit to lead," I snap. "Go get cleaned up."

Grabbing the bag of fruit my aunt packed me, I follow Amora, leaving Stacy still whimpering behind us.

Mina's been with me for two weeks, refusing to leave now that she knows I'm alone, and packs me the best lunch every day, forcing me to eat more fruit.

It's been strange, to say the least, but in a good way. It almost feels like having a mom, but better. Every day we talk more about the past, and each time, I let a little bit of the hurt go. According to my aunt, none of what happened had anything to do with me. A narcissistic mother and a busy father. The affair my mother had was bound to happen, and I got caught in the crossfire.

Mina told me that even as a kid, my mother needed everything to be about her and claimed having kids was her literal nightmare.

"She looked me dead in the eyes before her wedding with your father and said if he ever wanted kids, she would leave. She

couldn't imagine sacrificing her body, let alone her time, to take care of something as soul-sucking as a child. Some people are just like that, mija. It has nothing to do with you."

"And your father. He was a nice man, but he wanted a family after a while. When your mother had you, she handed you off so fast your dad's head started spinning. He didn't want to be a single dad with a wife in the next room. But then she started drinking." My aunt paused, taking a deep inhale before continuing.

"Your father still loved her back then, so he took her away to some rehab, I'm guessing, out here in Washington. They said her triggers were family-related, so he kept me away, thinking I would come and cause your mother to relapse. I guess after your mother's affair, he left, and since he was the only way I got to talk to you, I lost you and had no way to find out where you were. He sure as hell wasn't answering my calls."

I'd questioned a lot, but was most curious as to how she finally got my number. Turned out it was as simple as seeing a real estate ad on TV with my father's face. She saw it and called right away. He didn't tell her I was alone, probably because he doesn't know.

The man may have loved me once, but now it only extends to monetary gifts. Which honestly, I would take any day over having two people like my mom.

I yawn, stretch my arms, and walk into the locker room. Soon enough, the girls clear out, leaving me to soak under the hot water and breathe the steamy essence of my lavender soap.

After we shower, Amora convinces me to visit a new coffee spot up the street. Something about a hot college guy she wants to sink her teeth into. When we get there, I find a place in the back, slightly secluded. It's a dark shop lit by low-hanging lamps that bounce the light off dark brick walls. It's pretty cozy with old worn sofas and chairs instead of plastic ones, and the smell of fresh ground coffee beans swirls in the air, calming my racing nerves.

I've decided to tell Amora a few things. Mainly about Spencer and me. After everything that happened in the pink room, I could use a little of her carefree yet frank advice.

My heart flutters at the thought of our mouths connected, his warm body pressed against mine. What it would be like to give in. Could we really come back from how far we've fallen?

"Earth to Lily. Girl, what the fuck are you thinking about up there?" Amora sets my drink down, flopping into the seat across from me. Her long ponytail swings behind her, slapping against her shoulder.

"Sorry," I murmur, wrapping a hand around the warm paper cup. The heat burrows into my skin, skirting up my arms.

"So, what did you want to talk about?" Amora lifts her coffee, taking a tentative sip.

I chew on the inside of my cheek, wondering where I should start, what she might say. But her support has always been ironclad, even more so after the incident with my mom.

Butterflies take flight in my stomach, coasting around until I feel nauseous. "Erm. Spencer."

Amora's rose lips curl, her perfect pearly whites peeking through.

"About fucking time, bitch."

I STARE AT AMORA, whose mouth has yet to close. She's stayed relatively quiet the entire time, only asking questions sparingly for clarification. The barista sets a second steaming coffee cup next to her, but she doesn't move to touch it.

Just as waves of unease unleash like a tidal wave through my gut, she huffs, leaning back into the soft upholstery. She runs her tongue over her teeth before tilting her head to the side. "So, all this" —she waves a hand around— "was because you think he didn't reciprocate your feelings, and you thought he was using you for a little summer fun?"

I chew on the inside of my lip until a bitter metallic taste coats my mouth. "Yes."

Her eyebrows furrow. "And what did you think when he asked to move here?"

"Well, I figured he was eating his words since I" —framing my face, I give a tight lip smile— "Got a little sexier."

Amora scoffs, picking up her now tepid drink, icy blue eyes rolling dramatically into her head. "I see. Well, honestly, Lil, I think it was a legit misunderstanding. And I got to say, he's handled all the shit you've thrown his way really well. Any other guy would have had you gutted like a fish by now."

I cringe inwardly at everything I've done—all the wasted time. Things could have been so different...

"What are you going to do?" She takes a sip, wrinkles her nose, and lifts a finger to beckon the barista.

"What do you mean?"

"Bitch, it's clear you've got some seriously repressed sexual tension with the guy. That much is obvious, but do you still care about him?"

"No." *Yes.* Shit. I do... my stomach curdles, and I push my drink away.

Her face jerks back, eyes widening as her brows shoot

into her faint hairline. "Well, then, at your next little meeting thing, apologize and move on. It's the last one, right?"

"Yeah..."

The realization settles over me like a cloud bearing the next flood. Gripping my necklace, I observe Amora as she flirts with the college guy that's come to the table. She effortlessly laughs and touches him like he doesn't light her skin on fire. It must be nice. Not having someone you hate and want to rip their clothes off at the same time.

Fine.

After all, I've done, a little apology wouldn't hurt, and then we can move on... well, I guess the Band-Aid needs to be ripped off sooner or later when I leave for Kentucky.

Either way, Spencer and I are long overdue for some closure, and it's time we both acknowledge that.

TWENTY SIX

One more meeting, three more finals, and five more days. If I can just last that long, things will get better. At least that's what I tell myself for the millionth time while I pace the small room waiting for Lily.

She's consumed my every waking thought, plaguing me with her words like a fucking virus in the body. They've attached to each cell, multiplying and moving through me, making me sick as hell.

I've forgotten to eat on more than one occasion, guilt swelling in my stomach when I think of what went through her mind when she heard me that day. How she *felt.*

Lily had shit parents—a dad that put work before his kid and a mom that locked herself in her room like it was an ivory tower. She would tell me I was the only one that understood her. Understood how it felt to be forgotten. To mean nothing to someone who was your world. Though our situations were different, I *did* understand her. And I did everything I could to show her just how important she was.

So for her to hear me say that she meant nothing... I

scrub my face with my hands, agony swirling in my chest, seizing the muscle beneath.

All the shit these past few months seems trivial in comparison to how she must have felt. Because unlike her, when we parted ways, I still had a family that loved me. Parents that cared about me and pushed me. Lifted me up when I fell, gave me tough love when I acted out. And Lily...

She was alone.

The door handle jiggles, shoving my heart into my throat, and I press my body into the back wall to keep steady when it opens.

She steps through the door, eyes downcast. Her cream sweater hangs from one shoulder, draping loosely over a pair of skintight torn black jeans. She's frustratingly beautiful, and today, she looks a little less... cruel.

Lily sits down softly at the edge of her seat, keeping her bag draped over her side rather than hanging it off the chair.

She doesn't intend to stay long.

I sigh, taking the remote from my pocket and flipping on the last color—an emerald green. The timer ticks away, and the air around us thickens, filling with our mingling scents and shuddered breaths.

My hands tremble at my sides, and I have to physically push my weight onto my heels to keep from moving. Anxiety works its way up my spine, firing electricity through my brain like a lightning storm. There's so much I want to say...

As if she's counted the seconds in her head, she begins a fraction before the timer goes off.

"Hey." Her voice is hoarse, cracked like she hasn't spoken all day.

"Hey."

"How was your day?" Still, her eyes are stuck on the

table, and never in my fucking life have I wanted to stare at those stupid ass contacts so badly.

"Busy," I rush out, eager to get to the open-ended segment. "How was your day?"

Lily's throat bobs, and she shifts in her seat, crossing her feet at the ankles. She keeps her back straight, but her shoulders deflate a little when she answers. "Okay. How are you feeling?"

"I'm sorry." The words tumble out before I can stop them.

Her head snaps up, her eyes finally connecting with mine, stealing my breath. Her mouth opens and closes twice before she mutters, "For what?"

Gripping the nape of my neck, I squeeze, unable to look away from her. "I...should've tried harder to figure out what happened to us. I shouldn't have let you think that you meant nothing."

Lily scoots back in her chair, folding her arms as if to hug herself. "No. Spencer..." she swallows, a light blush creeping across her face. "I think we both could have done things differently. I, for one, didn't have to do all those things to you."

"I understand, though. If I were yo—"

"Don't." Her voice is firm, and she arches forward to clench her knees, her knuckles blooming a bright white.

"Don't what?" I breathe.

"Act like you understand anything about me or the reasons I've done things. You don't know *anything*."

I scoff, leaning back into my chair, slight irritation trying to push away the guilt I felt seconds ago. "I know all about you, Lily. I know you still dance in the windows like nobody's looking and that your ears turn bright red when you lie. I know your favorite food is popcorn, but it's also your least favorite because the kernels get stuck in your gums. Yo—"

"Stop. That's superficial shit, Spencer. You are completely clueless as to who I *am*. The shit I've gone through..." Her voice trails off, but her nose flaring tells me she's on the verge of crying or screaming. I'm not quite sure which.

Annoyance and frustration bubble up into my throat because, really, I *want* to know. I want to know everything. All the shit she's had to go through and make up for all the times I wasn't there.

But I know better.

What's done is done.

I rub my temples, trying my best to push away the thumping against my skull. "I see you plenty, Lily. But what's the point of doing this? It won't change anything."

Her breath hitches, and she blinks a few times as if I've said something off-kilter. A couple more blinks, and she's able to grab at her calm composure. "Smartest thing I've ever heard you say. Are we done here?"

I suck in a bit of air, letting my pulse gain some type of rhythm before nodding. This is not what I had planned. Definitely not what I fucking wanted.

"Hmhm." My answer is slow, drawn-out, only because I know what will happen when she walks out.

It will be the last time she does it. This will be the last time we are confined within the four walls, forced to fucking talk to each other.

This is it.

We will become two strangers with a few shared memories and a tragic backstory.

And I'm going to let her walk out because I'm not the type to force someone to stay. Or maybe it's because I am a little weak after all. Unwilling to really fight for people because in the end... they can easily forget who you are.

But as I stare down at my twitching hand, and listen to my aching heart, rattling in my chest like it's threatening to stop beating once she's gone, I know.

It's the first time I've been able to admit it. I *don't* want her to go.

But I do.

I always fucking do, and today... I accept that whatever we had, is done.

SOMEHOW, I made it through the week and aced every fucking final.

Little by little, I've cleaned out my locker and connected with all my teachers making sure everything was good to go. Now, all that's left is to—

"Hey, you." Remy slides next to my locker, a soft smile curling the edge of her lips. Somehow she's managed to pull half her dark locks up into a lopsided bun, and she looks more like a librarian than ever.

"Hey."

"All cleaned out?" Her voice is low, somber. She tucks a stray piece of hair behind her ear before rotating to put her back against the cold metal.

"Yeah." My voice cracks, and I clear my throat in an attempt to cover it. "Look, Remy, it's only till spring break."

She sighs, hugging her latest romance read closer to her chest. "Yeah, I know. And it's imperative. I'm just going to miss you."

The slight burn in the back of my nose flares, hitting the

brim of my eyes. The mix of feelings I've been having with finally letting go of Liliana and this impromptu trip with my parents has put my emotions into overdrive.

Dad says Mom is too far gone, and it's becoming more dangerous to leave her at home every day, even with a nurse. They visited some places a few weeks back, and she's checking in at the end of March, so Dad wanted to clear some stuff on her bucket list while she still remembers.

By this time next week, I'll be in Niagara Falls, a week after that, I think Barbados, and then somewhere in Europe right after.

"I got you this." Remy shifts to take her backpack from her shoulders, opening it and pulling out a bag. "It's a few disposable cameras and a Polaroid. That way, you don't forget to take pictures. Maybe give her a few, so she can look at them and..."

Her voice trails off as I grab her, wrapping my arms around her tiny shoulders. Despite the heaviness in my stomach, the comfort of her hug makes the air a little warmer somehow and the upcoming trip a little less bleak.

"I know I won't be able to talk to you much, but please, for the love of all romance books, please don't do anyone stupid while I'm gone."

She rubs her eyes with the back of her sleeves and cranes her neck to look at me with furrowed eyebrows. "You mean *something*? Oh! Spencer, jeesh."

Remy backs out of my hug, slugging me in the arm. Our bodies shake in unison as our laughter bounces through the empty halls. I'm going to miss these little moments with her. When the bell rings, it signifies more than just me going on a vacation.

It's the last time I'll hear it and head to a home where I'll still have my mom. Losing someone while they're still here is something I wouldn't wish on anyone.

It evokes a type of pain deep in your bones. You feel it when you move, when you rest, when all you're doing is fucking breathing. It wears away at everything else until all you want is to feel nothing. To be numb.

Hell, I'd sacrifice ever feeling happiness again if I didn't have to hurt like this anymore.

But life isn't that kind. It takes just as easy as it gives, and in my case, it's taking everything.

Just another thing I've come to accept this week.

TWENTY SEVEN

"You want to look at what?"

My aunt Mina whirls around the kitchen smoothly, as if she's been cooking in it for years. Having her here has become my favorite thing in life, even when she makes ridiculous suggestions like this one.

"Let's look at the lights."

"Like drive around and look?"

She sighs, slapping the cutting board on the counter before unsheathing a knife from the block a little too slowly. "Sweet girl, please give me this one thing. I missed so much of your childhood."

There it is, and with those magic words, I cave like Andy's toys when they hear him coming. I hold my hands up in defeat. "Okay, okay. But Blaze has to come."

"Of course, he doesn't have a choice." She beams over her shoulder, her ruby lips stretching into a perfect smile.

Blaze moves behind her, skirting around to reach in the refrigerator for a soda. He tosses me one before opening his, the crisp pop of the can cutting through the stinted silence. "Yeah, sure."

He tries to act as though it's the most unimportant thing in the world, but he can't stop that gray eye from speaking his truths. It twinkles in excitement, betraying his nonchalant attitude.

"Don't forget, I have to be gone for about a week the day after Christmas," she reminds me, slicing into the carrots.

"A week?" Blaze and I say in unison.

"Yes, mija. And now my second child, Blaze. I'll be back as soon as I close everything up. I have to move a few things over that I can't do here." She leans across the bar top, pinching my chin between her thumb and forefinger. "And then I'm never leaving you again."

It's strange, the ache radiating across my chest. I didn't have this woman in my life for over a decade, yet in just a few weeks, she moved mountains in my chest, breaking every rock I tried to hide behind. She's been so honest, so pure in everything she's done, and I found myself clinging to her like my life depends on it.

Hell, maybe in a way, it does.

Being with her has shown me I am enough. Enough to move across the country for, to give up your entire life for. Enough to love.

"But she's leaving us." Blaze tips his can at me before chugging it back, a grin just visible behind the rim.

Asshole.

I hadn't told my aunt about my plans for Kentucky. Really, I just wanted to enjoy the next six months and make up for as much lost time as possible. But sure, why not rip off the Band-Aid now.

"Kentucky," I clip.

"Why?" My aunt straightens her spine, her soft features scrunching as though she's in physical pain. "Your father mentioned you'd be local, but he didn't tell me where."

Solace.

"Yeah, I wanted to, but I can't afford it, and I don't want to give him something to hold over my head later. *I may not be in your life, but I paid for your education,*" I mock what I think my dad would say.

It's dumb, I know. Amora has told me time again to use the man for his money and call it a day. She suggested opening my own practice and paying him back, but what's the point? He won't accept it, and in the end, I'll still feel like he's contributed in some way. I don't expect my aunt to understand.

So it surprises the shit out of me when she does.

"Entiendo. I get it, I do. So what's in Kentucky?"

"Cheer."

Mina's eyes widen, the honey lining them sparkling under the fluorescent kitchen lighting. "I see."

I bite the inside of my cheek, not sure what to make out of that. I know I can go anywhere for cheer, but I wanted to prove that I could make the cut when I chose Kentucky. Ride with the best of the best. Prove my mother wrong.

Hell, It's not like I haven't played with the idea of going to a community college and just scrap my plan altogether, but something about it felt like failing. And I've worked too hard to have failure creep into my garden, poisoning all the other plants.

"Well, it's fine. I'll help you pick out your dorm stuff, and you'll come back on holidays and stuff, right? And I mean, I can always visit."

Blaze and I exchange a glance, and right then, I see it.

The shine in his gaze. The silent nod of approval. And that's all I need. Tears pour from my eyes like sheets of rain. My heart jackhammers in my chest, making me vaguely wonder if I'm having an anxiety attack.

Mina whirls around the bar, embracing me in her arms, squeezing every last salty tear from my head. Blaze's large hand meets the small of my back, and he rubs in little circles as my aunt rocks me back and forth.

It's overwhelming to feel such pure, real love oozing out of people. There's a type of vulnerability you have to have to receive it properly. You have to be willing to open your heart and trust that those people won't stomp all over it.

But that's the thing about love. Even if you *hav*e been hurt by it before, the majority of people are willing to crack open their chest and try again. Because once you've felt it, you crave it.

My eyes shift of their own accord to the dark house in the backyard. The aura surrounding it feels different. It's unusually dark, and something as equally cold as the snow outside drifts overhead.

Maybe it's because of how we ended things last week. There was a sort of finality to everything. To us.

But I do wonder... would Spencer Hanes be willing to open his chest again? Would I?

"MERRY CHRISTMAS." Amora's extremely high tone pierces through the down comforter covering my face. The bed shifts as she pounces on top, narrowly missing my ankles. "It's like ten, Lil. Why are you still asleep?"

"Because I'm eighteen years old, and I don't have presents waiting for me under the tree."

"Yeah." She yanks the soft cotton from my face. "But you do have a badass aunt that just made us breakfast."

I groan at the sudden influx of light, but then the smell hits me, and my stomach does a somersault, jolting me upright. It's sweet—definitely bacon and syrup are involved.

My aunt Mina's been a dutiful caregiver during her four-week stay, and to say I'm excited it's becoming permanent is the understatement of the century. She works for a marketing company, and luckily the majority of it is done by emails, phone calls, and random turnaround meetings. The one day she had to take a trip to Oklahoma, I just about lost it. It felt like a year since the last time I had to cook a meal, so Blaze and I ordered out instead.

He's been around a lot too. Spending the night in our guestroom down the hall, soaking up every bit of maternal love Mina's giving out. She must sense he needs it because she takes care of him like he really is my brother. She even fussed at him for barely passing one of his finals. So it's no surprise that when I finally roll out of bed and make it down to the kitchen he's already at the table shoveling an absurd amount of pancakes down his throat.

"Caveman," Amora clips, climbing on a barstool.

Blaze ignores her and instead lifts his eyebrows in greeting to me before turning back to his feast. My aunt spins merrily in the kitchen, plating an equally insane amount of food on our plates.

I've never been a stickler about the food I put in my body, but I've always try to be at least a little cautious. Workouts after eating junk food sucked, and I usually puke at practice.

My aunt must notice my face and sighs. "It's Christmas, mija. Stop worrying about it. It's one day."

I poke at the side of my hip, where there used to be only bone. Now my finger sinks in an inch before reaching it. "Yeah, you said that five pounds ago, Aunt Mina. You know what five pounds can do when girls have to toss you?"

She groans again, cutting my rations in half. "Okay, I'll be more mindful, chica flaca."

My eyes roll in the back of my head, but I take the plate and join Blaze. I sit at the opposite end and can't help but look across the backyard.

There hasn't been smoke coming from Spencer's chimney the entire break, and not once have I seen him at his window. He also has a pretty nonexistent family since his parents are both only children and much older. I'm fairly certain he only has one living grandparent, so I don't think they went anywhere.

A knot swells in my throat.

What if he moved back to Idaho?

Blaze cuts through my thoughts, kicking me under the table. "Close your mouth, Lil."

"Hush," I hiss, turning to my plate of food, but my appetite is gone.

He chuckles, leaning back and running a hand down his stomach, clearly pleased with his ability to eat his weight in pancakes. "You want me to go over? See if he's there?"

Blaze does me the courtesy of keeping his voice low, but I still glance over my shoulder to make sure my aunt doesn't hear. It's not that I don't want her to know per se, but she's got a spicy attitude, and I wouldn't be surprised if she marched over in the snow to Spencer's house to have his neck. Or maybe she would scold me for being so quick to jump to conclusions about him in the first place. Either way, I'd rather not broach the subject with her yet.

My eyes flit back to Blaze, and I shake my head. He chuckles, threading a hand through his dark hair. "He's too weak for you, Lily."

"Excuse me?" I have no idea why I'm offended, but I am.

He leans forward, interlocking his fingers and putting his elbows up on the table. "How many times has he let you walk away from him now? How many times has he let you pull that bullshit on him without handling you like he should have?"

I swallow around the burn now suffocating my sinuses. I don't mention how he tried to be invisible when he first moved here or the countless times we were alone, and he could have *tried* to talk to me. To dig deeper.

"When a guy wants something, he'll do whatever he needs in order to get it." With that, he stands, and meanders over to the sink, and starts doing the dishes.

"Such a precious boy. Thank you." My aunt beams and sits next to Amora. They become engrossed in a conversation about Amora dyeing my aunt's hair when she returns from Florida.

I shift back to the dark house, pushing the food around on my plate as I play with Blaze's words.

He'll do whatever it takes.

He may not have meant the words he said to William that day, but I am sure of one thing—Spencer doesn't want me now.

He *hates* me... and for some reason, I hate that.

TWENTY EIGHT

January

School's been in session for a couple of weeks, but I haven't seen Spencer once. Not at lunch, not with Remy during passing periods, nowhere. I even decided to start going back to Mr. Jones's science class and... nothing. The teacher doesn't even call his name for attendance, and reality begins to settle in the pit of my gut.

He must have moved.

Blaze's words from Christmas loop in my ear on repeat. He was right. I mean, I already figured that, but to know Spencer left without so much as a *fuck you* twists my stomach in knots.

Knowing I *care* makes me nauseous.

The way he'd held on to my face, the desperation that dripped from his words, I almost thought he meant them.

Thought that even after all the shit I'd thrown at him, he still found a way to see under the facade—the hurt.

I had this naive notion that maybe this time, he would come after me.

But then Spencer performed the infamous disappearing act I'm so familiar with.

It goes without saying at this point, I'm conditioned to expect certain things from people. First and foremost, they are selfish. They think about what the relationship (be it a friendship or otherwise) can offer them. They need to know it will be worth the effort required to make it work, whether it be social status, a good lay, or compliments to feed their ego.

And there's not one thing I can offer Spencer. Nothing that matters to him anyway. He couldn't give two shits about where he is on the social ladder. He's handsome enough to get any ass he wants, should he actually try. And his grades probably feed his ego more than anything I could ever say. So logically, he has no reason to want a friendship with me.

Still, I thought maybe one thing he said might have been true, so I held on to it.

But as the days turn into weeks, the gnawing sensation in the back of my head grows, filling me to the brim with a truth I've known since the day I overheard him with William.

He'd said he loved me.

And I think out of all the lies I've ever heard, that was my favorite one.

"WHAT THE FUCK are you doing here?"

I stop midway up the path to my house, terror stealing the air from my lungs.

That's my mom's voice coming from inside. She hasn't come by in months, and to be honest, she hasn't crossed my mind at all. Even at school, she works the night shift, so I'm gone before she arrives.

I rush to the door, pressing my palms against it, unsure if I should go in or stay put. Her voice sounds like a growl and angrier than I've ever heard it.

But when my aunt Mina speaks, it's level, and there's a strong authoritative tone lacing every word. "No, the question that needs to be answered is, what are *you* doing here?"

"This is my house, puta. Yo—"

"Let me stop you right there. This hasn't been your house since the day you left a child to raise herself. Second, if you call me another name, *hermana*, I'll be mopping your blood off the floor later."

My mom scoffs, and I hear the faint sound of spit hitting the tile. "You have no business here. Where is the little chocha?"

"Again. I'm going to ask you to watch that mouth of yours. My patience is wearing incredibly thin. You're drunk, and I don't want my dear niece coming home to her mother in pieces on the freshly polished linoleum. So why don't you leave?"

A cackle erupts from my mom, churning my insides like butter. It's the same sour laugh I've heard too many times before, usually after having my ass thrown against the wall. Still something I haven't had the heart to tell my aunt about. I was scared she would do something drastic.

"Hmm... I need to see my daughter." Her words are slurred, and she mutters something I can't make out.

"I don't care. I've been here since Thanksgiving, and she hasn't mentioned you once. She doesn't want to see you. Leave. *Now.*"

There's a clack of heels followed by the muffled sounds of something hitting the ground. I wonder vaguely if my mother tripped in her stupor or if my aunt pushed her.

"I'll be back, big sister."

"You won't. And if you do..." I push my ear painfully close to the wooden door, straining to hear my aunt's hissed warning. "I'll make menudo from your guts."

I wince at the thought of my mother's intestines floating in broth. This time though, my mother makes no sound and instead stumbles toward the front door. I skirt back, my pulse in my throat, and wince as I trek through the snow to the side of the house.

Not one time did I ever consider what things would be like if my mom showed up. I've been happy living in this new bubble, pretending nothing else existed. It's like I had replaced Mom altogether, so caught up in absorbing every ounce of love my aunt gives that it purged out my mother's hate, like an antidote to a poison.

But that's not how it works, and of all people, I should know better.

The pain my mother inflicted isn't surface level, easy to push out in a few months. No, my mother's toxins run soul deep, twisting in the pits of my gut, to the lining in my heart, curling around my brain stem and piercing into my cerebellum.

Her words, the physical pain, her absence—all of it, are embedded in my every hesitation, every negative thought, every foul action.

And just now, the placebo effect my aunt had on me is

gone, replaced by the realization that no matter how happy I am now, it isn't real. Not in a way that lasts because it can be ripped to shreds at the drop of a hat.

The door slams shut, and after a few minutes, when my heart returns to a fairly calm rate, I enter through the back door.

Mina is on her knees, sweeping up dirt from a plant that must have been knocked over. Her shoulders are shaking with a silent sob, but when she hears me shuffle behind her, she snaps up, a calm grin on her face.

"Ah, how was school, mi amor?"

"It was okay," I whisper, grabbing some napkins and joining her on the floor.

"Clumsy me." She motions to the mess, but I don't look away from her. Her dark amber eyes scan my face, searching for something before I grant her a soft smile, not wanting to lie. I wrap my arms around her neck, pulling her closer.

It hasn't been easy watching my mother become lost to alcohol, but to be honest, I never really knew her in the first place. She was always locked away in her room, treating me like I was an annoying house guest. But my aunt Mina? She knew her before her first sip. When they were kids who probably loved each other more than anything in the world. So the pain currently coursing in my veins, squeezing my heart in the process, isn't for me. But for her.

Mina's silent cries reverberate through her body, sprouting goose bumps along my arms and a shiver down my spine.

We're both hurt, just in different ways.

The daughter who wasn't good enough to love, and the big sister who couldn't save her.

"How many gifts did you get, Amora?" A genuine laugh erupts from my mouth as I take in the pile of presents and assortment of flowers she's attempting to balance.

Valentine's Day came fast, and while the flowers and parading of love used to just annoy me, now it twists the muscles in my chest until breathing's a chore. Amora suggested a break by heading out for lunch.

"Come on, Lily. A little help."

I roll my eyes but grant her an olive branch by opening the back door to my car and taking the top bags from her pile. It's not a secret Amora's had her fair share of guys, but the truth is, she hasn't slept with any of them. Well, maybe sleep is the wrong word. She definitely enjoys the pleasure of their tongue between her thighs, but her slight obsession with Blaze has left her waiting on him to dick her down.

I've told her more times than I can count that she and Blaze are too polar, but she has this notion that opposites attract. Opposites, sure, but not in the way she and Blaze are different. Amora needs someone who will take the shit she throws, add a little spice, and toss it right back. Someone with a tongue sharper than hers and the patience to reel her in.

All of which Blaze is not.

After loading up way too much shit, we head up the street for lunch. The drive-through lady takes our order and has us park while we wait. Amora adjusts in her seat, facing me.

"So, how's Mina? Does she need a touch-up yet?"

Amora dyed my aunt's strands a shade of honey and platinum that make her look like she walked out of a magazine. It damn near looks like a professional job.

I sigh, leaning back and stretching my hands above my head. "No, but we do have our first family therapy session coming up.'

"Seriously?"

"Yep." I'm extremely excited about it too. My heart flutters when I think of going and finally healing the way I need to.

My aunt and I are fine, better than that, actually. But just because that piece of my garden is pretty doesn't mean the weed growing in the corner can't overtake it someday. We've decided to tear it up by the root, and for that, we need a little help.

"That's really good to hear, Lil. How often?"

"Once a week at first and we'll go from there."

Being able to tell Amora about therapy openly does something to me. It chips away at the barrier I've held in place for so long, not allowing others to truly see me.

Amora smiles, grabbing my hand as the worker appears at the driver's side window with our food. "I'm proud of you. I still want to call the police on that crazy bitch of a mom you got, but this is good."

The corners of my mouth curl. "Enough about me." I poke my thumb in the direction of all the presents. "Who got you what?"

And just like that, I learn about the fourteen guys that

think they stand a chance with the Duchess of Emerald Falls.

THE THERAPIST'S office resides in the middle of downtown, at the top of a fifteen-story building. Walking inside, it feels more like a business meeting than a place to let loose and delve into all my secrets. Not to mention the high windows give me pause. I wonder how many people have looked out of them longingly.

When I used to dream of running my own practice, I was going to buy a home on some land. Make it comfortable and inviting, have a playroom for kids and a couple of therapy animals.

This place is sterile, like a hospital, and every piece of furniture is hard plastic. We've been sitting in the waiting area for fifteen minutes, and the entire time I've become entranced with watching the aging secretary twirl a set of pearls between a fresh manicure. She told us the doctor would like to see us separately at first and finish up with a joint meeting at the end.

Finally, the door creaks open, and a tall woman steps out. Her inky hair is brushed into a taut bun and she's wearing an equally dark, fitted linen dress. Small black spectacles sit on the bridge of her skinny nose, held in place by a silver chain wrapped around her neck. When her neutral tinted lips stretch into a smile, it transforms her relatively sad face into a ball of warmth.

"Miss Conley. I'm ready when you are."

My aunt squeezes my hand, leaving a whisper of a kiss on my temple as I stand. I follow behind the doctor into another sterile room. It lacks personality, with only a few diplomas, abstract art, and a couple of dying ferns scattered around. One wall is floor-to-ceiling windows, letting in too much light for comfort.

No part of the space makes me want to bare my soul, and I vaguely wonder how many people stopped seeking help because they felt so out of place here as well.

The doctor strides behind her desk and sits, tapping her computer, so it whirls to life. That simple act leaves me feeling as though this is an interview, but I force my mind to hold on to her warm smile and shove away the nagging wall that's trying to rise up and shield me.

"Miss Conley. My name is Dr. Floren. It's a pleasure to meet you."

Swallowing around the knot in my throat, I plaster on my cheerleader smile. "Lily is fine."

Her dark eyebrow raises above the rim of her glasses. "So not Liliana? Got it."

She types into her computer, and I shift in my seat, suddenly hyperaware of the chill in her room. It sprouts goose bumps all down my arms even though I have on a thick sweater.

After a few more seconds, the doctor grabs a notebook from inside her desk drawer and shoots her chair around, sitting a few feet to my left.

"Alright, Lily. How are you feeling today?"

It's a simple question. One that people literally ask one another every day. But being asked in a room that I'm not sharing with *him* cuts through the air, slicing into me despite my emotional barriers. Despite her impersonal office, tall windows, and lack of therapy animals.

It punctures my chest, letting everything seep out and pool on the floor beneath me.

The truth is, I'm not okay, and pretending to be is becoming too hard. Burying my issues seemed easy, but after each rainstorm, everything just floated back to the surface, leaving me to repeat the process. So instead, I bury my nails in the dirt and rip up the ground. Taking out every little thing for me to shove on a table to be dissected and picked at. Scrutinized and judged.

I hate my mother. I hate that she carried me for almost ten months and felt absolutely nothing when I was born. That she was able to throw me aside, and nothing I did was enough for her attention—enough for her to leave that goddamn room. That I've let my mother turn me into a monster like her.

I hate my father. I hate that he left me with someone he knew didn't love me and found himself a new family instead. He's a coward that couldn't fight for me.

He's a coward that couldn't fight for me.

Spencer.

I fucking hate Spencer Hanes. I hate that he left me, again, when all I wanted him to do was stay.

My eyes reconnect with the doctor's, and my smile fades to a grimace. I tell her what I wanted to tell *him* every time he asked. "I'm pretty fucking sad today."

March

JENNY'S SMOOTHIE SHOP.

Still a relatively new place not too far from Emerald Falls stadium, and it's dead as a doornail on a Thursday night. Blaze suggested we stop by after our stint at the gym. One of the many things my therapist suggested.

"Find a way to relieve some of the tension. Instead of focusing only on cheer and helping other people, try focusing on *your* body."

It turns out you really can't judge a book by its cover. Her plain-Jane office had nothing to do with her incredible personality. Every session, she milks more out of me than a dairy farmer. I try to pass some of that on to Blaze, but I'm not quite sure if any of it is sticking yet. He's got a soft spot for me only because we share the same bruise. Not sure if he'll ever let anyone else see it.

When we walk inside, Remy's face is buried so far in a book that she doesn't even hear us come in.

Blaze stiffens and nudges my shoulder. "Grab me a banana mango. I'll be in the car."

Instead of questioning him, I nod and strut to the counter.

When I'm three feet away, I clear my throat, waiting for her face to pop up.

The customer service smile she wears fades quickly,

replaced with furrowed brows and twitching lips. She snaps the book closed. "Lily, what do you want?"

I bite my tongue. The temptation to spew a harsh comment or quick insult is strong, but it won't get me what I want, what I *need*. Instead, I shove my hands in my back pocket and rock on the balls of my feet.

She raises a brow, drumming her fingers on the cover of her book, her patience clearly wearing thin.

Forcing a large breath through my nose, I relent. "Two mango, banana smoothies. Also, did Spencer move?"

"Why do you care?" she clips, and the nerve in my temple tics.

This girl has been a frustrating conundrum since the day I learned of her existence, and it's clear that won't be changing. I clench my jaw a few times, swallowing the dozens of retorts that nearly slip before finally answering, giving her the simplest answer I can muster. "Because I *do* care, Remy."

She scoffs, rolling her eyes before snatching her book off the counter and away from me. Almost as if I could taint her precious romance with my words. She rings up our smoothies and shifts to make them, keeping her back to me. "Yes, and I believe you like I believe in Santa Claus."

Like you believe in those romance novels. I bite my cheek again and focus on keeping my tone neutral; after all, she's seen me do some not-so-nice things to her friend. "No need to be sarcastic when I'm being honest."

"Lily, you've done nothing but make his life miserable. Why should I believe even for a second that you give a crap about him?"

"Look, Remy, I don't know what Spencer's told you, but..." I pause, searching for the right words.

She twists, dropping two smoothies in front of me, and

tilts her head, narrowing her eyes as if there's nothing I could tell her she hasn't already heard. Maybe she does know the whole thing and sees no fault on Spencer's part, but that doesn't make my hurt any less valid.

"We all handle our pain differently. Out of all the books in the world, none of them agree unanimously on how we have to deal with our traumas. I think you need to make amends for any hurt you may have caused someone and let it go."

I replay Dr. Floren's words. I overreacted with my treatment of Spence; that much was evident even when I was lashing out. And now, it's time to right my wrongs the best I can and close the chapter properly. For the both of us.

The thought of letting him go *completely* feels like swallowing a rock straight out of a volcano. It sears my insides, leaving scars I'm unsure will ever mend. But at this point in my healing process, it needs to be done.

Remy taps the counter, and I realize she's waiting. "Just need to clear a few things with you."

She ignores my comment and instead asks a question that surprises me. "How were you ever best friends in the first place?"

My brows knit together, and I think about her question for a second. It's not her place to ask and my business to keep, but a small part of me wants to tell her. To make her realize just how amazing Spencer is, so she doesn't mess up his friendship the way I did.

I latch on to my necklace and begin pulling it back and forth. "For me, he was the light in the dark. He made me feel important, funny... loved. Out of all the superficial friendships I've had, he was the only one that felt real. He would stay up with me till three o'clock in the morning in our treehouse, reading stories to me after I had a bad day. Even when he had to be up at six to go fishing with his dad."

A swell of emotions bloom in my chest at the many memories we shared throughout seven summers. Amora, with all her funny quirks and fearless attitude, to Blaze, my broken knight in shining armor. No one has ever made me feel the way Spencer did.

I try to swallow down the knot that's now tripled in size, making it difficult to breathe, and find Remy's natural hazel eyes on mine. She pushes up her hexagon glasses and nods, pursing her bee-stung lips. "He'll be back for the fair."

He's coming back?

The temptation to drill into this small girl and gather as many details as possible is overwhelming. Almost as perfuse as the excitement lighting my nerves on fire. Instead, I take a quick breath and grab our drinks. "Thank you."

"The love he has for you is going to ruin him. So please, just..." She sighs and looks behind me out the window. "Decide what you want and stick with it."

Has. Present tense.

I tell myself not to read into that, not to let the small flicker of hope turn into a full-blown inferno.

But I've never been too good at putting out fires.

TWENTY NINE

"William, Just text her. And for the love of all things virgin, don't let me have to beat your ass. And also, don't take all day. Remy has lots of other shit to do besides tutor your dumbass."

"Hmm. You've mentioned my buns of steel twice. Got them on your mind, Hanes?"

"Fuck off, Will." I grit my teeth, wondering why the hell I just sealed my dear friend's fate with the likes of William. He needs to retake his SATs if he wants any chance of going to school anywhere in Washington, and if anyone can help him, I know it's her. She's got the patience of a shepherd herding sheep and the ability to help just about *anyone*.

My mother's peppered hair catches the light and reflects in my periphery. "Hey, man. I got to go, but I'll call you soon."

"Yeah, but, hey. Good luck tomorrow. I know you busted your balls over that project. It's going to be great."

I mutter a quick thanks before ending the call and

bounding over the couch to my mother. She giggles, her thin shoulders shaking as she places a frail hand on my chest.

The trip was the best thing I could have imagined. My dad had me waking up at five in the morning to get schoolwork done, but the rest of the day was something out of a movie. We went sightseeing, kayaking, bungee jumping, and sailing. We ate foods from Greece to China, exploring every nook and cranny the world has to offer and marking off literally every item on my mom's bucket list.

Out of the twelve-week trip, she only had an episode twice. *Twice.* The least amount she's had in years. But Dad had to remind me on more than one occasion that it didn't mean anything. He said there could be a plethora of reasons she was managing so long but warned that she'd continue to deteriorate as soon as we came back.

Sure enough, on the plane ride home, about ten minutes in, she couldn't even remember my dad. The walls of excitement—of hope, came crashing down in an instant. It reminded me how fragile life is, how nothing is permanent.

It taught me the one thing I've forgotten since my mother's diagnosis.

Hold fast, hold steady isn't just a coping mechanism she taught me to keep my cool. It was something my mother would recite when things got tough. When I needed a gentle reminder that nothing is easy, and everything required consistency and work. When the waters get crazy, hold on, ride it out.

And whatever you do, don't fucking give up.

"Are you excited?" Her soft voice pulls me back to her.

"Yes," I lie.

The long-awaited science fair is this weekend, and the bus leaves in about thirty minutes. I'm not sure if *she's* going, but I would be lying if I said I didn't want to see her. I thought about her more than I'd care to admit, mainly about all the things I regret.

"You're going to win. Don't you worry about it." She leans into my shoulder, and I wrap an arm around her back, cherishing the ache between my lungs.

Today is the day. Not only for the fair, but my mom's departure, and no amount of preparation could have got me ready for the train wreck of emotions that are flitting through me. She'll only be an hour away. Fifty-three miles, to be exact, but it's not the same.

It's not like I'm going off to college and leaving her at home. No, I'm taking her to the place she's more than likely going to die. Alone. Surrounded by people she doesn't know, mourned by people she doesn't remember.

Tears prick the back of my lids, the small ache now radiating to every cell in my skin, leaving me wishing I could rip it off. We've said goodbye twenty times, and still, it's not enough.

"Honey." My mother leans back, craning her neck to look at me. "Please don't forget what we talked about."

We talked about plenty, but I know she means Lily. My mom's never met her, but even when I was a kid, she would say she can see Liliana in my eyes, tied to my soul in a way that only true love is.

When we were in Niagara Falls alone while my dad got us some ponchos, I told her everything. There had been something about the way the water rolled over the cliff, crashing into the water beneath that reminded me of what was going on in my chest. Because when it came to Lily, everything was erratic, a contradiction... torrential.

But after my mother had time to digest my words, she

pointed out something else. Like the waterfall, Lily and I were also passionate, graceful poetry with a full roar.

"You don't give up on something as world-altering as a waterfall, son. And if you loved her, even when you hated her, that's all you need. Because when I was angry with your father, love was nowhere in sight. That's when I knew he wasn't the one. Now, make things right, and get your girl."

"I love you," I whisper into her temple, leaving a whisper of a kiss on each one and wiping the lone tear that fell from my face to hers.

She leans into my chest once more before lightly pushing me back to examine my eyes. "I love you most. Now, go win, and I'm not talking about just the fair."

My lips twitch with a smile, but I don't give in. Not when there's so much pain coursing through my veins. "Yes, ma'am."

I kiss her again before she ushers me out the door, fussing about being late.

When I arrive at the school, I make out the small silhouette of Remy bouncing on her heels, peering at her watch, and saying something to Mr. Jones. His eyebrows are threaded together, and he, too, is checking his watch.

I swing into a spot, grab my bag from the back and haul ass toward the antsy pair.

"Sorry, Mr. Jones. There was traffic."

Remy's face splits in a huge smile, and she runs to greet me, throwing her arms around my neck. It soothes some of the ache from earlier, but Mr. Jones is quick to break it up.

"Alright, Mr. Hanes, come now, let's go. We'll be late for check-in."

He escorts us on the bus and points to an empty seat near the front. I keep my eyes down, careful not to search for her. But I don't need to. I can feel her. Her eyes burn into the side of my face, leaving me shifting in my seat.

Just do it.

My knees move first, turning to the aisle before I twist my body. My pulse thrums against my neck, accelerating to an uncomfortable pace. But when my eyes meet hers, everything stops.

There are no contacts.

Lily's big chestnut orbs glow with the wide grin curling up the ends of her lips. Her beautiful sun-kissed skin shimmers from the light peeking through the bus window and illuminates a few freckles across her collarbone I never noticed before.

She's sitting in the seats one row back on the opposite side, but I can make out her lavender cream even from here. It fills my nostrils with its hues of lemon until she's all I can smell. My head feels high, dizzy as it becomes intoxicated with the scent. I didn't realize how much I missed it.

Remy clears her throat. "Go. Sit with her."

Guilt rams into my chest, and I snap back in my seat. "I'm sorry, Remy. That was rude. Talk to me. How were midterms?"

She rolls her eyes. "Boy, I've talked to you every week. Really. It's a three-hour ride. We'll have plenty of time to catch up."

"Exactly." I push my back into the seat, twisting my knees so they face her.

Every nerve in my body is on fire, pulling me, begging me to talk to the brown-eyed girl two feet away, but I don't. Not yet. I need to wait until I know exactly what to say and when I'm a little less high on her smell because this time, I'm going to get it right.

Remy gives me a once-over and sighs, resting her head in the crook of my shoulder. "Isn't today...?"

She doesn't have to finish for me to know what she's talking about. I nod, letting my head fall on the top of hers. "Yeah."

We sit in silence for a moment, and the next thing I know, a dark veil closes over my eyes.

THIRTY

By the time our bus pulls into the hotel, the back of my neck is raw from the friction of my necklace, and my nerves are shot to hell. The entire three hours, I had to text my support system to keep from jumping over the seats.

Another suggestion from Dr. Floren.

"Create a small circle of those you trust who you can reach out to when you are feeling overwhelmed or upset. Sometimes even when you feel extremely happy. These people can help you calm down or talk to you in order to help find a solution."

Mr. Jones rises, holding up a hand to silence the dozen students all buzzing with excitement. My eyes drift to Spencer and notice he's leaning to the side and can easily see me out of his periphery.

It forces my spine to straighten, and the hair on my nape stands at attention.

"Alright. We're running a little behind, but you all have practiced repeatedly over the past few weeks, so I'm confident you have your data memorized by now. We're in section

45 B. I'll call you by partner groups, give you your badges, and then I need you to hurry inside. I'll also give the team leader your hotel key for the night. Remember, we'll have dinner after and breakfast in the morning at eight sharp. Good luck, Bulldogs."

Team leader?

Mr. Jones must've forgotten that Spencer is no longer teamed up with a guy. I make a mental note to tell him later as I pack my things inside my purse. He begins calling names, and as luck would have it, Spencer and I are the first called.

He reaches Mr. Jones before me and grabs our lanyards, exiting the bus before I've slung my bag over my shoulder. I stumble after him and down the steep stairs.

Spencer stands at the bottom, leaning against the bus, with his hands in his dark jeans. His chocolate locks are a little longer, curling around the shell of his ear. My heart thumps violently in my rib cage, and I'm almost certain he'll be able to see an outline of it if he looks down.

"Hey." His voice is throaty, and my breath falters.

I swallow, reaching out for my badge. "Hey."

"How are you?" he asks, handing me the lanyard.

Our fingers brush against each other's, and a shock sparks the length of my forearm. I clamp down on my bottom lip to keep my smile from stretching too far. "We aren't in the color room, you know."

One of his shoulders hitches up, and his dimple appears with a smirk. "Yeah, but I still want to know."

I open my mouth to answer, but Remy appears at our side, her partner following close behind. She eyes us for a moment before tapping me on the shoulder. "Let's go, you guys. Time to win some money."

Some money?

Spencer nods and turns, but waits until I'm next to him before leading the way.

It's strange. We wrestled as kids, shared the same bag of popcorn, and slept cuddled up in a treehouse. Yet being six inches away from him right now feels like I'm a breath away from the sun.

Stop.

This is about closure. Letting go so that I can move on.

I repeat the phrase three times before we enter the hotel.

To say the fire marshal would be disappointed is an understatement. The entire floor of the lobby is packed, overflowing with students and projects, and men in white jackets with clipboards. They are all moving to a room behind the tall reception area. The majority of everything inside is glass or reflective steel. The nearby elevators are see-through, all full of onlooking spectators. The ceiling in the hotel is enormous, at least twenty feet, and has a complete slanted skylight. A light sprinkle has started, and I watch as the water beads and rolls down the windows. Soon enough, it picks up, and watching it feels almost like being on the inside of a waterfall.

Suddenly, a firm hand wraps around my wrist and weaves me through the crowd. When I look down at Spencer's fingers locked on me, every nerve in my body ignites, and my core throbs in a way it hasn't since our time in the colored room. I squeeze my eyes closed and remind myself.

Closure.

Finally, we reach our section, and he finds our table quickly. His trifold is set up next to a plethora of others, and honestly, pretty badass. There is data and graphs, pictures, and studies. He even has a binder with colored tabs, which I assume have more in-depth information on his color study. That's when I noticed the title.

COLORS AFFECT HUMANS, BUT TO WHAT EXTENT?

I huff. Of course. How the hell hadn't I put that together?

Spencer leans in, his breath tickling the stray hairs on my neck. It sends a shiver down my spine. "Thank you."

My eyes connect with his, and instantly the world around us is drowned out. He's right next to my face, one deep breath away from his lips touching mine. And for some insane reason, I actually consider rising on my tiptoes and closing the distance.

It would be so easy.

There was a time I thought maybe we just needed to get all the tension out of our system. Just one good fuck to make us feel better. And right now, with his gaze on my lips, his deep erratic breaths, and the clench of his jaw, I think he may feel the same.

Sex. Then closure. Yeah. Totally possible.

"Colors." The husky voice of an older gentleman draws us apart.

Four men, who I assume to be judges according to their large badges, step closer to us. I back up, giving the floor to Spencer, and mouth my good luck.

I feel bad I can't really be of assistance on this part, but that guilt only lasts five seconds. Watching him explain the depths of our experiment leaves me in awe. He uses terms and vocabulary about the brain I had no idea existed. He's intelligent as hell and listening to him sends a heaviness between my thighs that makes me clench my knees together. By the time he's done, I'm fairly certain I have taken at least two college courses about the psyche, and that's when it hits me.

Dr. Floren doesn't use too many colors because of how the brain can react to each one differently. Leaving her room clean and neutral lets the brain decide what they want to feel without exacerbating it.

Thinking about it, how I still have so much to learn, sends excited shivers down my spine. I can't wait to be in my field. Helping those that think they are alone... forgotten. And be a haven for managed souls tormented by abusive parents.

Mr. Jones appears as Spencer makes his final remarks and asks them if they have any questions. "Miss Conley. Your room key."

He places the card in my hand, still staring at Spencer. "How's he doing?"

"Amazing." The word tumbles out, but it's the truth. He's incredible.

"I knew he would do great—an absolutely wonderful idea. Alright, don't forget. We're ordering pizza and meeting in room 734."

"Oh, Mr. Jones," I stop him, remembering to remind him that Spencer and I will be sharing a room, but instead, like any conflicted teen, I don't.

I'm supposed to be amending my past with Spencer. But I don't recall Dr. Floren saying how that needed to be done. "Never mind."

He nods, smiling briefly before running off to the next table. When I turn around, Spencer is leaning against the table, his mouth slightly ajar.

"What's wrong?"

He shakes his head, those deep brown eyes honing in on me. "They said we are going to place."

"Seriously? They can tell so soon?"

"I guess. I mean, they got our reports a week ago. This is more for show and presentation. Lily... I didn't tell you about the prize."

Lifting my chin, I move closer, fiddling with the edge of one of the binders. "What is it?"

"Scholarships to any of the sponsor's universities. Ten thousand, to be exact, for the last place. The full first year paid for winners."

"Oh shit. That's amazing." I knew Kentucky wouldn't be on the list of Washington fair sponsors, but my curiosity piqued. "Any schools I know?"

"Solace."

Of course.

The dream school I didn't have enough money for. Without my permission, my brain starts doing the math. Maybe if I stayed home and commuted to school, it could work. I could always continue cheering there, perhaps even teach cheer at the local dance academy on the weekends. My mind continues to spiral, wondering if perhaps I could have my cake and eat it too.

A saying I never really understood after all. Because what's the point of giving me a cake if I can't eat it?

My eyes drift back to Spencer, and I think for a second what it would be like to not have to let him go. To not move on and see what could be.

To close our past and move on to our future.

THIRTY ONE

"Where are you guys going?"

A few of the guys from class suggested taking our pizza to go and hanging out in one of their rooms to celebrate. By some fucking miracle, the universe decided I was due a win, and I actually pulled it off.

First fucking place.

It was close as shit, and I had to answer more questions than I was mentally prepared to, but I killed it.

I called Dad to give him the news and instantly regretted it. Mom was having an episode, I'm sure linked to the stress of her arrival, and didn't know what fair I was talking about. Hearing her say that twisted the organ in my chest, squeezing it empty of all the pride I felt moments before.

She was the inspiration behind the whole thing, after all, and I hate not being able to tell her we did it.

My father, a cardiologist, always thought I would follow behind him, but everything changed after my mother's diagnosis. I needed to dive into the circuit board that is the brain. Inspect the wiring and find out how it can be fixed, so no one would have to suffer the living loss of a loved one.

Which brought me to my science project. Colors have been used in studies before with Alzheimer patients to spark memories, but seeing as the individual episodes are linked to other things, I decided to perform it on the average brain. Make notes, comparisons, connections, and a conclusion.

And it was worth drowning in research that took weeks to shift through. Not only did I land mine and Lily's (even though she doesn't want it) first year of Solace paid for, the department chair of biology intends to meet with me next fucking week. About what? No clue, but I'm borderline having an aneurysm thinking about it.

Remy's eyes narrow as she waits.

"To celebrate Spencer!" my classmate, Collen, yelps, snapping me from my daze and grabbing another box of pepperoni.

I try my best to give Remy a reassuring smile, but she purses her lips and eyes each guy beside me in a warning. Ever the pure soul.

Collen tugs on my arm and leads the way down the winding hall. When we make it to his room, I can smell the liquor before he even opens the door.

I STARE at the impossibly small screen, trying to read the text from Lily. She told me our room number is 915.

Our.

I have no fucking idea how Mr. Jones made that mistake, but I'm feeling pretty thankful as I trail the halls looking for the door.

Something was different about Lily today. Aside from the missing contacts and the vintage anime tee she wore, her general vibe toward me lacked the usual accompanied loathing. And when I had stooped down to say thanks, a fraction of an inch away from her ear... her eyes lingered on my mouth, and a blush coated her nose. In that moment, she *wanted* me, and not in the normal, angry, hateful, sex-type way.

I groan, remembering how I had to hide the bulge in my jeans only reignites it, and now I'm hard as a fucking rock.

Finally, I stumble upon our room and rap on the door as soft as my heavy hands allow. I hear a muffled sound behind it before the locks click, opening to a towel-clad Lily.

If eyes could physically dislocate from their sockets like the cartoon, I'm pretty sure mine would be a foot out of my skull. Her olive skin contrasts with the bright white cotton of the towel, and I thank my lucky stars she's not fresh out of the shower because I'm pretty sure seeing her skin dripping wet would be my undoing.

I don't miss her smirk as she backs up, allowing me inside, and shuts the door behind her. I pass by a cloud of steam flowing from the bathroom and into the open living room. Shucking off my jacket, I twist, leaning my ass against an upholstered chair.

"You're drunk?" She tilts her gorgeous fucking head to the side, amusement dancing in her eyes.

I nod, holding up my thumb and index finger about an inch apart. "Maybe a little."

She scoffs playfully and turns back toward the shower. "Well, if you'll excuse me, I was on my way t—"

"Come here," I spout the command before I can stop it,

and it comes out much more hoarse and forceful than intended.

Her eyes widen for a second before she regains her composure and pops a hand on her hip. "I'm getting in the shower."

"That can wait," I clip.

Lily huffs, her wet mouth parting, and I think I may have shocked her. My tongue darts out, sliding along my bottom lip as I consider the few times I've gotten to taste hers. Their sweetness holds a rent-free space in my head, and the desire to lick her becomes overwhelming.

As if she can feel the hunger rolling in my gut, she shuffles on her feet, a telltale blush creeping up the side of her delicious-looking neck. "How are you feeling over there?"

"I'm hungry."

Her breath falters, giving away the fake calmness that's currently slipping between her fingers. "I'm sure there are leftovers downstairs. Or if not, there's a room service menu on the nightstand."

My thumb comes up, wiping the corners of my mouth as my eyes home in on hers.

"I don't want what's on that menu." I eat up the distance between us, stopping when her breasts are rubbing against my chest with her inhale. The air between us mingles, an intoxicating mixture of mint and liquor, pushing me into another level of high.

Her staggering breaths get worse. My dick presses painfully into my jeans, but I ignore it, taking a step toward her.

When she finally speaks, I have to strain to hear her whisper. "What do you want, Spencer?"

I thought she'd never fucking ask.

"You."

THIRTY TWO

Spencer Hanes just told me he wanted me. Through all the shit I've thrown at him, and after the hot and cold that is my screwed-up heart, he said *he* wanted *me.* And even though it shouldn't excite me as much as it does, my pulse accelerates, thrumming through my body with anticipation.

Never mind I'm ninety-nine percent sure it's only sex-related, I still let my mind take the three-letter answer and run with it. At least for tonight.

Just this one time.

After that, I can do the whole closure thing and move on. We just need to get it out of our system.

I keep my face as neutral as I can, tilting my head away from his. "Who says I'm on the menu?"

He laughs. It's low, gravelly, and sexy as hell. It connects with my core, sending a pool of desire soaking into my thin underwear. I rip myself out of our bubble and force my feet to the bed where my pajamas are laid out. Instead of looking at him directly, I speak over my shoulder. "I'm taking a shower. You need to get some—"

A sharp gasp steals my words.

Spencer presses into my back, letting one hand snake up to the front of my throat and the other holding me by the waist. He tightens his grasp, and suddenly his lips are on the curve of where my neck ends and shoulder begins.

My skin tingles under his mouth, and I lean into him, unable to fight how good it feels. His hand that was holding my waist moves up, untying my towel and letting it fall to the floor. My moans echo in the air as he twists me around, his lips nearly touching mine.

His eyes somehow darken even more. "I said, I'm hungry."

With a light shove, I'm on the bed, sprawled out for him to see. His eyes rove the length of my body, an index finger following behind his gaze, lighting my skin on fire in the process.

In those two seconds, any logic or reasoning behind not enjoying this moment dissolves, and I reach up to grab his collar. He collapses on top of me, his mouth on mine, gentle at first, but then his tongue slips through and takes control. We stay like this for what feels like forever, exploring and tasting, kissing, and nipping.

Lost in time, we make up for all the kisses we should have shared and all the ones we won't in the future.

But unlike our farewell in the green room, there's no finality to it. This feels like an introduction.

One of many.

He breaks our kiss, and my mouth mourns its loss, but it only lasts a moment. His warm lips trail down my body, his lashes fluttering across my skin like butterfly kisses as he descends.

Shivers wrack through me as I watch him, anticipation coiling low in my belly. I writhe beneath him, thrusting my body into his until he takes one large hand and holds me in place.

I groan my disapproval, and he smiles against my thigh. He gently removes my panties and gives me a warning. "Try not to move."

Spencer's face disappears, and a second later, I throw my head back into the pillow, his warm mouth shocking my nerves into overdrive. His tongue moves quickly, prying my pussy open and finding my throbbing clit immediately, forcing my back to arch.

A growl rips from the depths of his throat as he grabs both sides of my ass, pulling my body closer to *actually* feast on. One hand reaches up, pulling my bra down, letting my breast tumble out. He rolls the pebbled nipple in his fingers with surprising expertise while his other sneaks down below his mouth and slides inside my soaking channel.

My eyes flutter shut, unable to look any longer, and a long moan spills from my mouth.

"You taste too fucking good," he groans.

His fingers curl while his tongue continues its assault, moving in rapid circles until stars light up the inside of my eyelids. My muscles tense, lightning bolts of pleasure spreading through my body, from the tips of my toes to the ends of my hair. Every inch of skin tingles until finally, with one last suck of my sensitive bud, the orgasm rips through me. My back arches from the bed, and my hips move of their own accord, chasing Spencer's mouth as my pussy tightens around his finger, drawing it deeper inside.

It's not until I'm greedily gulping air that I realize I was holding my breath. He laps at my orgasm, draining my cunt of every drop until I finally come down, and my eyes trail along my bare stomach to a grinning Spencer.

He pulls his fingers from my pussy with an audible squelch and samples each one, closing his eyes as if it's the best thing he's ever tasted. After he's done, and a blush has worked its way up my entire face, he threads a hand under my back and scoops me up like a doll, placing me at the head of the bed. I grab the top sheet, sliding it over the both of us as he settles in beside me.

Realization starts to sink in, and my pulse increases, screaming the millions of ways this will explode in my face. My body vibrates from the erratic thoughts, and a horrible chill takes over.

None of this is what I expected. It wasn't angry or aggressive. It was passionate, and specifically just for me.

Why would he do that?

As if he can read my mind, he kisses my bottom lip twice. "Stay with me. Whatever's going on up there, ignore it and just be here in this space with me."

I nod, and the softness of his voice pushes away the stress, at least for now.

Spencer rests in the crook of my arm, draping his own across my waist to pull me closer. The temptation to play with his hair is strong, so I decide not to fight it, threading my fingers in his soft locks.

He glances up and kisses the tip of my chin before laying back down and sighing. "Do you remember that time when it was raining, and I came over, and we stayed up all night in the treehouse?" His voice is low, still filled with sex, as his hand trails up my naked stomach. Every spot his fingertips touch lights the skin on fire underneath, and suddenly my core is aching all over again.

I bite back a laugh. "That was every day for half our summers. You'll have to be more specific."

He huffs through his nose. "Good point. But this time was different. You asked if I'd been crying."

There was only one time that ever happened. We were in sixth grade, and the storm outside was one for the books. When Spencer sent me the text, asking to meet, I didn't hesitate. I think a piece of me knew something was wrong.

His eyes were red and puffy—a look I wore more than I ever let on. So when he told me he wasn't upset, I knew it was a lie. I didn't push him, though. Instead, just brought out my laptop, and we watched a movie he had been begging to watch for weeks. When he fell asleep, I cried, cuddling him until I didn't have any tears left.

"I remember."

He pinches my nipple softly, and I gasp. "I lied."

Nodding, I tug his hair to make him look at me. "I know."

He flips over, resting his forearms on either side of my head. His chocolate eyes search my face, and I melt under the golden flakes swirling in them.

"It was when we found out my mother's treatments weren't working, and she was advancing to near moderate stages of Alzheimer's. It was still early, but they knew it wouldn't be long." He presses his lips to mine.

Once.

Twice.

"You made me so happy that night. I knew you didn't want to watch that show. But you did it anyway. That was the third time I knew I loved you."

"The third?" My brows furrow, but he doesn't respond.

Instead, he lies on his side, returning to his previous position. His eyes flutter shut, and he just murmurs a soft, "third."

A few moments later, his breath becomes steady and heavy, filling the room with his tempo. I lay still for what's probably hours, listening to his rest.

I want to stay like this forever. Forget the world and just exist here in our own private bubble. But the shower water that's still running won't let me.

Forcing myself to get up, I gently move his arm and hop out of bed, meandering to the bathroom. When I pass the front door, Spencer's backpack catches my eye. It's open, and half the contents are sprawled on the ground. I bend down, sticking the items back in, when something catches my eye.

I examine it slowly, and within a second, an idea materializes.

I'm supposed to be closing things here, guarding my heart against ever breaking again.

But hey, what's one more time?

THIRTY THREE

It's the warmth of the sun on my face that wakes me up. Deep yellow rays penetrate the thin hotel curtains, blinding me with its light. The world's natural alarm and the most annoying thing to see after a hangover.

I groan, rolling over and drawing the sheets over my face. Why I decided to let them talk me into some tequila World of Warcraft game, I'll never know. Since I don't play the damn game, I was the first one to drink. Every. Single. Time. After my sixth shot, I bowed out.

Then, there was that fucking dream.

Lily.

Like the juice of the forbidden apple, it still coats my tongue in its sweetness. It's the type of taste you can't get enough of, easy to get addicted to... to love. The memory of her warm body writhing beneath me, arching into me like she couldn't get enough, and her orgasm... *Fuck.* It was amazing watching her completely unravel, shedding years of built-up anger in a single moment.

Right before Lily came, her toes curled so tight, three of

them popped. And when I looked up, her nose was scrunched up in the cutest way—I actually had to look back down to keep from smiling.

Groaning again, I roll on my side, releasing my throbbing dick from being trapped under my thighs.

And then I hear it. A light stifled giggle.

My body tenses and everything I thought was a fucking dream slaps me in the face.

"Hey." Her voice isn't too far, and it's a tone I haven't heard from her. Light, sweet, dripping with affection.

I'm in the fucking twilight zone. I know it.

"Hey." My voice, on the other hand, is hoarse, what I imagine a zombie would sound like rising from the dead.

"How are you feeling?"

That evokes a throaty laugh from the back of my throat. I throw the cover off and let my eyes focus.

Lily's sitting in the armchair next to the bed, legs clad in skintight ripped jeans, crossed, and a slightly oversized band tee draped off one shoulder. Those blonde locks I'm coming to like, are tied into a messy, yet adorable bun on the top of her head.

And her eyes. Seeing the chestnut hue for the second day in a row feels like winning the fucking lottery. They are lighter than I remember, and for the life of me, I can't figure out how she doesn't love them. But when she tilts her head, she reveals dark shadows beneath them. Like she didn't sleep... at all.

"Are you okay?" I try my best to hide the sudden alarm tightening my vocal cords.

What if she regrets everything? I know where she stands with me and how much I care, but the same can't be said for her. She may have gotten me out of her system and is ready to move on.

Forget.

Thankfully Lily speaks, pulling me from the thoughts trying to drown me. "I did a midnight run to Wally World. And I made you something."

What?

I rewind and replay what she just said at least seven times before letting my brows furrow. She squirms like she's nervous. Lily Conley. Queen of Emerald Falls. Nervous.

"It was a real invasion of privacy, so I'm really hoping you don't get pissed off. But I really wanted to do something special. To kind of close the chapter of who we were before yesterday."

There's a full blush across her cheeks, but it stops right before her ears. She's being genuine. She grasps her necklace and draws it back and forth, chewing on her bottom lip.

Now she whispers. "We missed breakfast, so everyone is getting on the buses in about ten minutes. I'm going to load up. So hurry down."

She's up and out the door before I even have a chance to get up. The combination of the lingering liquor, the fact my dream was real, and what just happened has my head reeling, to say the least.

I stretch my arms above my head, reveling in the way my back cracks down my spine. When I stretch across to grab my phone on the side table, a note rests on top.

Pulling it toward me without getting up yet, I unfold it and read Lily's script.

First and foremost, please don't be mad. They were lying on the floor, and I got this idea and kind of ran with it.

Second. I'm sorry. I'm so sorry, Spencer. I've wasted so much time hating you when we could have been something else entirely.

Anyway, I made these last night, one for you and another for her. I know it won't absolve me of all my sins and the way I treated you, but I do hope it can start the healing between us.

XO

Liliana.

P.S. Just so you know, I know what I want. What I've always wanted. And it's you.

I read the letter several times over, letting the words seep into my bloodstream and carry the euphoric tingle throughout my entire body. There's no way this is real, no way I'm not still asleep.

Finally, I sit up and notice two leather-bound books under my phone. Moving it, I grab the top one and open it to more script.

To remember her love, always and forever.

My hands are shaking, and my heart is in my throat, but I

flip the page. And the moment my eyes settle on the first picture, the world crashes down around me.

It's a scrapbook. A fucking scrapbook of my bucket list trip with my mom. Standing on the Great Wall of China. Shoveling our face with pitas from Rome. Posing under the waterfall in Niagara. Every single picture. Printed, cut, glued, and labeled.

The amount of time it must have taken her to fucking do this, *twice,* is unreal. I needed one sign. Just one. No matter how small, that I was still somehow in her heart. And she gave me two galaxy-sized signals. My heart speeds up, hammering in my chest like it wants to jump out, find her, and burrow itself behind her ribs.

I grab the second book, and it's identical to the first. The only difference is the writing on the front.

To see his love even in times, you don't quite remember.

Hot tears flow down my cheeks, that same erratic heart now swelling so big I fear it may actually bust through my sternum. But I push through, flipping every page and tracing my finger down my mother's beautiful face.

Any wall, any fucking reservation or hesitation I might have had, crumbles into dust. Liliana was always there, deep beneath the mask, even when I started to doubt it myself. And there is no way in hell I'm giving that up again.

I shove my things in my bag, doing quick work to get dressed and brush my teeth. My leg bounces the entire elevator ride, and when the door finally slides open, I haul ass outside.

Lily is talking to Remy, her back to me. But the closer I get, her spine suddenly stiffens, as if she can feel me, and she swings around.

I don't wait, dropping my bag and keeping my pace. She jumps at the perfect moment, my beautiful little cheerleader, and lands right in my arms, wrapping her legs around my waist. Our mouths collide in an unapologetic, hungry kiss. I steal every breath she has, squeezing her as hard as I can to make sure I'm not dreaming.

"Mr. Hanes. Miss Conley." Mr. Jones clears his throat.

Lily smiles against my mouth, unlatching her legs and sliding down my waist. I hold on to her hips, helping lower her down until her Converse hits the pavement. There's a fresh burn of tears teetering on the edge of my eyes.

The ends of her lip curl and she brushes the wayward hair from my face. "So, you liked it?"

"Fucking loved it. Thank you... so fucking much, Lily."

"Language, Mr. Hanes. Now, let's go."

I kiss Lily again before turning to grab my bag and climb on the bus. We sit in the seats next to Remy, who holds her hands out impatiently. "I have to see this. Gimme, gimme."

"Yeah, of course."

Lily scooches next to the window, resting her head on the glass, watching as I pluck out one of the books. Remy takes it, opens it, and gasps. "It's so beautiful, Lily, oh my goodness. Oh, Spencer, what's that?"

She's pointing to a tapestry from a workshop we went to in India. It's a kaleidoscope of colors, handcrafted by some of the most incredible women. I explain it to her, then she flips the page and asks about another. Soon, I'm lost in the conversation, describing the details I tried to on the phone but couldn't.

When I look back at Lily, she's asleep, her chest rising and falling in a steady tempo, soft hums coming from her button nose. And it's right then, I know.

This is the thirty-sixth time I know I love her.

WHEN WE ARRIVE at the school, I reluctantly part ways with her and promise to meet her tonight after my celebration dinner with my dad.

The dinner is nice but depressing as hell without my mother. He didn't want to get her since it was her first weekend there, deciding to let her settle in and calm down. My dad spends the whole time talking, excited about the future, while I push my food around, taking small bites here and there. I try my best to smile when needed and maintain at least a semi-content mood. But after spending three months as a family, to have it disappear in twenty-four hours... it didn't really mesh well with my chicken marsala.

Still, I try my best to wear a smile, nodding my head when needed, mutter thanks after compliments and answer questions in full sentences.

When we get home, I shed the dress clothes at my door, tugging on something comfortable, and drift to the window. Lily's light is off, and I wonder vaguely if she crashed earlier, still tired from being awake all night.

I open my window, and the smell of damp earth and ozone blows inside. It's hard to see in the dark, but heavy clouds hang overhead, painting the black sky with fluffs of gray and hues of purple. I contemplate just letting her rest and texting her tomorrow when I hear it.

It's low at first, muffled through the brick exterior. But then it comes again, even louder.

Was that a scream?

Just then, fissures open up the sky, drowning our backyards in a blanket of white as lightning rips through it. The rain pours through, pummeling to the ground as if its plan is to drive right through to the core.

I grab my phone and call Lily, a sudden overwhelming sensation of dread working its way up my spine into the darkest part of my thoughts.

No answer.

Calling again, I shove on boots and grab my windbreaker, pulling on the hood.

No answer.

Another crack of lightning pierces through the sky, stretching its electric fingers in every direction.

Fuck.

I leap from the window, ignoring the harsh winds slapping across my face on the way down.

Sirens.

Fuck!

I'm through the back gate, around the side, and in the front door within seconds. I don't really know what I was expecting, but it wasn't this.

Lily is against the wall, holding her stomach and sporting a fresh raw bruise on the right side of her chin. Her mother, the head custodian at Emerald Falls High School, is on the ground, screaming in Spanish, struggling under the knee of a... she looks like an older version of Lily. Her long blonde hair has streaks of white that whip back and forth as she struggles to keep her down.

Her big brown eyes flash to me, then to Lily and back

again. She yells through the screams of Mrs. Conley. "Spencer, I need you to take Lily. Now!"

I jolt upright, not thinking twice, and scoop Lily up in my arms, cradling her to my wet chest, and push out the back door.

The rain thrashes against me as I run to the closest place I know will make her feel safe. I somehow manage to climb up the wobbly stairs and into the treehouse.

Shuffling on my knees, I take her to one of the beanbags, but as I set her down, she clings to me, shivering violently. "Lily, I have to get you some clothes."

She shakes her head against my chest, bunching my jacket's soaked fabric in her tiny hands. I relent, rocking her back and forth, waiting until her breaths are even.

The storm rages on outside, the sirens sailing through the air for what feels like forever until finally, they stop. That's when Lily releases me, leaning back into the beanbag, one hand still wrapped around my jacket. Her face is puffy, eyes rimmed in a deep red, and mascara streaks down her face. My heart aches for her, anger and confusion swirling around my chest as I work out what the fuck I just witnessed.

I damn sure don't ask though, instead I unzip my jacket. "I'm not going to leave you, but at least let me get you a blanket. Do you still have some in the crate?"

There was a chest we used to keep under the sealed window for our sleepovers out here. It also had some battery-powered lanterns and dish towels for any spills. The chest is still there, but the new paint job makes me wonder if it houses the same items.

She nods.

Thank fuck. I move quickly, opening up and pulling out

all the contents. The lights are set up in seconds, and when I turn around, Lily is already coming out of her clothes.

I suck in air, heat creeping up my cheeks. Part of me wants to look away, but the other part...

Then I see it.

The necklace that's always hidden.

It's the heart charm that belongs to a bracelet I bought her three years ago. I left it up here the day she told me not to move to Emerald Falls.

She fucking kept it.

THIRTY FOUR

He sees it.

The charm to a bracelet I found a couple of years ago when Amora and I made over the treehouse. It became clear immediately it was from him, and I think it was the second time my heart broke.

I hated him for what he did, but I missed him so damn much I couldn't bring myself to throw it away. It felt like I still had a piece of him here, comforting me when I was surrounded by the dark. When I was lonely and broken at the hands of my mother. So I kept it, attaching it to a delicate chain long enough to keep the small charm hidden, right next to my heart. Every time I feel overwhelmed, upset, or sad, I latch on to it, and it always anchors me.

After a few lingering seconds, he snaps out of his daze, moving quickly and wrapping the blanket around my shivering limbs. He strips off his hoodie and sweats in one fluid motion, leaving him in basketball shorts and a dry white tee.

Spencer flops down on the beanbag beside me and hoists me closer, draping my legs over his lap and my head into his chest. Even through the blanket, I can feel his warmth. It reaches through and encircles my body, acting as a second cover. He returns to stroking my hair and rubbing the goose bumps from my arm.

Everything about what he's doing fuels the fresh rain of tears streaming down my face. I never told him when my mother would hit me. I was too embarrassed and thought maybe things would get better.

I guess that's why it's taken me so long to feel the effects of my mother's abuse.

Like the frog in tepid water—merrily swimming inside, not realizing the temperature is slowly rising. Then all at once, the water is in a rolling boil, and the frog is dead. I was almost the frog tonight.

My aunt found herself a date. A nice banker guy that set up her new account and went out—the first time since making her stay here permanently. And since the bed was calling my name after being up for over thirty-six hours, I went to it, drowning in the sweet bliss immediately.

When I woke up, the smell of smoke encroached on my airways. Not like the house is on fire, but like a basic pack of Marlboros smokes. I crawled down the stairs, cautious, the tiny hairs on the nape of my neck standing at attention, not really knowing what would be waiting for me. Whatever it was I imagined, had nothing on what I found.

My mother, dressed in her nicest black dress, was dancing in the kitchen. Her hair combed back in the perfect bun, a pearl necklace dangling from her thin body as she moved. A cigarette stuck out from the corner of her lips, a cherry appearing at the end as she took a long drag.

She heard the stupid stairs creak from my weight, and she snapped her face up to meet my gaze. My lips pulled into a vicious snarl, anger licking up my spine and settling between my shoulder blades. "Why are you here?"

My mother looked at me, wiping away a streak of mascara I hadn't noticed before, and smiled.

After that... everything blurs into punches and kicks. And it wasn't me who was at the receiving end this time. I'm relatively certain I blacked out, succumbing to the built-up rage that resided beneath my skin, waiting for its chance to wreak havoc.

But then, my light, my sun, the guy that's taking over my life, appears at the door, leaving the rest to be forgotten.

When my mind returns to the present, Spencer is kneeling in front of me, his glorious eyes searching my face, trying his hardest to read my thoughts. I decide not to speak and instead reach up, planting my hands on the side of his face and drawing him to me. His lips cover mine in the sweetest, softest kiss yet.

He's hesitating. As though he's scared he's going to hurt me.

It strikes a match of irritation, and I push into him, deepening the kiss and nipping at his lip. He moans in my mouth, and my core tightens.

"Love me," I whisper against his mouth, too caught up in his web to worry about the missing 'make' and 'to' in my request.

"I already do, baby."

We freeze. His hands are locked in my hair, mine are wrapped around his back. Our lips are inches apart, the staggered breaths we exhale whirl between us, drowned by the storm surging outside. So many reasons to keep going and never look up, but we stop. Our eyes look into each other's as if they hold all the answers in the world.

And maybe they do.

At least the questions I want answered.

We are what we need more than anything in the world. Today, yesterday, tomorrow, and I'll be damned if I waste another minute not wrapped in his love.

I reconnect our mouths, arching, so my body is flush against his, our lungs taking and receiving the same small puff of air, making me dizzy. Grinding into him, I hook my hand in his shorts, pulling them down, greedily searching for his length currently pressed into my leg.

He hisses when my cold hand wraps around it, smiling into my mouth. It's wide as hell, and for a second, I wonder if it will hurt. Besides some fingers, nothing else has been inside me.

Shit. Am I supposed to tell him...

No. Well, maybe I should.

But what if he stops?

"Where's your head? Come back to me." His throaty whisper travels right to my core, turning my thoughts into incoherent whimpers.

He kisses my chin. Once. Twice, and then descends to the column of my throat, taking care to be as soft as possible. My pulse throbs under his tongue until it moves down, sliding between the valley of my breasts and then down to my navel.

I keep my eyes on him as I take his dick and drag it through my soaked folds, trembling when he growls below me.

"Lily," he hisses through clenched teeth, moving back up to nip at my bottom lip.

Whether it's a warning or challenge, I'm not quite sure, but I'm ready to find out. Lining him up with my entrance, his beautiful eyes snap to mine, dark, hooded, needy. His eyelashes flutter, and a shiver shakes through him as I tilt up, pushing the tip of his head inside.

"Fucking hell." Spencer slides in more, digging his hands in my ass. My eyes flare, a little pain spiked with immense pleasure as I stretch around him to accommodate his width.

Then, out of nowhere, he pulls out. Chocolate eyes flitting back and forth, brows furrowed with what looks like rage. My body mourns the quick loss of him, and I automatically reach out, pulling him back to touch me.

He sucks in a quick breath, his throat bobbing from his harsh swallow. "Lily. Have you had sex before?"

I groan, tilting my pussy up, so it rubs against him. "Why does it matter?"

His eyes disappear, rolling in the back of his head as he feels me. His words are strained, and it's easy to see he's holding on by the thinnest of threads. "Please, just answer me. Have you?"

"If you promise, you won't stop," I clip, wrapping my hand around him again. He's somehow harder now, and it's pulsing under my fingertips.

He nods.

So I answer.

"No."

THIRTY FIVE

She's a fucking *virgin*?

I literally turn off my brain, refusing to let my thoughts run away and take me out of this moment. Instead, I lean against her, propping myself on my elbows. "Are you sure?"

She grunts, her face tensing as if she's the most annoyed person in the world. But then she narrows her eyes, and I know if looks could kill, I'd be a fucking goner. "If you don't put it back in, I will."

And she means it. She bucks her hips, and my head slips inside, the slickness of her cunt letting it glide right in.

"Okay, but slow."

She grits her teeth, but nods, nonetheless.

I push back in, and much to my agony, slow, reveling at the way her tight channel squeezes around me, pulling me in further. She's nothing but wet, coiled muscles, and her moans into my biceps are almost my fucking undoing. I want to ask her if it hurts, but she answers the unasked question, jerking her hips back and meeting my next thrust.

Fuck. She feels so fucking good.

She buries her teeth into my arm, reaching to pull me closer. "More."

I want to take it slow, cherish her for giving me something so fucking important, but she backs away again and shoves herself up, taking my dick all the way to the hilt.

Fuuuuuuckkk.

Gripping her ass, I sit up, letting her legs wrap around me like a vice, and drag out to the head. I lean forward and push back in. She throws her hands above her head, stifling a scream. Working up a rhythm, I lose myself and whatever control I had, moving in tune with each moan spilling from her lips.

My eyes flash to the window where the rain and lightning still attack the earth, drowning every other sound with its winds. I reach up, hooking a finger under her chin and tilting it so she can look at me. Her chest is flushed, pebbled nipples peek from behind a lacy bra, and rain droplets shimmer on her skin as she rocks her hips. Everything about her is breathtaking.

"You're so fucking beautiful. Don't hold back. I want to hear you."

Her eyes widen, and she nods. I reach up, tearing the fabric of her bra down, and find the pert little nipple with my tongue. Biting softly, I coax a whimper from her before rolling it around until it's unbearably hard. My other hand works its way down, finding her sensitive clit waiting. Rubbing in small circles, I start slow but accelerate as her moans get louder, hungrier.

"Come for me, Lily."

Lily's legs tighten around my waist, and her muscles tense, her impending climax consuming her. Her pussy flutters before her body finally seizes beneath me, her orgasm ripping through her body. She screams her release into the next strike of lightning and roll of thunder at the moment I can't fight anymore. My balls tighten, a surge exploding through my body as I come. Colors crash behind my eyelids, black, blues, silvers, and white. I have to find her lips with mine to ground me. To bring me back down to earth.

When our breaths finally sync, the high rolling through our bodies coming to a close, we slump into each other. Exhaustion takes over, and for the first time in five years, she sleeps in my arms while the world rages on outside, and I know what I've known all along.

I'm in love with Lily Conley.

MONDAY USED to be just a typical day. Not one I hated and not one I was excited about. But today, knowing I'll see Lily puts an extra pep in my step when I pull up to the school.

Yesterday, she spent time with the woman I found out was her aunt, at the police station and later with her family therapist for an emergency meeting. Both pieces of information I acquired over text. Though what actually went down on Saturday is still a mystery, Lily has all the time in the world to tell me.

Something I've learned about people, especially those who shoulder a significant burden, is that words are easier to write, or in this case, text, rather than talk about face-to-face. It's difficult when the strong have to be vulnerable, and however she wants to tell me these things, I appreciate it. She's given me so much already...

My mind drifts to Saturday night, when the world was

crashing both outside and inside the treehouse. The place we spent years laughing, crying, playing, loving. Seems kind of poetic in a way that it all came back full circle to where it started.

"Hey you." Her voice cuts straight to my core.

I spin around, grinning like a dummy from ear to ear, but it soon evaporates. We haven't talked about how things are going to be. We made out in front of some kids from AP science, but I hadn't put much thought into how her group of people will react.

Lily's lips are on mine before I have a chance to finish my thoughts that now don't even fucking matter. My hands wrap around her waist, lifting her and spinning in a full three-sixty before placing her back on the ground.

She giggles into my mouth, kissing me once, twice before backing away.

Her face, as beautiful as ever, glows today. Her rose lips stretching into an endearing smile, lighting up her aura from a thousand miles away. She's wearing my windbreaker from the other night over a cropped white tee and painted on black jeans.

But it's not the mouthwatering outfit, flowy hair, or lack of contacts that puts my heart in my throat. Nope. It's the necklace.

It's not hidden today, dangling from her neck like she couldn't be prouder to wear it.

I thread my hand through hers, and she leans against my shoulder as we walk, or maybe float is a better word, toward the entrance.

As soon as we pass the school threshold, I feel it. Every single person within our vicinity is staring at us. Some are stifling laughter, others are whispering comments I can't quite make out, but the air is thick and putrid, reeking of something I can't place.

My back tenses, unsure if it's me, or if she feels it too. But when I look down, her eyes are already on mine, a confused look pinching together her delicate features.

Amora and Remy surprise us, appearing out of fucking thin air.

Remy is worried, her big hazels darting back and forth between Lily and me as if she's on the verge of tears but also waiting for some big thing to happen. She rocks on her heels, her chest heaving.

Amora, on the other hand, is fucking pissed. Her nose flaring, eyes bulging, and teeth bared. She doesn't even look at me and instead holds out a balled-up piece of paper for Lily to take.

When I look at Remy, I notice she, too, has a wad of flyers in her clutches.

Lily releases my hand and grabs the flyer, unraveling it as I take one from Remy.

The world stops. Completely and utterly. All sound ceases to exist, while all colors fade to a gray scale.

Holy. Shit.

It's a picture of Lily, fall of her senior year, I'm guessing. She's all bright white teeth and perfect hair. Her eyes twinkle somehow, even beneath the contacts. There's a thick layer of makeup covering her naturally beautiful face. The true mask of the Queen of Emerald Falls.

But next to that is a mug shot. Fresh off the fucking press of Lily's mom from Saturday. It's not hard to see the resemblance as they share the same heart-shaped face, small nose, and slightly pointed ears. But if you didn't know they were related, the big, bold black caption underneath does it for you.

Lily Conley, the PEASANT of Emerald Falls

The same words I told her when we were in the pink room. Lily doesn't miss a beat. Whatever was there just moments ago crumbles into dust, replaced by the girl in the picture. Her lips flip up in a snarl as she homes in on me with a sharp red stiletto. "Are you fucking kidding me?"

"Don't." I know where this is going, what she's fucking thinking, and there is no way in hell I'm going to let her spiral. Let her think *I* would do this.

Reaching out for her, she recoils immediately as if I'm trying to burn her. I ignore the intense pang in my heart and step forward.

She steps back, one hand raised. "So this is it, huh? Your big revenge for everything I've done." Her laugh is bitter, echoing through the now silent hall as spectators crowd around us. "Get close to me, *fuck* me, then humiliate me?"

"Please. You *know* I wouldn't do this." I try for her again, just barely grazing her elbow before she rips it away. She has to be able to hear the truth in my voice, the fucking fear. It feels like I'm holding a pile of dry sand, and I'm watching it slip through my fingers, unable to catch the tiny grains.

I can't lose you. I just fucking got you. *Please.*

She closes her eyes, taking a few steady breaths, her brows knitting together as if she's trying to think of anyone else that would know about Saturday. That would know her mother works here. She's trying to make it make sense. She doesn't want to believe it's me. I can see it.

"Stop it, Spence. I'm going to fall," Liliana screeches at the top of her lungs.

She wanted to see the meteor shower, and me, thinking I'm something like Aladdin, have her follow me to the roof of the tree-house, perching on my shoulders. I can't resist tickling her pretty pink toes dangling so close to my hands, so I run the tips of my fingers down the arch. I don't tell her I love the way she squeezes closer to me, holding on like I'm the only thing keeping her safe. Instead, I recite the movie, twisting it to fit us now.

"Liliana, do you trust me?"

She peers down at me from a curtain of dark lashes, her chestnut eyes shimmering in the first pass of a meteor. Her smile fades, replaced by something in the deepest part of her heart. Like this is the most honest thing she's ever said. "I'll always trust you, Spence."

Then, as if the sky was waiting for this moment, dozens of little stars streak across the sky, and I make a new wish on all fifty-three. After that, we made it rule number one on our contract. Always trust your best friend if they ask.

"Liliana, please. Trust me."

Her eyelids pop open, and whatever, *whoever,* was there ten minutes ago is gone. She grasps the delicate necklace around her neck and wrenches it free in a powerful snap, throwing it at my feet. "It's Lily, *dog*. And I never want to see you again. Stay the *fuck* away from me."

She turns on her heels, Blaze appearing from fucking nowhere with an impassive look on his face as he follows behind her. My heart sinks into my gut, dissolving in the stomach acid as I watch her leave. It's as if my feet are stuck in quicksand, and I know I'm fucked either way.

Thrash and run after her, I'll only sink faster.

Sit and do nothing, I'll still sink.

Without thinking, I reach out, grasping the edge of Amora's arm. Surprisingly, she doesn't pull away and instead regards me with sad striking blue eyes. Her mouth opens and closes twice before she grabs onto the words she's searching for. "I don't know you, and I have no fucking clue how I know this, but I know you're not stupid enough to actually have done it."

With that, she disappears behind her friends, leaving me reeling in the middle of the hall.

Hold fast, hold steady.

But even doing that won't stop the sand from rising and swallowing me fucking whole.

THIRTY SIX

I make it around the senior lockers and into the art hallway before my feet give out. Luckily, Blaze was behind me, scooping me into his arms and taking me straight back to my car. He drives me home, making quick work of explaining everything to my aunt, and tucks me into bed. I notice when he tells her, he leaves out the part that it was Spencer's doing.

That he ripped my fucking heart out of my chest and waited for the perfect time to throw it in a blender.

And it was perfect, really—extremely smart planning on his part.

Play this little victim, come up with some story to make me feel like a dumbass for getting so mad at him all those years ago, then leaving conveniently for three months. Letting me stew over everything and realize that I miss him. That I lo...*love* him.

Then he does all that stuff at the fair, which makes me rethink my entire future in the blink of an eye. Makes me consider rearranging things so I can have the future I wanted while doing what I've come to love. But that wasn't enough. He dug so deep under my skin, I gave myself to him. All of me. Every tear, scream, and orgasm.

I trusted him. Fucking *trusted* him.

And at the precise moment when it would hurt me the most, he dropped the other foot. Five days before regionals. Spencer knew it would fuck up my head, mess up the hierarchy of the squad, and ruin any chance I have of winning.

I scream, throwing pillows across the room and letting obscenities tumble from my lips into Blaze's face. And he just waits. My wonderful, broken little knight just waits. Not once does he ask me if I want him to take care of the problem (Spencer), which pisses me off more. Instead, he merely watches until I'm blue in the face, depleted of any more tears, and utterly spent. That's when he moves in, humming his song until I'm asleep.

He doesn't leave for the next three days. And neither does Amora. She comes later that night bearing gifts in gallon-sized ice cream containers and horror movie classics. Neither she nor Blaze says anything about the rumors I know are running like wildfire or why they keep getting up and going downstairs and returning empty-handed.

Finally, when Blaze heads to a basketball game, my aunt and Amora force me to get up and have a spa night with them. My toes are stretched out with little foam separators, my face is nearly frozen in a mask, and I'm slightly tipsy on some wine my aunt brought up, but I'm content. I think.

"Lil." Amora's just washed off her mask and sits next to my aunt, grabbing another handful of popcorn. "I need to ask you something?"

I nod, not wanting to break the charcoal mask quite yet.

Her eyes are averted to the pile of popcorn sitting in her

lap, while one of her hands fist the hem of her shirt. Her words rush out, like if she waits too long she'll tell me to forget about it. "I hate to bring it up, but it's bothered me for months. Why didn't you tell me about your mom a long time ago? Didn't you trust me?"

It's not often I see Amora be vulnerable, so when I do get the rare opportunity, it drives guilt into me like a sledgehammer. She's right, after all. She's been through the thick of it with me when it wasn't borderline domestic violence anymore, but straight abuse. But like Dr. Floren has brought to my attention, I have some issues with fully releasing trust in relationships.

You know, abandonment issues and all.

Instead of apologizing, I decide to be honest. "I didn't want you to know for two reasons. One, you would have definitely stayed after school one day to confront her. And the other... I thought if we ever fell out, you would use it against me."

Amora's face contorts, her features pinching together as though I've offered her a month-old glass of milk. She stands, her hands clenched in fists. "First off, yes. I would've gotten the bitch fired off the top." She glances at my aunt, an apologetic grimace before returning her sharp gaze to me. "Second, is that what you think of me, Lil? That fucking low that I would expose something like that? Bitch, I am your girl. Through thick and fucking thin. Your friend twin flame. Or is that not what you think of me?"

Now I'm standing, ignoring how ridiculous I must look with the charcoal mask on my face cracking. "Yes. Of course, I know this. I have issues, Amora. Ones I didn't even know I fucking had until recently. Yeah, I was a little standoffish, but I didn't know how deep my mother's poison actually went.

How it embedded in me so deep I couldn't feel it. It's not an excuse. It's an acknowledgment. I'm so freaking sorry. Everyone I've ever trusted has fucked me over, and I love you so much I didn't want to give you or Blaze the chance. I wouldn't be able to come back from that."

My body shudders as the tears cut through my mask, dropping fat black droplets on my white rug. It's the truth. Dr. Floren has shown me that we all deal with trauma and abuse so differently. In my case, I chose a mask.

But it's one I've never taken off. One that I never let slip, even with the people I trust the most. It's no fault of theirs, but I hope she can understand, or at least try, and realize it was never to hold her at arm's length because of anything she did. It was because, really, I was terrified of the mess I'd be without her.

Her arms wrap around me, engulfing me in her lemon hues and floral undertones. She smells like a field full of daisies blooming under the sun. After a few moments like this, she pulls my face into her hands, and I nearly fall into the depth of her blue ocean eyes.

"Lily. Listen to me and listen good. I am not going anywhere. Ever. Even when you're off in Kentucky, living your best life. Especially not then because helloooo, football players."

I laugh through my tears, accepting the wet cloth my aunt materialized out of nowhere to wipe my face.

Amora waits, sitting us back on the bed, crossing her legs. "Also," she starts, grabbing a vial of Juliette Rose Gold Nail polish and taking my aunt's hand. "I don't think Spencer did it."

"Same here," my aunt chirps in.

My face snaps to them so fast my neck actually cracks.

"What?"

Mina sighs, resting her head against my pillow. "That boy is torn up. He's been by every damn day trying to talk to you. I can see it in those little puffy eyes of his."

I threw my phone across the room the Monday I came home and haven't picked it back up since. There was no way I could take the millions of notifications and texts asking about the scandal, and I knew he'd blow up my phone. Instead, I became a recluse, ironically kind of like my mother, only leaving my room to pee or take a quick shower. It's irresponsible, given regionals is literally this weekend, but I had to. For my own sanity and extremely brittle heart. "No one else knows who she is, and besides. When Spencer and I fought, he called me a peasant. That's not a coincidence."

"Someone has to know. By chance, maybe. Someone who has it out for you may be watching you." My aunt examines her freshly polished nails, nodding in approval for Amora to finish. "And the name isn't that random. You are the queen, Lily. Peasant is the literal opposite."

I shake my head, refusing to allow their words to fill me with the little hope that's dangling by a thread. My heart screams its piece, telling me to listen and go talk to him. Don't jump to conclusions like I did the day I overheard him with William.

But my head. My stupid head does what it does best. Inflicts reason in order to save my mangled heart.

Spencer Hanes isn't the pawn, I thought. He's the rook. The manager of the board, a flexible piece that smart players know how to use for their strengths. He moved quickly, in a straight path right past me.

And he just called checkmate.

"Ready?"

I drove by myself to meet the girls in Richland, where regionals are. It will be the first time I've seen them in a week, and while part of me feels like shit about that, I know they were in good hands with Amora. Not to mention we had drilled the routine in their heads since the beginning of the year, so there wasn't anything they needed from me that she couldn't offer.

Still, guilt restricts my windpipe the closer I get, and by the time I pull up, I can't breathe.

Amora leans against my car, eyeing me with those piercing blue orbs that I swear can read my mind. "I've already talked to the girls, no one gives two fucks about your shitty ass Mom. They know the team wouldn't be half of what it is today without you. You got to have more faith in them."

Even though my throat is dry, I still attempt a harsh swallow. Over the past few days, it's settled in that I don't really care how I'm perceived in terms of the hierarchy at Emerald Falls. I created a facade of being distant to keep everyone away in hopes of never feeling neglected. When really, I never had to worry about it in the first place.

The people that *matter*, the ones that show up every day, have taught me what love is. How it looks when times are tough, and you need a kick in your ass. Or when you need the help of a doctor. Or when you're being stupid and giving up that once-in-a-lifetime type love.

So while I'm glad the girls are fine, not bothered by my parentage, I'm even happier that they are ready to show out, despite it.

"Yeah, I'm ready," I finally answer, grabbing my pom-poms and joining Amora inside.

The colossal stadium is packed. Bodies squeeze past one another to find seats in the college basketball stadium. The smell of popcorn wafts through the air, along with accidental taps of blow horns and chatter, making it impossible to think.

I catch a quick glimpse of the mat in the center of the court. It's double the size from last year, I assume, to accommodate the new outrageous routines, and it lights up like the Radio City Music Hall.

Amora jerks my hand, weaving us through the bodies into the honeycomb hallways overridden with cheerleaders. Colors of every combination clash, reflecting off the polished walls. Music of all kinds stream in between the bodies, counts are recited, and girls dry heave into paper bags.

When we finally get to our room, a giant EMERALD FALLS sign is posted on the door.

But when we pivot inside, the room is quiet. Dead silence, actually. Stacy stands with her back to the entrance. A frail hand on her hip, the other gesturing in the air. Tonya catches us in the corner of her eye and slips a quick finger over her lips.

"Are you serious right now? No one fucking cares that this peasant son of a bitch is going to *lead* us out there? We'll be the laughingstock," Stacy scoffs, both hands on her hips now.

My stomach somersaults, landing with a sickening thud, while my blood turns into nothing more than boiling liquid, flowing through my veins so fast I start to see double. Nothing else matters except the vision of red, swaying her hips in front of me. All I need to hear, all I need to know is—

"So I did all that work, exposing the little bitch and it was all for nothing!?"

That's all I needed.

"Stacy." That's her only warning because, frankly, I don't give a *fuck* why she did it. There is not an excuse in the world that could justify her sticking a knife in my throat when I have done nothing but help groom her to take over next year.

She turns, her red pony swinging before her primped face connects with my fist. There's a crack in the air, echoing through the narrow hallway, and then the pop of her ass hitting the floor.

I may have put the past eighteen years of neglect in that one punch, sprinkled with some of the abuse. And maybe a little bit of the closure Dr. Floren talked about.

Even though I'm seventy percent sure I fractured my hand, the relief is immediate. It spreads through my limbs, relaxing the muscles like the best dose of endorphins I've had in a week. But it's a short high. I'm not stupid. Without Stacy, we are missing a near vital part of the crew, and our stand-ins won't be enough. Dread creeps in. I let the girls down, in one weak moment, when I couldn't control my emotions. They've worked so hard, and just like that...

"Wherever your head is at... stop. Focus." Amora leans in with her whispers, the heat of her words combating the chill working its way through my body. "Fuck her. She deserved it. We got this."

I muster the best smile I can, turning to the crew that's bright-eyed and bushy-tailed. Amusement dancing in their eyes, excitement in their bouncy steps. Amora is right, and after we win, I'm racing home to get my damn man.

"Alright, ladies. Showtime."

THIRTY SEVEN

To say I've been a fucking wreck the last five days is the understatement of the century. Sleeping, eating, hell, even thinking has become a daunting task I have to force myself to do. There's no way I can prove I didn't do it. Hell, it makes perfect sense that it *would* be me. But that's not going to stop me from fighting tooth and nail trying to prove my innocence until the truth does come out.

Too many times have I have let this girl walk out of my life, with me in the rear, willingly letting her.

Not this time.

She needs to know that without a shadow of a doubt, she is for me. I am for her. And that's it.

Which explains why my dumbass drove out to regionals as one last grand gesture. I have no fucking clue what to say or how I might persuade her, not to mention I'm a ball of nerves. This *also* explains why William drove me, lecturing me the entire way. It wasn't until we pulled up and saw the flock of cheerleaders that he relaxed a little.

"She's hot, no offense." He holds his hands up, a silent

surrender to the wrath he dealt with after he mistakenly kissed her during a Halloween party. "But jeesh, man. How many signs are you going to need from the universe before you grab some new snatch?"

"Are you done?" I ask over my shoulder, meandering through the dense crowd.

He always brings up how long it took me to get her out of my mind back in Idaho. How long I moped around until I finally found something to keep my mind busy. But I never moved on, and those girls were only a distraction. She's it for me.

My heart knew way before my head. But now that they are on the same page, there's no going back.

William stops at least four times to pick up a few numbers before we find our way to the front. Lily's aunt Mina stands, waving us over. "Where in the hell have you guys been? They're up."

Will tenses beside me, wide green eyes stuck on Mina. He has no shame as his gaze trails down the length of her black sundress, then finding its way to her lips.

"Oof." He huffs as I jab him in his side.

Mina ignores him altogether and sits, tugging on my shirt sleeve to follow.

Even though our circumstances weren't ideal, it's been nice getting to know her. She's always been kind when she's had to turn me down from seeing Lily. *"She's not ready. Just give her some time. She has to figure it out herself. She needs to know without a shadow of a doubt, or else it will be forced. She'll come around."*

I lean forward, resting my elbows on my knees when the announcement is made.

"Three-time reigning Regional Champs, Emerald Falls

High School." The announcer booms and the entire stadium erupts. The bleachers shake, my ears pop, and our bodies vibrate with palpable excitement.

The Emerald Falls cheer squad exits from behind a hidden curtain, trailing in military style. Each step is perfectly in tune, matching that of the person in front of them. The three in front carry black and gold pom-poms, one of which is Lily.

My heart stops, just as the noise around me fades. It's only been a few days since I've seen her, but it feels like a lifetime. I clench my teeth, fighting the burn prickling at the back of my eyes.

Every nerve in my body is pulling me toward the sizable blue mat.

My leg shakes in front of me until Mina places a tender hand on my knee. "It's going to be fine. Just got to hold fast."

I look to her, my nostrils flaring with a burn coiling in them. Her ruby lips curl into a soft smile before she pats my leg twice.

Before I have time to think, the music starts.

The girls break off, moving in unison before bunching up in groups and lifting another, tossing her in the air incredibly high. The flying girls twist, some flip, but they all land on their feet with unbelievable grace.

After that, stunts are done one after the other in unison, it reminds me of those synchronized swimming competitions. Everything is fluid, as if their muscles have the memory of every move they've ever practiced, and their bodies are on autopilot.

It's incredible to watch. And Lily is a fucking masterpiece. She commands the mat, and though her eyes are facing the front, I catch the small orders and compliments she gives each of the girls when they move and rotate. *She's* incredible.

My gut twists. This is the first time I've ever seen her in her element. And now I regret all the missed time I could have seen this. Seen how absolutely made for this she is.

No more wasted time. Ever again.

Lily sticks the final landing of an outlandishly high jump, and the crowd erupts. Even William stands to applaud.

After everything calms, groups of other teams file out onto the floor, all clustering up. Some sit in tight circles, others are in loose staggered sitting groups.

"This is for the winners," Mina whispers in my ear.

"This soon?"

She nods, raising her eyebrows and bunching up her shoulders. "I'm so nervous."

I'm not. Even though I didn't get to watch any of the other teams, there's no fucking way EFH didn't win. They fucking killed it. My eyes find Lily standing on the outside of their circle. Their hands are interlocked, and she's speaking to all of them with their heads inclined toward her. I make out the words *proud* and *phenomenal*, and I couldn't agree with her more.

The announcer's voice echoes through the stadium with his announcements. "First, we would like to give a round of applause for all the performances here today—amazing job, ladies and gentlemen. We would also like to thank our sponsors for making this event possible and continuing to support the cheerleading community. At this time we would like to announce our third place winners... Astigo Valley High. Nice job, ladies."

The team with sea-foam green stands, waving at the

crowd before moving to the front of the mat to accept a pretty impressive trophy.

"Our second-place winner... Coentuga High. Great job, ladies."

This time a red team stands, bouncing to the front to accept an even larger trophy.

My eyes leave the red team and snap back to Lily, whose eyes are on me. Her face is impassive, and while that scares the shit out of me, I don't care. I mouth it anyway because I want her to hear it from me first. "You won. Congratulations. You killed it."

Her hand lifts to her mouth before rubbing the tip of her nose. But that's it. My heart jackhammers in my chest, but I don't allow my thoughts to wander. To doubt. Instead, I hold on to my chair's armrest and focus on the announcer's voice.

"And your RCA, Regional Champs in the northwest division, with a ninety-three point seven five, Emerald Falls High School!"

The crowd erupts, even louder than when they were introduced, and the everyone in the stands jumps to their feet, myself included. The Emerald Falls cheerleaders jump, celebrating their victory, and in the middle of it all, my eyes find her.

A shot of cannon confetti sounds in the air, raining down as my heart thunks in my chest, begging me to go to her now.

I want to jump over the fucking railing, past the judge's table, and grab her.

So I do.

My hands grip the cold metal railing, and my muscles tense as my feet leave the ground. I land the three-foot jump and bound past the long table, ignoring the hollers of Mina,

William, and a group of security guards now trailing after me.

I reach the mat and jerk to a stop. My chest heaves, adrenaline shooting through my nerves with a force so strong my body shudders. The group of girls doing the small celebration look at me, mouth ajar. Lily rotates, eyes connecting with mine.

Everything I had planned to say evaporates in the heat swirling between us. The part of me that always lets her choose what she wants to do rears its head—whispering how stupid I am. How this isn't going to work. To turn my dumbass around and walk back to the stands.

But I don't. Not this fucking time.

"Lily. Since the day I first saw you, with that yellow ribbon tied in your hair, flying behind you in the wind, I knew. Right then and there. But if I didn't, you showed me the next week when I went into that treehouse and never wanted to leave. You've been with me through the roughest times of my life, even when you weren't physically there. You're so many wonderful things bundled into a spicy little ball of fire, and fuck, Lily, being without you feels like being without the sun."

Lily's eyes slowly well with a wall of tears, or maybe it's my own eyes, but she doesn't stop me. She just stares. Everyone stares, waiting. I greedily swallow some air before saying what I should have said the day she told me not to move to Emerald Falls.

"I would never hurt you, Lily. I need you to trust me when I say that because it's always been you. Yesterday, today, tomorrow. For the rest of my fucking life. It will always be you. And I am so in love with you I—"

"I love you too."

"Lily, I promise you I didn't... wait. What?"

The ends of her perfect lips curl, those chestnut eyes glimmering with amusement. "I said I love you too, Spence."

Is it possible that your heart can explode with happiness, but you somehow live through it? Because mine does. It swells in my chest and pushes so hard into my ribs, I have to hold a hand to it to keep it inside. Relief, euphoria, bliss. Everything surges through my body until I feel the tear slide down my cheek, matching the ones trailing down hers.

I scoop her in my arms, the sudden screams and cheers of the crowd finally registering as we twirl around, her giggles muffled in my neck. A second round of confetti cannons ring out, showering us in the gold and black of Emerald Falls. And when Lily leans back, hands clenching me as if she may fall at any second, I see it.

Her purest form. The one from before, before she needed to put on the facade.

My future. Wrapped in her chestnut eyes.

Our love. Raining down in foil confetti.

This new Lily isn't some horrible girl, hell-bent on making my life miserable. She's a fighter, resilient and strong. Lily's the product of thousands of pounds of pressure molding her into the diamond I couldn't see. I thought all this time she had lost herself, but really she was blooming into what she's always been since the day I laid eyes on her.

A queen.

EPILOGUE

"Oh, you look perfect, mija."

My aunt Mina beams at me from the bottom of the stares. Her wide brown eyes sparkling with tears that slowly release down her cheek.

I wasn't going, but two weeks ago, she helped me pick out the dress. It's an A-line, long sleeve, and floor-length. The deep emerald stands out beautifully against my skin, which is only showing at my chest with the low V-neck, and at my right leg from the slit that reaches just under my thigh. The heavy fabric is divine, and I purposely didn't show Spencer so I could see the look on his face right now. And it was so worth it.

His own tux is black, tailored to show every bit of his muscle, and the emerald green pocket square ties it together magnificently. His thick locks are combed back, but a few strands fall over his forehead in a sexy Johnny Depp from Cry-Baby type way, so I won't dare fix them. His mouth is parted, and I have to bite the inside of my lip to keep from smiling at how fast his chest heaves and falls.

When I've made it to the end of the stairs, he still hasn't spoken and my aunt Mina jabs him in the ribs. "Boy, if you don't—"

"I'm sorry, it's just," he pauses, his smile finally splitting his face and bringing his delicious dimples out. "It's just when I don't think you can get any more beautiful, you always make me feel stupid and show me you can."

His words swirl in my chest before blooming on my cheeks. "You are many things, Spencer Hanes, but stupid isn't one of them."

I reach up, kissing him on the edge of his mouth. His hand snakes around my back, holding me in place so he can admire me up close. He lowers his voice to a whisper. "As long as one of those things is being yours, I'm happy."

"Bet your ass you are."

He laughs through his nose before releasing me and digging into his pocket. "I got you something. I wanted to give this to you our freshman year because I planned to add to it..."

He pulls out a large white square box before turning it to face me and pops it open. Inside, resting on a pillow of fluffy black velvet is a gorgeous medium twist charm bracelet with two charms. The first is the one I've been missing for months since I threw it at him. The second is a small masquerade mask. I feel my eyebrows furrow as my finger traces over the intricate piece of silver.

"Because our prom is masquerade-themed?"

He chuckles, taking it out of the box, and holds his hand out for my wrist. "Purely coincidental. It signifies the mask you wore. It's something I don't want you to forget because it takes a truly strong person to endure everything that you have in your life. It helped you shield your heart from any more hurt, keeping it intact until I came back." His hand connects with mine, sending shivers up my forearm.

I'm thankful my sleeves are long, so he doesn't notice the gaggle of goose bumps. He clasps it on before locking our fingers together. "But I'm here, and it's my job to protect it from now on."

He smiles at me once more before turning me to face my aunt. She has a large camera covering her eyes, but the tears flowing from underneath and her shaking shoulders reveal what's happening behind it.

"Mina."

"Just smile, you silly girl."

So I do. We take at least thirty-five pictures, in way too many poses, before finally, she comes from behind her shield, a blubbering mess. I wrap my arms around her, squeezing as I rock us back and forth, humming one of Blaze's tunes that always calms me down.

She cries a little more before grabbing onto my face, but careful not to mess up my makeup. "I am so, so, so proud of you, mija."

I can feel the prickling at the back of my eyes, threatening to mess up my mascara, so I kiss her cheek and smile. "Thank you. For everything."

She shoos me away with her hand, grabbing a tissue from inside her shirt. "Hush hush. It's my job. Now, here. Don't forget your masks."

Mina hands us our half-black masks. Mine is lace with hints of the same emerald green as my dress, while Spencer's is matte. His phone rings just as Mina finishes securing it around my face.

It's hard for me to grasp just one emotion that's flitting through my body at this moment. But there is one I notice a little more because I haven't felt it ever before.

Peace. There's a serene aura swirling around me, almost lifting me off the ground. It's knowing that life is full of shitty things, and even though I could handle it by myself, I don't have to. Not anymore.

Mina gives me one last once-over before Spencer leans in, kissing her on the cheek. "We won't be back late. Promise."

She laughs. "Oh, I know. Or else I'll have those testiculos of yours and feed them to the dog next door."

We walk outside to a rumbling black truck that vibrates my entire driveway. For a second, I wonder how in the hell I'm even going to get inside. As though Spencer can read my mind, he squeezes my hand and winks. "Easy stunt to a frequent flyer."

My heart flutters, and I lean up to kiss him. Ever since regionals, he's come to every practice and watched all of my recorded tapes. I have to force myself not to look at him at performances because it trips me up every time I do. He looks at me as if I'm the most magnificent thing he's ever seen, and it melts my mind into mush.

One of the dark tinted windows rolls down, and a green-eyed devil appears. William has since taken an interest in being Spencer's shadow, and it was surprisingly easy for us to forget our past encounters. Especially with him popping up almost every weekend and he never misses a chance to ogle my aunt. Luckily though, he disappears when Amora's around, unable to put up with her sharp tongue before getting worked up.

"Heya sugar. You look goooood. You too, Lily!"

Spencer rolls his eyes, and I laugh as we pile inside. Remy sits tucked away in the back seat. A phenomenal bloodred sleeveless dress that sparkles in the low light of the truck and clings to her like a second skin. "Remy, you look hot."

Her small face turns nearly the same color as her dress, a timid smile sweeping across her face. "Thank you. You too, Lily. You guys look perfect."

"Alright, alright. Let's blow this popsicle stand. Score me some..." William clears his throat, looking at Remy in the rearview. "After I get you home, of course."

She grins for a moment before hugging herself around the middle. I wait until we've pulled off, and the boys are talking about potato distribution before turning to her.

"Hey, so I read a lot of manga when I was younger and haven't really had time for it lately. But with summer around the corner, I thought about opening my reading horizons and wondered if you could give me any recommendations."

Remy's face lights up like the fourth of July. Her hands wave around as she talks, and she goes off on at least four tangents, describing six different genres until I pick one. "Oh, I think I like the broken alpha one. That sounds interesting."

She beams, her cheeks swelling so much her eyes seal shut. "Yes, that's one of my favorites."

By the time we reach the school, she's ordered three books online and created a buddy reading schedule, totally forgetting how uncomfortable she was. Spencer pauses and shoots me an appreciative smile, but I wave it off. In the short time I've gotten to know her, it's easy to see why he became friends with Remy. She's a pure type of person. The bright light that will sit with you in the darkest of rooms until you get up and walk to the door.

We pile out of the car and walk toward the school, which is booming—spilling music, and light into the dark parking lot, leading us into the good time it promises. I notice Blaze standing at the entrance across from the last-minute ticket booth. His dark suit is tailored perfectly, and for once, he doesn't look so broody. I lean into Spencer, reaching up on my tiptoes. "I'll be right back. Get the ticket for William, and I'll meet you right inside."

He nods, capturing my lips with his. The stampede of butterflies never gets old. They flap around with excitement until I'm dizzy from his smell.

Finally, he releases me, and after catching my bearings, I meet Blaze with a hug. "You look handsome."

"And you are stunning."

I don't want to, but I grit my teeth and ask what I'm wondering. "Waiting on Stacy?"

After her confession of trying to ruin the team tat I busted my ass for she lost her spot as next year's captain and decided to just quit. Waste of talent, if you ask me, but not being associated with the team gave Amora free rein when she ran into her late after school one day. I told the girl to let it go, something I excel at thanks to Dr. Floren, but she's a firecracker through and through. Once you light the fuse, there's no turning back.

"Amora, actually."

My head snaps up so fast it pops. "What?"

He grins, pushing some hair away from his face. "It's not like that. She wants to make some dude jealous."

My eyebrows furrow as I try to figure out who Amora would want to make jealous. Shit, the only guy she can't get her nails into is Blaze. Just then, I notice the blue in Blaze's eye twinkle. It's subtle, but his jaw tightens, forcing me to follow his line of sight.

Remy.

Whipping back around, his face becomes impassive. And I can tell he doesn't want me to say anything. So I don't. But I know what I saw. It was a crack.

Once there is a crack in the masks we wear, it's only a matter of time before the whole thing shatters, exposing who we really are. The ugly, filthy truths we hide underneath. And if anyone can love Blaze's bruises and show him how to love them.

It's her.

He clears his throat, shifting on his feet. "So, Solace, huh?"

I nod, wiping a stray piece of lint from his jacket. "Yep. The first years have been paid, and I've already started applying for scholarships after that. Plus, I'll be able to save everything I make from coaching cheer to the little league girls."

Blaze smiles again, and I remind myself vaguely to play the lottery later. "I'm proud of you, Lil. Now go have fun with your rook."

"What?"

He huffs, the corner of his lips curling up. "Kings are lazy. Make everyone else surround them and do all the work. Can't protect their queen like a rook can."

I giggle, backing away just as a strong hand wraps around my stomach. Spencer leans in, his lips grazing the shell of my ear, and sends a violent shiver down my spine. "Can I show you something first?"

My teeth sink into my bottom lip as I nod.

He leads me inside the side door, down the dark hall, up a flight of stairs, and toward the room we used for our experiment. When we get to the door, he turns, his darkened eyes focus on me, a playful smile twitches the side of his mouth. "There was one color we didn't get to try. Will you try it with me now?"

My heart thunks in my chest, my hand shaking in his, and when I answer, my voice is barely a whisper. "Yes."

Spencer's dimples deepen as a grin slips across his mouth. He pulls the door open and pulls me behind him inside.

It's black, not like pitch black, but a weird muted color that somehow lights the walls up. That's when I realize the desk and one of the chairs is gone.

Spencer yanks our connected hands, forcing my body flush against his, and takes my chin in his thumb and forefinger. "I am so fucking in love with you."

Before I can respond, his lips are on mine, and his tongue dives into my mouth. His hands waste no time, trailing down between the valley of my breasts, setting my skin on fire under his fingertips.

We enjoy the push and pull for only a moment before I feel his hand slide over, tugging the fabric away, exposing my pebbled nipple to the cold air. I gasp, and he breaks away from my lips, moving down to capture it in his mouth. His tongue teases over it, flicking it before rolling it between his teeth, sending jolts of pleasure into my core.

My head falls back as a moan escapes my lips, and I push

my body closer to him, leaving no space where we aren't connected.

A low, deep groan comes from the back of his throat, leaving my pussy throbbing. My hands find his hair, tugging it aggressively. He laughs against my skin but finally sits down in the chair, gripping my hips to follow him. He trails a hand down my exposed thigh, sending shivers through my body.

"Spencer." It's a desperate whisper.

"You're so fucking beautiful." He pulls the draping of my skirt to the side and hooks a finger inside my drenched panties.

Spencer squeezes his eyes shut, and he takes a deep breath before pulling hard, snapping the thin material. Before I can even breathe, his thumb connects with my clit, rolling it in circles, making my entire body convulse.

"Hey. How are you feeling?"

My mouth drops open, unable to focus on anything other than the waves of nerves shooting through my core.

"If you could be doing anything right now..." He pauses, slipping two fingers in my channel while his thumb continues its assault. "What would you be doing?"

"Spencer Hanes, if you don't shut up and fuck me—"

"You'll what?" he toys, curling his fingers and stealing my words.

Suddenly his fingers and the pressure on my pussy vanishes. My eyes snap down at the same moment his cock comes free of his slacks. He drags it through my slippery folds, hisses through his teeth.

"Spe— Fuckkkkk."

The threat I had vanishes as he impales me, filling me to

the hilt. His fingers dig into the fabric, pulling me up and down in a rhythmic tempo until I'm lost in the abyss. Heat pulses through my body until it rushes south and coils low in my belly.

"Fuck, I love you, Spencer."

He smiles, letting his teeth graze against my jaw before he presses a thumb on my clit. "And I love you, Lily."

He circles it twice, and my pussy flutters, the tingle of ecstasy spreading through my limbs like lightning across the sky. Not giving two shits we're in the school, I scream his name as I shatter into pieces around him.

He fucks me through my orgasm before releasing his own, shuddering beneath me as he comes undone. I fall against his chest, greedily sucking in the air I deprived myself of. He strokes my hair, letting our heart rates return to normal as we come back down to earth. Suspended shivers still work their way through, and every time I shake, he laughs.

Truthfully, I could just stay here and skip the dance altogether, but I know Blaze will kill me when they crown us, and I'm not there to relieve him of the mystery of standing onstage alone. As if he can read my mind, Spencer stirs, letting me get up before he fixes himself. "Do you remember that contract we made?"

I stifle a laugh. "Yeah, I still owe you a punch to the gut for breaking rule two."

He scoffs playfully, pulling me closer as we exit the room. "So you remember rule thirteen?"

Of course. I remember every damn thing on the sheet. Nodding, I curl into his chest. "Yes."

He smiles. "Just making sure. Now, let's get my queen to the prom."

13. If Spencer and Liliana ever exchange cooties of a kiss, they agree to forever be bonded by such cooties and will marry no later than their twenty fifth birthday.

The End.

PREVIEW

I love when a brat is good with her mouth.

Scratch that. I don't *love* anything. That requires the capacity to open one's theoretical *heart,* which is literally the stupidest shit I've ever heard. It's a vital organ that merely pumps blood through your body so you can continue to breathe. Yet, people seem to place some imaginary power that it has the capability to feel based on another human being.

Don't get me wrong. I feel things—hunger, annoyance, pain. Real things. Real *feelings*. Not *attachments*. Which is all love is. Well, that and hate. It's all connected, both emotions twisting around each other until they're nearly indecipherable.

That being said, I do take pleasure when a woman is on her knees, hair coiled in my fist, sucking the soul from my dick. Current case in point: a redhead I've snuck off with at my father's fundraiser. A gala for the richest in Washington state. All here to measure whose cock is bigger based on how many zeros are in their bank accounts.

My father, Mr. Steel F. Barot—CEO and founder of Clean Source Energy Incorporated, doesn't have to prove anything to the piranhas circling. He's the great white who enjoys watching them fight it out, eating one another alive, donating everything they can, leaving my father with more money than he makes in a day.

No matter how fucking horrible these things are, as the future heir, or *pup* as my father loves to spit, I'm expected to attend. Typically, my friend, Lily, accompanies me and provides an entertaining distraction, but she has some therapy sessions, leaving me stranded in the infested waters alone. Every Tom, Dick, and Harry thinks they can butter me up and get in good with my father. Little do they know, not even *I'm* in good with the old man. Still, it's something I use to my advantage quite often.

Like now.

This little lady was one of the many things that caught my eye under the dim candle lighting, and not in a good sense. Her red dress is the color of a fire hydrant, clinging to every bone that sticks out from her thin frame. There's at least four coats of makeup covering her face, and I'm relatively certain she came with her husband or maybe fiancé.

Even so, Sheila, or perhaps Stephanie, eye-fucked me the moment I walked in, and I've never been one to turn down a pouty set of lips. One of her surprisingly rough hands wraps around the base of my shaft, while the other digs into my hip. She's attempting to steady herself from the long strokes, and I'm beginning to grow tired of keeping her upright. She underestimated my size, and that in itself is annoying enough.

But instead of letting that ruin the fun, my eyes drift to a near close like they always do, and suddenly the red hair in front of me dims to an inky black.

The same black hair I think of far more than I should and can't seem to get off without. It's been two years since I've seen her, yet she's all I see when I find myself balls deep in someone warm.

Those oversized hexagon glasses that frame almond-shaped eyes that make it feel like I'm staring at a sunflower in the brightest grass. Her slightly toned arms from carrying piles of books everywhere she went. And that fucking halo floating over her head, that was a constant reminder that she was too good, too pure for the likes of me.

Remy Solace.

ACKNOWLEDGMENTS

First, I want to thank you! My readers. For taking a chance on a new author, who has some pretty crazy ideas swimming in her head. Out of all the books in the world, and you read mine. You will never know just how much that means to me! Thank you!

My'chal. Timon. Bae. NONE of this, not one sentence, would be possible without you. You corral the kids, take on dinner, yell at me to call Garnet when I can't get out of writer's block. You keep me going. You are my NUMBER ONE hype man. You talk me down from the insanely high rooftops and I will forever be grateful that our stars aligned. Because your love...it's something out of a storybook.

To Hailey, Aaron, and Christian. My Sun, Moon, and Stars. You made mommy the person she is today. Thank you for telling mommy to keep going and for showing me it's never too late to achieve a dream.

Garnet Christie. Girl. Where would I be without you? Probably still curled up in a ball letting imposter syndrome eat me alive, if I'm being honest. Our daily talks, venting, plotting, ideas...I can never repay you for not only your kindness, and love, but encouragement, and believing in me when I didn't think I could do it. You are a gem, and I love you!

To the girls: Greer Rivers, Emily McIntire, Kayleigh King, and Sav Miller. Where do I even start. From Emily's ability to cull the weak to make the strongest story possible, or Greer's positive light that shines even in the darkest of holes. Y'all paved the way for me and told me about the speed bumps so I could see them before they happened. If it wasn't for you ladies, I'd still be sitting around waiting on an agent. Instead, you encouraged me and pushed me to this very publication. Even when I said, what do y'all think about a female bully? Y'all said YES!! And that was all she wrote. Y'all are amazing, and I will forever be in your debt.

Beta readers! You wonderful ladies made me feel less crazy, and pulled me out of my head! It wouldn't be what it is right now without y'all's encouragement and awesome feedback! Hope y'all are ready for Blaze

Garnet Christie, Greer Rivers, Emily McIntire, L.L. Lily, M.L. Philpitt, AC Powers, Bella Grace, Kautharmm, and Jeanie Robinson.

To my cover designer, AJ Wolf of AJ Wolf Graphics. GIRLLLLLL. I don't even know what to say! I struggled with this damn cover, and wanted something that stood out just like my trope. You dealt with my back and forth, my horrible drawings, and my second-guessing. THANK YOU! You made a dope ass cover and I am so excited for what we do this year.

Now. To my editor, Ellie, and proofreader, Rosa, at My

Brother's Editor. YOU LADIES TOOK A CHANCE ON ME! I mean WHAT?! How I got so lucky, I will never know, but damnit THANK YOU! You wonderful duo gave me that last nod I needed to know that this is it. I did it, and it's ready to see the world!! Thank you for making it pretty, for being patient with me, and your kind words.

ABOUT THE AUTHOR

Lee Jacquot is a wild-haired bibliophile who writes romances with strong heroines that deserve a happy ever after. When Lee isn't writing or drowning herself in a good book, she laughs or yells at one of her husband's practical jokes.

Lee is addicted to cozy pajamas, family game nights, and making tents with her kids. She currently lives in Texas with her husband, three littles, and fluffy cat, Olaf. She lives off coffee and Dean Winchester.

Visit her on Instagram or TikTok to find out about upcoming releases and other fun things! @authorleejacquot

Made in the USA
Coppell, TX
06 March 2021